Katey Lovell

I grew up in South Wales and now live in Sheffield with my husband David, son Zachary and our friendly moggie Clarence. If I'm not writing, I'll most likely be found with my nose in a book or reviewing on my blog Books with Bunny.

www.kateylovell.blogspot.co.uk
@katey5678

Praise for Katey Lovell

'*Magical and sparkly short stories, highly recommended*'
Sky's Book Corner

'*I'm so glad I picked this up, it's gorgeous*'
Rather Too Fond of Books

'*Swooning all the way through*'
Reviewed the Book

'*An absolutely wonderful debut*'
Little Northern Soul

'*Quirky, cute and utterly romantic*'
Bestselling author Rebecca Raisin

'*Sweet, romantic, perfectly formed coffee break reads. I loved them*'
Bestselling author Carmel Harrington

The Singalong Society for Singletons

KATEY LOVELL

A division of HarperCollins*Publishers*
www.harpercollins.co.uk

Harper*Impulse* an imprint of
HarperCollins*Publishers*
1 London Bridge Street
London SE1 9GF

www.harpercollins.co.uk

A Paperback Original 2016

First published in Great Britain in ebook format by Harper*Impulse* 2016

A catalogue record for this book
is available from the British Library

ISBN: 9780008217679

Set in Minion by Palimpsest Book Production Limited, Falkirk, Stirlingshire

Printed and bound in Great Britain by
Clays Ltd, St Ives plc

MIX
Paper from
responsible sources
FSC™ C007454

FSC™ is a non-profit international organisation established to promote
the responsible management of the world's forests. Products carrying the
FSC label are independently certified to assure consumers that they come
from forests that are managed to meet the social, economic and
ecological needs of present and future generations,
and other controlled sources.

Find out more about HarperCollins and the environment at
www.harpercollins.co.uk/green

For my lovely Mum. Thank you for everything.

The Cast List

The Singalong Society for Singletons

Hope Brown
Monique Brown
Liam Holly
Isadora Jackson
Ray North
Connie Williams

Supporting Roles

Justin Crowson
Amara Lin

The Musicals

Wicked
Frozen
The Lion King
The Sound of Music
Grease
Chicago
West Side Story
South Pacific
The Rocky Horror Picture Show
Les Misérables
Singing in the Rain
Fame
Rent
Oliver!
Walking On Sunshine
Mamma Mia
Mary Poppins
White Christmas
Shrek – The Musical
The Wizard of Oz

Prologue

I've always considered myself a modern woman. That's why I'd planned to ask Justin to marry me that night.

It would have been a risk, me being the one to do the asking, because in many ways he's an old-fashioned guy. A traditionalist – well-mannered, sweet, polite. But I'd been so sure that the time was right for our relationship to shift up a gear that I'd been willing to take the chance.

After all, we'd been together since our last year of secondary school. We must have passed each other in the corridors hundreds of times before that and we'd even been in the same maths class for a while, but we hadn't exchanged so much as a word until that fateful April day in Year 11 as we waited to audition for the annual summer show. That year it had been *Guys and Dolls* and I'd had my heart set on the role of Sarah. Miss Adelaide might get the show-stopping numbers, but Sarah was quieter, calmer. Prim and proper, but determined beneath the façade. Truth be told, she was a lot like me.

I'd been nervously wringing my hands together as I waited to

1

sing the audition piece of 'I've Never Been in Love Before'. I can still recall the twisting sensation in my stomach, churning like one of those Slush Puppy machines at the seaside.

Justin had been sitting next to me and he'd seen how worried I was, how badly I'd wanted the role. Musicals were my 'thing' and if I was cast in a minor role or – heaven forbid – not at all, my confidence would be severely knocked. Justin had spoken to me in a tone that was immediately soothing, telling me I'd shine as Sarah. He'd been the perfect distraction, listening intently as I waffled on anxiously about how I thought I might throw up on my shoes. He didn't recoil at that frank revelation, instead smiling reassuringly until it was my turn to perform on the makeshift stage in the sports hall that reeked of floor polish and sweaty feet.

Thanks to Justin I'd kept my cool, holding myself together to pull out a performance to be proud of – one that got me the very role I'd been coveting. I'd been over the moon.

In contrast, he hadn't gone through with his audition in the end. Being as tone deaf as he was, it was probably a blessing. I'd never been a Brando fan, but even *his* version of 'Luck Be a Lady' was far superior to the adaptation Justin had mumbled under his breath as he sat next to me that day. At least Marlon got the words in the right order.

I later found out that the only reason Justin had planned to audition at all was to spend time with me. That was a relief on two counts – firstly that he'd considered getting up and making a twat of himself in front of half the school proved he was serious about our fledgling relationship; and secondly because it showed he wasn't one of those deluded people who can't hold a tune for toffee but secretly thinks they're going to win the next series of the Saturday night talent show on TV.

Ever since that audition day we'd been together; through the stressful last term of school, into sixth-form college and sharing the first five years of our twenties. Things had become increasingly serious, the single drawer of 'essentials' that Justin had in my cosy bedroom at the house Issy and I shared on Cardigan Close had, over time, turned into a whole *chest* of drawers. Justin had practically been a fixture or fitting himself; as much a part of the furniture as the sofa that took up half the lounge, or the comfy armchair in the corner of my bedroom which I refuse to get rid of despite the threadbare material on the armrests (much to my housemate Issy's chagrin).

He was my other half, the love of my life, and that's why I'd steeled myself up to pop the vital question. I couldn't envisage a future in which we weren't together.

Justin and Monique.

Monique and Justin.

We were meant to be. I knew it.

As we'd left the house that evening, hurrying out onto the cobblestoned street and into the dome-roofed Hackney cab that took us to the city centre, I remember thinking it would be a night to remember for all the right reasons. But I was wrong. Boy, was I wrong.

We had tickets to see a show at City Hall, a touring production of *Wicked*. I knew nothing about it other than it was linked with *The Wizard of Oz*, but I'd fallen head over heels in love with the song 'Defying Gravity' and was desperate to see it performed live. Justin hadn't been as keen, but then he only ever came to the theatre because he knew I loved it. Dramatic numbers weren't really his bag, but that night, in particular, he seemed out of sorts, tetchy almost. I'd stupidly put it down to him being tired after a long week at work, that and the fact he'd rather be watching the darts on the telly with a pint in his hand. Just as I was nuts over musicals, he was obsessed with sport. It didn't matter if it was the Golf Masters or the Cricket World Cup, if it was a major sporting event Justin would be glued to the screen, willing on his chosen team.

I'd convinced myself he'd come round as the night went on.

3

After all, I'd got a plan to stick to. We'd walk through town, the Sheffield Christmas lights strung out along Barker's Pool hanging underwhelmingly over our heads as we made our way towards the enormous (yet sparsely lit) Christmas tree in front of the imposing Victorian town hall. From there we'd stroll arm in arm to the Peace Gardens, a popular meeting point in the centre of town, where we'd giggle fondly as we reminisced about how far we'd come since sharing our first kiss there one balmy Saturday afternoon, back when we were fifteen and free from care.

In my mind it'd been wonderfully romantic, like something from a black-and-white film. The fountains and cascades would be on and the fairy lights wrapped around the spindly trees would make a stunning and dreamy backdrop for my proposal. In my mind it was going to be magical. In my mind it was going to be perfect.

In reality, the evening itself had been nice enough. Therein lay the warning, I suppose. Nice enough isn't magical. Nice enough isn't perfect.

We'd gone for drinks at one of the upmarket bars in town, Justin opting for his usual beer whilst I'd splashed out on a Manhattan. I'd used the excuse that it was to celebrate reaching the end of term without collapsing in a heap with the other teaching assistants amidst the rush of Christmas parties and visits from 'Santa' (who was actually Mr Thomas, the headmistress's husband), when really the alcohol was Dutch courage, pure and simple. I'd been turning the question over in my mind; it had taken all my efforts not to blurt it out before heading to the show.

Wicked had been brilliant, a glorious spectacle of a musical, and the cast had us captivated as they belted out the amazing show tunes. The wannabe performer in me wished I wasn't sitting in the plush gold velour seat – how I longed to be up on that stage, the glaring white spotlight shining on me just as it had on a much smaller scale in that school hall during *Guys and Dolls*!

4

Musicals have the power to transport me to another world, whisking me away from my mundane life. But as soon as the house lights came up in the auditorium a nervous niggle had started gnawing away at me. No matter how hard I'd tried to push it to the back of my mind, I hadn't been able to shake it off.

I felt cold to the core as we walked down the venue's sweeping stone steps and it wasn't just the December chill clawing away at my skin. It was something worse. Justin seemed as though he was holding back, his face hidden under the fur trim of his parka. His hand was loose around mine. He was distant. Barely there.

The rows of festive decorations strung out before us, a twinkling ladder across the sky. It was the only part of the image I correctly predicted, and we silently sauntered through the streets whilst revellers enjoying five-too-many 'Mad Friday' beers fist-pumped the air as they sang along to Slade's Christmas classic 'Merry Xmas Everybody' at the top of their lungs. Looking back, we'd been the odd ones out, Justin and I, sober in both body and spirit.

We reached the fountain, although it wasn't turned on because of the gusty weather, and sat near by. All the while Justin looked awkward. Fidgety. On edge. He took a deep breath, a visible cloud appearing from his mouth as he exhaled.

I swallowed uneasily. Something was up.

'I wanted to speak to you,' he'd said finally. He had this funny lop-sided grin plastered on his face, unfamiliar even though I'd been swooning at his smiles for a decade. He looked different, somehow, and for one brief moment I'd laughed, convinced he was building up to asking the same question I'd been preparing to ask him.

My stomach lurched with hopeful anticipation and I wondered if he might produce a ring. At the time, it had seemed entirely possible he might, but looking back everything about that night made me feel foolish.

I'd been dreaming. Only momentarily, but a lot can happen in a moment. I'd even wondered whether the hypothetical, mythical ring would be a square-cut solitaire like the one I'd saved in the favourites folder on my laptop, or an antique he'd picked up from one of the quirky antique shops on London Road or Sharrow Vale. Justin knew how I adored anything vintage.

Seconds later my world crashed down around me. I was dizzy, stunned, confused, and all it took was three little words.

'I'm going away.'

Justin had looked excitedly out at me from beneath the safety of his hood, the weird enormous grin peering out as he waited for my response.

I'd not understood what he meant at first; not known that those three words said it all.

'What do you mean?' I'd stumbled finally. I genuinely didn't understand the statement.

He was going away, he'd said brightly, heading to America for a year to work at the Chicago-based head office of the bank he was a slave to. He oozed gleeful delight, prattling on about how it was a wonderful opportunity and what an honour it was to be considered a suitable candidate. I could go with him, he'd said, his puppy-dog eyes full of expectation.

I was so shocked I couldn't even formulate a simple sentence.

'When?' I managed eventually.

He'd proudly told me January 4th and that it was a year-long contract. He'd been specially selected by the Big Boss when the person they'd lined up for the role backed out due to ill health. That was why it was such short notice, he explained. Justin had been put forward as the best possible replacement, the opportunity a reward for the long hours he'd been putting in recently. It was too good an offer to pass up, he'd said, something he had to do now whilst he was young, before he was tied down by responsibilities and a family.

I'd wanted to scream at that bit. He had a family here who

loved him, his younger brother Benji worshipped the ground he walked on and aspired to be just like him. He had parents who doted on him and bought him everything he wanted, from designer clothes to a brand new car.

And me. He had me.

But Justin was radiant with excitement, unleashing all the joy he'd obviously forced himself to suppress earlier in the evening. He hadn't said a word about America as he'd slurped on the spag bol I'd thrown together as a quick tea to line our stomachs, nor as he'd tapped his fingers against the pint glass in the pub. He'd kept schtum in the theatre too, letting me believe everything was fine, when all the time he'd been holding a bomb.

He rabbited on about head office and career progression, his tunnel vision blinding him to everything else. I'd never felt more irrelevant. I wasn't even a Christmas cracker-sized spanner in the works. His mind was made up and that was that.

'I can't just drop everything,' I said, feeling a smidgeon of annoyance that he expected me to. I had my job at the school, for starters, I couldn't let them down by buggering off to the other side of the world. And then there were my dance classes, the ones I attended every Thursday night without fail. The six of us in the class had been dancing together since we were tots. They were my extended family, my safety net. I didn't want to leave them behind, but I didn't want to be without Justin either.

'It's a great opportunity,' he'd repeated, the light in his eyes not dimming despite my lack of enthusiasm. 'For me and for you.'

His hand had rested on mine and I'd flinched. I didn't pull away, even though the last thing I wanted right then was for him to touch me. I just didn't have the energy to move.

'Imagine it, Mon. Me and you in the big city, living the American dream.' His eyes were alight with a passion he normally reserved for Saturdays when the Blades were playing at home. I knew, then, that he was going to go regardless. His mind was made up. Nothing I could say would change a thing.

'I can't go,' I said. 'And I don't want to. It's not my dream. Anyway, there's no way I could get on a plane and go all that way. Have you forgotten the melt down I had on the way back from Corfu?'

I could tell by his expression that he had, but I hadn't. We'd suffered terrible turbulence and the pilot's attempts at keeping his updates humorous and light hadn't reassured me in the slightest. I'd ended up bent double, hunched in the brace position 'just in case', despite Justin's instructions to breathe in and out of the sick bag to regulate my panicked gasps. It's safe to say me and aeroplanes don't mix.

'I'm sorry, Justin. But if you go to Chicago, you'll be going alone.'

He'd looked guilty then. He was going to America with or without me.

As we sat on the cold stone borders that flanked the segments of grass in the gardens, I couldn't believe I'd ever thought this would be the most romantic night of my life. A bitter, biting wind whipped through the open space, an invisible slap in the face to accompany the sucker punch my gut had just taken.

Worst of all, everyone around us had been full of festive spirit, carrying on as though nothing had changed, whilst for me everything was about to change irrevocably. I wanted to shout, to kick up a stink right there in the middle of town, but my body didn't feel like my own. It was a terrible dream and I watched on helplessly as it played out around me.

'I'd hoped you'd come with me. I thought it'd be an adventure for us both.'

I shook my head. 'I just can't.'

He'd looked crestfallen, the joy he'd had earlier evaporating out of him into the dark winter night. 'It's not the end for us though, is it? Loads of couples make long distance work. And the world's a smaller place these days, that's what they say…' It was as though he was trying to convince himself.

'I suppose there's always Skype…' I said half-heartedly.

I couldn't imagine not being able to physically *feel* him. We'd always been one of those touchy-feely couples, the kind that makes everyone feel a bit uncomfortable. Our constant public displays of affection were legendary, but you can't touch someone through a computer screen. You can't hold them or kiss them or make wild, passionate love to them. There'd be no substitute for having Justin here with me.

'We can make this work,' he'd said, his voice full of a false yet hopeful confidence. 'If anyone can, we can.'

But even then, I wasn't sure.

*

He'd left, just as he'd planned to, on the day we'd started back at school after Christmas break. I'd been assisting the more able children, helping them write sentences about the gifts Santa had left under their tree while he was on a cross-country train over the Pennines to Manchester Airport, ready to start a whole new life on a whole other landmass.

That was the weirdest part of it all. I was still in Sheffield, with the same job and the same friends and the same bedroom in the same house; but with an empty chest of drawers sitting hollow in the corner instead of filled with a selection of Lynx aftershaves he'd been bought for his birthday by some well-meaning aunt and every Sheffield United kit from the last ten years.

I'm sure that outwardly I looked much the same as ever – a twenty-five-year-old woman of average height and naturally athletic build with a fluffy mass of unruly dark blonde curls – but inside I felt as empty as those drawers. I'd hoped that by forcing myself to raise a smile I'd fool people into believing I was fine. But I wasn't fine, deep down. Deep down I was breaking.

*

I still have a photo of me and Justin together on my dressing table, in a heart-shaped wooden frame. It was taken at a charity ball the summer before he went away. In it I'm staring up at Justin, who's stood almost a whole foot taller than me and my face looks like it might split right in two because I'm grinning *that* hard.

I can't remember the last time I smiled like that. As much as I try to show the world I'm the same positive, smiley Mon I've always been, it's not my face splitting in two any more. It's my heart.

Chapter One

'I've been waiting for this *all day*.' Issy sighs with audible relief as the ruby-red Merlot sloshes into the glass. 'Honestly, I can't tell you how ready I am. In fact, I'm more than ready. I'm a woman in need,' she adds dramatically.

'Only all day?' I reply with a laugh. 'Then you're a stronger woman than I am, Isadora Jackson. I've been waiting all *week*.'

My blonde curls bounce wildly. People say they look like a halo, but although I'm a good girl, I'm certainly no angel.

'Seriously,' I continue, 'the only thing that's got me through the madness that is reception class during the first week in September is the thought of wine o' clock. We've had so many children crying when their parents leave, the noise in that class-room is phenomenal. Phenomenal! Thank your lucky stars that the kids you teach are past that.'

Issy gulps her wine, raising her eyebrows in a challenge of disagreement. I know that look. It's the one that says whenever anyone plays the 'I work in the most difficult age group' card, Issy's going to take that card and trump it.

'Teaching Year 6 isn't a bundle of laughs, you know. All those raging hormones and that snarky pre-teen attitude…' She visibly shudders. 'Can you believe I had Ellie Watts in tears this lunchtime because Noah Cornall dumped her? They're only ten! And the bitching and backbiting that goes on – I've not seen anything like it. It's the *Big Brother* house, but worse. How many weeks to go until half term?'

'Another seven.' I pull a face, unable to believe I'm already counting down to the holidays. The six-week summer break had worked its usual miracle of helping me forget how exhausting it is working in a primary school and although I'd not exactly been jumping out of bed with delight when the alarm went off at 6.15 on Monday morning, I'd felt a quiet positivity about the year ahead. There's something special about getting to know a new set of kids, and there had even been rumours of new furniture for the reception classroom. Heaven knows, the tables need replacing. Years of felt-tip pens being carelessly smudged over their surface meant their glory days were well in the past. But just one week in – four days, actually, if you discount the staff training day – and I'm already totally drained of energy, as I always am during term time. People at work say I'm bubbly and bouncy and full of beans, but that's because I raise my game. How anyone who works with children finds the time for a social life, I'll never know. When Friday finally rolls around, all I want to do is climb into my onesie and sleep for a week.

'My class need to be the small fishes again,' Issy says with a sage nod. 'It's always the same with the oldest in the school. They get ahead of themselves. Too big for their 'let's-get-one-size-larger-so-you-can-grow-into-them Doc Martens." Issy looks so serious, which naturally makes me want to giggle. 'They'll be the ones in tears when they start at secondary school next year, just like your little angels in reception have been this time. It'll knock them down a peg or two.'

'It'll get easier, it always does.'

I know Issy thinks I'm being over-optimistic, but I can't help it. What can I say? I'm one of those people who naturally looks on the bright side of life, except when it comes to Justin. But that's no surprise, given that he'd gone from 'we can make long distance work' in December to 'perhaps we should take a break – not split up, but accept long distance doesn't work for us' in January. I think I've every right to feel bitter. I'm living in this weird love-life limbo.

'You'll be fine when they get to trust you,' I assure her. 'You said exactly the same about your last lot. Remember Billy Rush? You were convinced he'd turn you grey, and look, your hair's exactly the same murky shade it's always been,' I say with nothing but innocence.

'Hey, watch it you! My hair's not murky. It's salted caramel,' Issy replies, defensively stroking the thick, straight locks that tumble down past her shoulders. How she manages to look glamorous, even in her mint-green fleecy Primark pyjamas, I'll never know. She's one of those naturally well-groomed people whose skin always looks fresh and eyes bright, even when she's tired or has a stinking hangover. It's infuriating.

'Yeah, right. Whatever you say. 'Salted caramel.' Is that what they call it at the hairdressers?'

I poke my tongue out at her, but she knows it's all in jest. That's the great thing about our friendship. We tease each other mercilessly, but we can switch to drying each other's tears in a matter of seconds if needs be. And Issy, bless her, has done her fair share of being the shoulder to cry on this year, so it's important to remember to laugh about things as much as possible.

'They refer to it by number. But it's the darkest blonde they do,' Issy replies haughtily, running her hand over her locks once more. 'You'd see for yourself if we were in the right light. This house has terrible natural light, and you know it. It's the price we pay for living on the shady side of the street.'

She's right about that. Even in the height of summer there's a distinct chill in the lounge of the mid-terraced red-brick house we share. I swear we must've been the only people pulling down furry throws from the back of the sofa to keep warm during the one red-hot week that had passed as the British summer. Even long sunny days had done nothing to rid our lounge of its chilly gloom. And now, on an early-September evening, where it's still light outside, both of us are in pyjamas, dressing gowns and super-thick socks, a necessity if we're going to meet our annual challenge of making it to the half-term break without caving and putting the heating on.

'So, are you going to pour me a glass or that Merlot or what? I'm dying of thirst over here.'

'You're not exactly encouraging me to share when you're slagging off my hair and saying my job's easy. Maybe I'll keep the whole bottle to myself instead.'

There's a cheeky glint in Issy's eyes as she pulls the bottle to her mouth as though to swig from it. I know she's only messing around, but it's still enough to make me worry. It's Friday night. I need that wine.

'I never said it was easy,' I correct quickly. 'Just that you've not got the screamers and the over-anxious parents and the snotty noses and the pooey pants to deal with.' When the negative aspects of the job were all strung out like that, working as a teaching assistant in a reception class sounded *bad*. Like a cacophony of noise and hassle and bodily fluids.

Issy shoots me a look. 'You knew what you were getting into, you've got a degree in child development. It's not exactly a state secret that four-year-olds have accidents and don't know how to use a Kleenex.'

'I know, I know.'

And I can't imagine doing anything else. My oldest friend Connie's stuck in a hell-hole of an office all day and she hates every miserable minute of it. She's crying out to do something more worthwhile than filing and answering phones. School might be exhausting, but there are plenty of rewards too – some of the things the kids come out with are hilarious and it's great watching them grow and progress day by day.

'I do love the kids,' I add, 'especially the little ones. They're continually evolving and that moment when they grasp how to do something new – there's nothing like it. The pride in their faces…'

I place my hand over my heart, recalling the happiness on one child's face today as he counted to ten by rote. It had been a touching moment, and one that reminded me how much I love my job.

'You're going to set me off crying at this rate.'

Issy rolls her eyes, but the grin that accompanies it is the real giveaway – it shows she understands. I might be more of a people person than Issy, but she cares about the kids much more than she outwardly shows. She just does a good job of hiding her love and loyalty. Issy plays her cards very close to her chest.

'It's great being with the little ones. I wish they'd have a bit more independence sometimes, though.'

'Like you said to me, it'll get easier. You'll have them whipped into shape by the summer. They're used to being mollycoddled at home, that's all. Come on, you'll feel better after a glass of wine,' she chivvies. 'And at least there's no alarm going off at some ungodly hour in the morning, so let's put a film on and forget about work. I've got a Toblerone in the cupboard, too, if you fancy a few little triangular pieces of heaven?'

'Mmmmm.' My mouth waters at the thought. Toblerone. My favourite. 'That sounds amazing. What do you want to watch?'

It's a ridiculous, pointless question. We've watched the same film every Friday night for the past three months.

'Ooh, let me think,' Issy replies sarcastically, putting the tip of her index finger to the corner of her lips, as though there's actually a decision to be made here. Her nails are coated in black polish and there's not a single chip to be seen. Typical: Immaculate

Issy. After a brief, yet dramatic, pause, she announces '*Frozen!*'

I pull the shiny rectangular DVD case from the boxy Ikea bookcase as Issy snuggles into the corner of the settee, pulling the chocolate-brown throw over her knees in an attempt to get cosy, because when it comes to frostiness, 24 Cardigan Close can easily rival an icy Arendelle. Brr!

*

By the time Hans and Anna are capturing the brilliant white moon in their hands as they dance beneath the waterfall, Issy and I are both decidedly more relaxed. A second bottle of red wine's been opened and all that remains of the chocolate is the iconic triangular prism box and a screwed-up ball of silver foil strewn on the table. The cares of the week are slowly slipping away; the weekend has truly arrived.

Until the doorbell rings, rudely interrupting the peace.

Issy groans. 'Can't we leave it?' I know there's no way on earth she'll get up from that settee; she's set up camp for the night. Begrudgingly, I inch myself into a standing position while she chunters on. 'Who calls unannounced on a Friday night anyway?'

'Exactly,' I say. 'It must be important.'

'Or one of those door-to-door charity collectors.'

A ferocious banging follows, five loud knocks that it would be impossible to ignore.

'That'd have to be one desperate charity collector.'

I pull my dressing gown more tightly around my waist as I reach for my key from the small hook on the back of the door. The knocking continues, louder and more frantic than before, followed by a voice.

'Mon! Mon! It's me!'

The desperation in the high-pitched cries urge me into action. The voice is instantly identifiable. I fling the door open and my sister stumbles over the threshold, a bulging black sports bag slung over her shoulder and a wheelie suitcase by her side. Her face is deathly pale in stark contrast to her chocolate-brown hair, and her cheeks are stained with the snail-trail tracks of tears.

'Hope! What's going on?'

I'm shocked at the state of her. Actually, I'm beyond shocked. I'm not used to seeing my older sister like this. Hope's always been the stronger of the two of us, the one with the 'don't mess with me' attitude and a permanent look of disdain waiting in the wings to throw at anything or anyone she considers beneath her. But right now she looks fragile and vulnerable, like a frightened kitten in a thunderstorm.

'I didn't know where else to go,' Hope sobs. Her long, dark hair falls in front of her face as she hunches forwards, a protective veil to hide behind. I know the trick; I've used it myself.

'Start at the beginning.' I try to keep my voice calm, although inside I'm flailing. Placing my hand on my sister's back, I gently guide her into the living room. Hans and Anna are no longer singing about love being an open door. Issy's pressed the pause button at an inopportune moment; the close-up shot of the princess showing her eyes closed and her face contorted. 'What's going on?'

'It's Amara,' Hope says finally, before looking up and locking her bleary, bloodshot eyes with mine. 'She's thrown me out. She said she's had enough of me pressurising her into telling her parents the truth.' She pauses for breath, gulping the air. 'I've been patient, haven't I, Mon? It's been four years now, but she still won't admit to her parents that we're a couple. Four years! I'm sick of moving my stuff into the spare room every time they come over, pretending we're just best friends sharing a flat.' Her shoulders judder as the tears start to fall. 'All I want is for her to be honest. I don't want to have to hide any more.'

'What exactly did she say?' Issy interjects, moving to the edge of her seat. 'Do you think she means it? Or is she just angry at the situation and taking it out on you?'

17

'Oh, she means it alright,' Hope answers with a bitter laugh. 'She's ashamed to be with me. Her parents are coming up from London tomorrow and when I told her I thought it was time to come clean, she said that'd be 'impossible'.' Hope raises her hands, wiggling her fingers to indicate quotation marks. It's a move full of pain-drenched sarcasm. 'When I said I was sick of her pulling all the strings in our relationship, fed up of it being fine to hold her hand when we're clubbing on a Saturday night or walking around Endcliffe Park on a Sunday morning but having to outright *lie* when it comes to her family… she said she couldn't lie any longer either. She handed me my bag, told me it was over and ordered I pack and leave.'

Issy raises a perfectly shaped eyebrow and when she speaks her tone is disbelieving. 'And you did it without a fuss? I'm sorry, Hope, but that doesn't sound like the feisty girl I know. *She* wouldn't give up and walk out on the love of her life.'

'Can't you see? It's *because* I love her! That's why I've gone. If Amara can't tell her family that we've been in a relationship, then what's the point in being together anyway? I know I'm lucky. Mum was fine with me being gay, once she got her head around it. Amara's parents aren't like that. They're always on at her to find a nice young man and provide them with grandchildren. If she tells them she's gay, they'll probably disown her.'

'But even if she's not with you, she's still going to be gay,' I reason. I hand her my glass, thinking a sip of alcohol might calm her down. 'She's not going to suddenly start lusting over Daniel Craig just because you've moved out. So she'll still be lying to them either way.'

Hope winces as she sips the Merlot and it's only then I remember she's never been a fan of red wine, much preferring a crisp glass of refreshing Pinot Grigio. Ah well, beggars can't be choosers.

'I know,' Hope answers resignedly. 'But it's easier for her to call an end to it than tell them the truth. If she's on her own, she can make up excuses and fob off the questions. She'll say she's not found the right person yet or that she wants to travel or concentrate on her career. That'll be more acceptable to her family than the reality.'

'Concentrating on a career,' I snort. 'I've heard that one before.'

I grind my teeth, determined not to make this about me, but it's touched a nerve. I feel brittle, fragile. It comes over me like this every so often, and it makes me mad. These involuntary reactions are all little reminders that however much I profess to have moved on, I still catch my breath at the thought of Justin Crowson. He upped and left and broke my heart, but in just over three months he'll be back in Sheffield. The 'break' will be over; we can get back on track. I'm clutching tightly to that thought. It's been painfully hard having so little contact with Justin since Christmas, and I hate this feeling of being so distant. Going from inseparable to short, sharp emails and five-minute phone conversations has been like losing a limb.

'It's time's like this I'm actually *glad* to be eternally single,' Issy replies. 'You Brown girls sure know how to get shat on from a great height.'

Issy hasn't had so much as a one-night fling in the last eighteen months, let alone anything more. Drunken snogs are her speciality, but nothing ever goes further. She's adamant she's holding out for Mr Right, the man she'll marry and ride off into the sunset with.

'Well,' I say, cutting Issy off before she says anything that starts Hope off blubbering again, 'you can stay here for as long as you need to. The futon in the spare room's not all that comfy, but you're very welcome to crash on it. And right now I'm going to get you a glass of your own. Have some more wine and watch the end of *Frozen* with us. That'll make everything seem a bit brighter.'

That set Hope off crying again. She's never been an especially girly girl and in her current state, the thought of princessy Disney films was probably enough to push her over the edge.

'I'll need more than one glass of wine to get through *Frozen*, no matter how big it is,' Hope says.

'You make it sound like an endurance test rather than an animated film.' Issy laughs, but not unkindly, as I move into the kitchen to fetch a glass. 'It's hardly scaling Everest!'

'It might as well be. You two are bloody obsessed with that film. Even the kids at school have had enough of it now.'

Hope works with Issy and me at Clarke Road Primary, teaching the Year 4s. She never planned to go into teaching – falling into it out of necessity rather than a vocational calling – but jobs related to her degree in visual arts are few and far between. At least this way she's able to use her imagination in the classroom now and again, even if there isn't as much freedom as she'd like. Creativity's not exactly a priority in the curriculum these days but Hope's eye-catching display boards are always spectacular, a talking point with staff and pupils alike.

I peep around the doorframe, mock horror on my face at Hope rejecting my favourite film of all time. '*Frozen*'s not a fad, it's a way of life! It's a story of sisterhood and love for all ages. And it's one of the best films to sing along to. There's nothing like belting out 'Let It Go' at the top of your lungs to make everything better.'

'Excuse me if I've not quite got your level of optimism,' Hope mutters, just loud enough for me to hear.

I can see her shivering from here, and I've a sneaky suspicion that it's not just her body responding to the chilly temperature in the house. Maybe the realisation that she no longer lives with her gorgeous girlfriend in a modern, city-centre apartment but is crashing out with her baby sister in what is little better than student digs is hitting home.

'Anyway, I'm not sure the neighbours will thank us,' Hope says wryly. 'We're hardly Little Mix, are we?'

'Ah,' I reply with a smile, 'but that's the best thing about living near the university. Everyone else on the street is a student. Most of them aren't even back until the end of the month, and the ones that are will either be out in town or having a party involving something far more raucous than the three of us pretending to be Elsa.'

'I think you secretly love it,' Issy says breezily, attempting to stop Hope snuffling. She wafts a box of pastel-coloured tissues in Hope's direction. 'Even you've got to admit that despite being the bad guy, Hans is a hottie.'

Hope pulls a lemon-yellow tissue from the box, a rose-coloured fan appearing as if by magic to take its place.

'I'm a lesbian,' she states, in case anyone's forgotten. 'And even if I wasn't, I don't think I'd be resorting to animated characters.'

She blows her nose noisily into the tissue. It sounds like a steam train heading into a tunnel.

'I've always had a thing for Flynn Rider,' I admit, handing my sister the full-to-the-brim glass of wine I'd poured her. 'I think it's his chiselled jaw. Maybe if I grew my hair a bit longer and threw it out of my bedroom window I'd get someone like that to climb up it. Mind you, it'd take years to grow. It's the one major downside of curly hair, every centimetre in visible growth is actually three.' I finger a strand of hair ruefully.

'I don't think there are any Flynn Rider lookalikes wandering around South Yorkshire looking for plaits to climb up, so the slow growth of your hair is the least of your worries. Anyway, you're not looking for a man, are you?'

'I'm most certainly not,' I reply brusquely.

Issy's mentioned on more than one occasion that she thinks getting 'under a man to get over a man' might be a step forward, but it hasn't occurred to me. I've not so much as looked at another male that way. I don't want to, because no one else can possibly compare to Justin. How could they? We've got ten years of shared history. He's my first love. My first everything, in fact. Anyway, we're on a break, we're not broken.

'After what happened with you-know-who, I'm not putting myself out there,' I say. I'm not sure of my status anyway, there's no noun to describe someone who's on a break. 'I'm not ready to lay my soul bare to any man, not if all they want to do is trample over it.'

I've said these lines so many times that it's a well-rehearsed speech, but the doubtful looks on both Issy and Hope's faces make me wonder how convincing I actually am. Maybe I should say them with a bit more oomph.

'Come on, let's get this film back rolling,' says Issy. 'And is this wine mine?' she asks, gesturing to the full glass sitting on the mantelpiece. 'Because I can feel myself sobering up by the second, and tonight I plan to get very, very drunk.'

*

We're all glued to the television screen as the tinkly piano starts up and Elsa sadly climbs the snow-covered mountain, her purple cape trailing through the snow behind her. Even Hope's transfixed, although she'd never admit it.

'I love this song,' Issy says, pulling a cushion closer to her stomach. 'Even though I must have heard it a million times, it still gets me right here.' She points to the centre of her chest, pulling an over-exaggerated sad face.

'That's why Elsa's so popular,' I say. 'She gives up everything to be true to herself and doesn't give a damn what everyone else thinks. She's a much better role model than the sappy princesses of old. She's spunky.'

'Did you seriously just use the word spunky?' Hope shakes her head in disbelief. Her eyes already look hazy; the crying and the wine a lethal combination. 'That's cringe-worthy, no one uses that word any more. Plus, it's one of those icky words that makes my skin crawl. That and 'moist'.' She grimaces.

'But Elsa *is* spunky. It's the perfect word to describe her.'

'Whatever.'

The misfit princess runs through the snow-covered land singing about her new-found freedom and how she can finally be the person she truly is rather than who everyone else expects her to be, and before long all three of us feel every ounce of the ice queen's angst as we sing along to 'Let It Go'. Elsa removes her glove and conjures magical wisps of ice from her hands and we shout the rousing chorus at the top of our lungs, well past caring what the neighbours think. We're out of tune and Hope isn't entirely sure of the words, but we don't give a damn. It's fun.

'It feels good to sing, doesn't it?' Hope says out of the blue. Her cheeks are flushed now, the pinkish hue making her appear much less frail than she'd looked when she arrived. 'To let rip and shout. Kids do it all the time, but as adults we're expected to have found other ways to express ourselves. But the truth is, nothing compares to getting everything out of your system by having a good old yell.'

'Letting go,' says Issy solemnly, before realising what she's said and dissolving in a fit of drunken giggles.

'I read something somewhere about singing being good for the soul,' I recall. 'Didn't it say people who sing live longer? Or were happier? I can't remember, but it was all positive.' Funnily enough, I'm feeling better for singing too and my words are spilling out at an incredible pace. 'We've all had a tough year. I've been low since Justin went to America, even though the sensible part of me knows that taking a break was the only option. That doesn't make it any easier though, I'm still wondering if he's on a date with some American beauty or out on the pull. And Hope, who knows? Maybe Amara *will* come round and realise you need to be together in time, but right now you need to put yourself first. Don't look at me like that! I know you think I'm fussing, but I want my only sister to be happy.'

I reach over and squeeze Hope's hand, one small pulse that carries an infinite amount of love.

'And Is, I know you're happy being single, but I saw your face when your sister told you about her latest scan.'

Issy swallows, and part of me wishes I'd kept quiet. This is a sensitive subject. But it's too late now, it's already out there, so I carry on regardless. 'You're going to be the most amazing mummy one of these days, when the time is right. The best.' Issy's lips form an O, and I think she might cry, so I quickly move on. 'But for now, all three of us need to pick ourselves up and take control of our own happiness. It's like Elsa says, we're free! Who knows where we'll be in a month, let alone a year. We need to increase our happiness, channel the good emotions.' I'm on a roll, fire in my belly and well-lubricated by the wine. There's no stopping me now.

'And how do you suggest we do that, oh wise one?' asks Hope, her voice acerbic.

'A club, an informal choir. Make Friday nights a musical spectacular and sing ourselves silly! Think how good it feels to shout and laugh and forget about all the crappy stuff.' I beam, convinced it's a winning idea. 'We should make it a weekly event, a celebration of the weekend and being happy on our own rather than out in the meat market that doubles as town on a Friday night. It's got to be better than having your bum pinched by some drunken chancer out on the pull, and if it raises our spirits too then it's a bonus, surely? What do you reckon? Isn't it the best idea ever?'

I wait for their response, fully expecting them to throw back a string of reasons why it's a terrible idea. The pause is excruciating.

'Oh, go on then,' says Issy finally, knocking back the last of her wine. 'But no more people. The last thing I want is a house full of strangers on a Friday night.'

'And no more *Frozen*,' Hope adds emphatically.

'Okay,' I agree, knowing this is as much enthusiasm as my sister's likely to muster. 'But can I ask Connie if she fancies it too? Four people isn't too many and she could do with a boost. She's hating her job and she's fed up with being hit on by sleazeballs every time she goes out. This could be exactly what she needs.'

I grin and a small squeak of excitement slips out despite myself. I'm so looking forward to this. I haven't been part of a club since I left the Brownies.

'The Singalong Society for Singletons,' I say wistfully. 'To moving on and letting go!'

Chapter Two

Friday 16th September
The Lion King – Connie's choice*

'Are you sure we'll have enough food to go round?' Hope asks. She looks doubtful, which is ridiculous seeing as the table is laden – correction, *overloaded* – with snacks.

Seriously, there's all sorts of goodies spread out on it, from breadsticks to sausage rolls to the black forest gateau centrepiece (my idea – apparently they're due a resurgence, according to the supermarket magazine I shoved in my trolley on a whim last weekend). There are also four blue-and-white-striped cereal bowls overflowing with a variety of crisps and savoury snacks, three bottles of wine, the remnants of a bottle of Jack Daniels, a six-pack of Diet Coke and the token punnet of raspberries Connie insisted made an appearance if she was going to come. She's always been a health freak, although she goes wild on a Friday night and allows herself a small amount of carbs. How we've been friends for twenty years is beyond me. Junk food is too good to go without, in my opinion.

'Are you joking? There's tons. It's only us three and Connie, we're not feeding an army returning from battle,' Issy replies.

'And we're only five minutes from the supermarket if we need anything else. It's not like we live in the back of beyond.'

'You don't think I should just nip out and get…'

'No,' I answer. I ensure I'm using my school voice, firm and decisive. 'We've got plenty. There's pizza in the oven too, remember, and there's that tub of chocolates from the end of term on top of the kitchen cabinet if we want anything sweet later on.'

'Ooh, I forgot about those,' Issy says, licking her lips with anticipation. 'Bagsy me the coffee creams.'

'I don't think anyone'll be fighting you for those,' Hope replies, pushing forward onto her tiptoes to try and reach the metal container from on top of the kitchen cupboards. Issy had insisted they be put well out of the way to avoid temptation after the three of us had broken the seal and eaten a generous handful each during the culmination of *Frozen* last Friday. 'But I'm taking the toffee fingers out and putting them to one side. They're my favourites.'

She nudges the tin down from the ledge, her fingertips edging the container forwards until it tips and she has to quickly read-just her arms to stop it falling to the floor with a clatter. She looks puzzled as she shakes the tub. 'I'm sure there were more left than this,' she says, peeling back the lid to reveal a very sorry-looking layer of multi-coloured wrappers that barely cover the silvery bottom of the tin. 'Own up, who's been secretly raiding the choccies?'

Issy looks guilty and when she speaks her voice is unusually soft and meek.

'It was me. I couldn't help it. There wasn't anything else sweet in the house and I had rotten period pains. So I took them upstairs, got back into bed and ate them. I only meant to have a few, but it was last Saturday when I had that phone call from Penny. It scared me to death when she said she'd been bleeding – I couldn't get the thought that she might lose the baby out of my head. I needed something to cheer me up and a ridiculous amount of chocolate and the box set of *Friends* was my only hope.'

'You should have told me you were struggling,' I say. I'm trying to sound light, but it takes a whole lot of effort not to sound miffed. 'We're supposed to support each other. You could've come to me.'

'I couldn't,' Issy explains, twisting her silver ring around her finger. 'I wasn't up for talking about it and I'd have only felt guilty if you'd seen me pigging out. All I needed was a wallow and a sugar kick – you know how it is sometimes. Look, I'll go and get another box of chocolates now if you want. If we mix them in with what's left it'll be fine.'

'It's not about the chocolate!' My nerve endings are tingling, and not in a good way. 'If you'd told me what was the matter, I could have done something. I could have *helped*. There was no need for you to be cooped up alone in your room all day when I was here, willing to listen.'

Issy smiles sadly and it breaks my heart. 'But what could you have done, Mon? Nothing. All I needed was a duvet day and to stuff my face. I had a sleep, had a cry and then pulled myself back together. It was no big deal.'

'I could have listened,' I insist. 'Even if that's all I could have done, I could have listened.'

'But I didn't want to talk,' Issy answers patiently. She speaks slowly and deliberately, as though explaining something to a small child. Maybe the teacher in her is coming out too, it's obviously a quirk of the trade. 'It was too raw. It's nothing personal against you, but it was easier for me to hide away and cry it out. I needed to get my own head around it, that's all. Anyway, everything's fine with Penny now. It was just a scare.'

A wave of sadness floods through my body, as though my blood's running cold in my veins. There's nothing Issy wants more than to find the love of her life and start a family, and the news that her little sister is having a baby had hit her hard. That Issy hasn't got a partner at the moment is irrelevant, the maternal instincts are still chewing away at her. The constant pressure from the glossy magazines she greedily devours doesn't help either, what with their never-ending reminders of ticking body clocks and staged photos of celebrities parading their precious new arrivals around the flawlessly landscaped garden of their luxury mansions. I can only imagine how hard Issy finds it having such a desperate longing within her but being unable to do anything about it. It seems terribly unfair.

When Penny announced she was pregnant it had come as a shock to everyone. She's only seventeen, and a young seventeen at that. There had been no talk of a boyfriend, no late nights, no tell-tale signs of illicit secret liaisons. She's doing well at college and keeping on top of her studies – everything had been pootling along the same as it always had.

Then one blazing hot day at the start of the summer holidays Issy had received a phone call from a terrified Penny crying that she didn't know what to do, that her parents were going to kill her when they found out she was pregnant. She was already four months gone by that point, the hint of a bump just beginning to show on her tiny, child-like frame, and Issy had been torn between the need to support her sister and the all-encompassing desire to give in to the internal pain that demanded she shut down and hibernate.

But Issy's too kind-hearted a person to hold a grudge and when that natural mothering instinct kicked in, it kicked in hard. She'd gone with Penny to break the news to their parents, who hadn't managed to hide their initial distress and disappointment. She'd taken her to the GP, who confirmed the pregnancy and attended the first hospital appointment, where the trainee midwife had taken three vials of blood, and a scan which showed that, yes, Penny was eighteen weeks gone already. The radiographer had said he was ninety per cent sure the baby was a boy.

And Issy had smiled along, excited about the prospect of becoming an aunt, even though every one of these steps served to remind her of what she didn't have.

Then last weekend Penny had been passing clumps of dark-brown blood, convinced she was having a late miscarriage because she didn't have what it took to be a good mother. This was the call that had pushed Issy to attempt to eat her way through a tin of chocolates designed to keep a family's sweet tooth in check for a month.

'You've been incredible. More than incredible. You've been the best sister Penny could have wished for,' I assure her, although I'm scared I'm going to cry. I can feel those first tell-tale prickles. It reminds me of the time I had acupuncture for sciatica, the little needles making pinching sensations, but this time it's in my eyes rather than my legs. I concentrate on breathing in through my nose, not wanting my sadness for Issy to show. I can't break down. I've got to step up and be strong. 'And you're going to be the best aunt too. When that little lad arrives, he's going to want for nothing.'

'He deserves the best,' Issy says vehemently, 'and between us we'll make sure he gets it. Penny's going to go to special classes that prepare teenage mums for motherhood – how to change nappies and make up bottles and all that practical stuff – and Dad has put in a request to reduce his hours at work. He's going to look after the baby two days a week so Pen can continue with her A levels. It's not ideal, but we're making the best of it.' A glimmer of something that looks like sadness passes over her face, before Issy literally snaps herself out of it, closing her eyes tightly together and when they pop open again they are a fraction brighter than they'd been only moments before. 'She's not the first seventeen-year-old to get pregnant, and she won't be the last. It is what it is.'

'She's lucky to have such a supportive family. My mum would have gone apeshit if I'd got pregnant at Penny's age,' I say, imagining how horrified mum would've been if Justin and I had announced an unplanned pregnancy at seventeen. 'Who am I kidding? She'd go apeshit if I got pregnant now without a ring on my finger first.'

Issy sniggers. 'Well, we all know how much your mum loves a wedding. Anyway, keep taking those little round pills every day and you'll be fine. No babies for you anytime soon!'

'I'd need to have sex to run the risk of pregnancy and there's no fear of that,' I say glumly. 'I don't think there'll be anyone in the near future either. I'm just not ready to put myself out there again. The thought of getting naked in front of a stranger fills me with dread. I don't want some random guy looking at my wobbly bits and judging me! I'm going to have to wait until Justin gets back and see if he wants to work things out.'

Issy wrinkles her forehead in disagreement. 'You've not got any wobbly bits, except the bits that you want to wobble.' She jiggles her ample bosom to clarify her point. 'And you're utterly gorgeous. Any bloke in his right mind would kill to be with you, but for some crazy reason I don't understand, you don't see what everyone else sees.'

'You're only saying that to be kind.'

'It's the truth. You're right – I'd say it even if it wasn't because I love you – but it is.'

'I'll pay you later.' I laugh, embarrassed. It's hard to take compliments, especially now when I'm feeling so dejected, but at least it shows Issy isn't deliberately shutting me out. That's a small blessing.

However, I'm glad when the timer buzzes to indicate the pizza needs rescuing from the oven. Grabbing the oven gloves, I quickly whip out the pizza stone, noticing the cheese topping starting to turn a burnished crispy brown rather than the stringy golden goo we love.

'Phew, that was close,' I add, nodding towards the pizza.

'What time's Connie coming?' Hope calls through. She's in

31

the lounge watching *Coronation Street*, and I can see her through the open doors. She's propping up an enormous stack of cushions behind her, trying to get comfortable.

'She texted to say she was leaving work quarter of an hour ago, so she should be here any minute. Just in time to grab a slice of pizza,' I answer as I rummage around the cutlery drawer for the elusive pizza cutter. 'If she's having a wild night of carbs and cheese,' I add.

The doorbell rings as if on cue and I rush to greet my oldest friend. Not for the first time I'm blown away by her beauty. She looks radiant standing in the doorway with the peachy light reflecting off her long wavy hair, the early-evening sky a vivid orange wash behind her. Near the roots Connie's hair is the same dark shade it's always been, but the ends are dip-dyed a vibrant peacock blue. Last week they'd been scarlet. Colour suits her, but I wonder if this constant reinvention is a sign that Connie isn't sure who she wants to be. She's like a teenager playing around with her image to see what suits her best. I want to tell her that she doesn't need to change, that she's already incredible as she is, but know that even if I did she'd only play down my words as I did with Issy's.

'Hi!' we exclaim in unison, embracing each other in a warm, squishy hug.

The weekend was about to begin, and it couldn't start soon enough.

*

'I do love *The Lion King*,' Connie says with gusto as the disc whirrs to life in the DVD player. 'It's got so many catchy tunes. That's why when you invited me to join the Singalong Society it was the perfect choice. I can't believe how long it is since I last saw it.' Her eyes sparkle with anticipation, full of a childlike fervour.

'It's for *kids*,' Hope says derisively. 'I doubt there are any other groups of twenty-somethings spending their Friday nights watching cartoons. I'm telling you now, next week we're moving on to a *real* film. I've had enough saccharine Disney to last me a lifetime.' Her eyes narrow as she chunters on, her grudge against Walt and his successors in full swing. 'All that sappy 'happily ever after' piffle,' she tuts. 'It bears no resemblance to real life.'

'Disney isn't just for kids,' I answer defensively. Hope dissing Disney feels almost like a personal insult. 'It's for all ages. There's always a serious issue buried under the princesses and castles.'

Hope doesn't look convinced.

'This one was based on *Hamlet*, you know,' I continue, gesturing towards the TV. 'And no one would dare to call Shakespeare piffle. He's the greatest playwright that ever lived.' I pause, grabbing a fistful of salty peanuts from the small topaz-blue bowl on the coffee table that divides the room in two. Suddenly I'm starving. 'There's a reason he's on every exam syllabus going, why his work will always be a key component of any literature course. He's a storyteller, pure and simple. One of the best that's ever lived.'

I pop a pinch of peanuts into my mouth, crushing them between my teeth with a satisfying crunch. The burst of flavour dances across my taste buds.

'Yeah, yeah, yeah. Whatever. We all know you're a geek when it comes to this kind of thing.'

Her dismissive words are softened by the affection written on her face. Hope had never understood my love of literature. In fact, Hope probably couldn't remember the last time she'd read a novel, whereas I constantly had at least one book on the go, usually more. It was another reminder of how different the two of us are, yet the bond between us has always been undeniably strong despite that. We're tight. Unbreakable. Just as sisters should be.

'Keep an open mind about this one, please?' I beg.

I know it's ridiculous, but I feel under pressure to ensure tonight works out as planned. It's not just the four of us getting together to watch a film, it's a chance for us to take control. Plus, as the inaugural meeting of The Singalong Society for Singletons, it has to go smoothly. The whole point of the thing is to inject some joy back into our lives.

'Well, I've not seen it since I was about ten, so maybe I can be won over. But don't hold your breath. I'm a tough nut to crack.'

A piracy warning flashes onto the screen, signalling the film's about to start.

'And don't we know it,' I reply boldly, poking out my tongue in retort.

Issy tries and fails to stifle a giggle as she pours the contents of a share-sized bag of cheese and chive crisps into a bowl, whilst Connie looks impassively at the floor to avoid getting involved. Typical.

'It's my choice of film next week,' Issy says. 'I'll be sure to choose something that isn't animated, if it means that much to you.'

'Ssh,' I hiss in a stage-whisper. 'It's starting.'

The rousing opening note of 'The Circle of Life' roars from the television causing each of us to sit straighter in our seats. Captivated by the power of the Zulu chanting and the sun rising over the desert, we settle down, prepared to be transported to Africa via a cute little lion cub and a soundtrack full of belting songs.

*

'Aww, look at baby Simba! He's petrified!' Issy exclaims as the future king is held aloft in the showy presentation ceremony. 'Bless his little cotton socks. He looks like he's got the weight of the world on his shoulders.'

'If we knew what was going to happen in life, we'd all look like that,' Hope answers, wearing a grim expression. 'It's no wonder babies cry all the time. All that lies ahead of them is a lifetime of slogging their guts out at work, trying to please other people, and being shat on from a great height by people who said they'd love them forever.' She frowns and I frown back at her. After everything Issy's just said, she has to start talking about babies. Sometimes Hope's mouth runs away without her brain.

Hope turns away, offended by the insinuation in my look, and I'm instantly ashamed of being so hard on her. She might be abrasive, but my sister wouldn't purposefully hurt someone.

Poor Hope. She's done her fair share of feeling sorry for herself during her first week at the house. It's all been textbook behaviour for the broken-hearted – listening to sad love songs on repeat, pigging out on extra-large bars of Galaxy and moodily sulking around the place in her tartan flannel pyjamas. I know the drill, I've been living it myself for long enough.

'Pause it a minute,' Hope says quietly, opening the door to the square of carpet at the bottom of the stairs that we optimistically refer to as the hall. 'My bladder's about to burst and it's better to stop the film now before it gets going.'

No one dares mention the tears that are brimming in her eyes – we're all well aware that Hope hates to appear anything less than rock solid. She's spent her whole life coming across as strong and dependable, so I can only imagine how hard it is for her now, trying to keep up that front when she's so obviously crumbling.

'And I'm going to get some more nibbles,' Issy says, pushing herself up off the sofa. 'That glass of wine has gone right to my head. I need something to soak it up.'

'There's some kale crisps in my bag,' Connie offers. In Connie's mind this is a generous proposition, in Issy's less so. 'If you want something a bit less fatty, I mean. They don't taste the same as normal crisps, but they're much better for you. Feel free to help yourself.'

35

She tries to hide it, but I spy Issy's eye roll. She's not the type to buy into these faddish foodie fashions. If she wants crisps, she wants actual crisps, made from glorious carbohydrate-riddled potatoes and full of saturated fat that'll fuzz up her arteries. Like me, Issy believes junk food is one of life's guilty pleasures. And Friday nights definitely call for junk food, no two ways about it. 'We could always get take-away?' she suggests hopefully. 'I'm sure the Indian down the road put a flyer through the door just last week...'

I gawp in her general direction. Even I'm stuffed, and that's saying something because I've got a massive appetite, but the waistband of my jeans is digging into my bloated stomach and it's not a pleasant sensation. I'm tempted to undo the button, that's how uncomfortable it is. 'We've just had pizza!' I exclaim.

'And your point is?' laughs Issy. 'I could eat a horse right now. And I'm sorry, Connie, but your kale crisps aren't going to cut it, I'm afraid.'

'I don't fancy those either,' I confide in a conspiratorial whisper, scrunching my face up in distaste. 'I don't know how anyone can eat them. They look like crispy bogies.'

'We don't need a take-away,' Connie says resolutely. 'Let's eat what's already out.' She gingerly reaches for a Wotsit, the gaudy powdery orange flavouring smearing over her fingertips. She pulls a face as she nibbles it, as though it might bite her back. The cheesy puffs are a far cry from the kale crisps, that's for sure. 'If no one else is eating my crisps, then I will.'

'You're welcome to them,' Issy mutters, resigning herself to the fact she's been outvoted on the take-away. 'But hang on a minute. I'm going to get my dressing gown, it's bloody freezing in here tonight.'

A young Simba is frozen on the TV screen, surveying the vast pridelands with his father. He looks so small and insignificant against the sprawling savannah.

'This film always did make me sad,' Connie starts, nodding towards the screen. 'But I've got such an empty feeling in my stomach right now. Not hunger,' she adds quickly. 'I always felt a bit like Simba. My family fell apart when Mum died. She'd been the lynchpin holding us together and once she was gone, it felt like there wasn't any point any more. Dad tried his best, bless him, but he didn't have a clue how to deal with a pre-pubescent teenager. It was like he was waiting in fear for the moment he'd have to go to the chemist and buy me sanitary towels. And the rest of the family, my aunts and uncles, they were there at first, bringing lasagnes round for us to keep in the freezer and phoning on Sunday mornings to see if we wanted to join them for a pub lunch in the Peak District. But really, we were alone. Mum arranged all the family parties, the barbecues, the day trips to the seaside where we'd pile in the car with a cricket set and a cool box... Once she was gone, it all stopped.'

Tears pooled in her eyes, threatening to spill down her cheeks with the slightest of blinks and I instinctively reach out to hug my friend. As I pull her in close her heartfelt sobs reverberate through the both of us.

'I know it's stupid to cry over a film, but it touched a nerve, you know? Simba's so brave, setting out to face the world alone. Look at me! I can't bring myself to leave Sheffield. I even stayed here for university when everyone else buggered off to Leeds and Manchester.'

'Simba was running away,' I correct, brushing a tear from Connie's cheek with the pad of my thumb. 'And so was everyone going to university too, really. It's not the same thing.'

I think back to my own three years at university. I'd not wanted to go in the first place and I could have got a job in a school without the degree and the student loan that came with it. But I'd blindly applied to the same cities as Justin because I hadn't been able to bear the thought of being away from him. Which would be laughable, considering our current situation, if it wasn't so downright sad. As it happened we'd ended up staying in Sheffield too, so Connie certainly hadn't been alone.

Connie wipes the end of her nose against the cuff of her chunky-knit lilac cardigan, and takes a deep breath as through preparing to swim underwater. 'I needed to stay here for Dad, you know? He's not good at looking after himself. I dread to think of him trying to keep on top of the washing pile, and I don't think he knows how to turn on the hoover. He probably doesn't even know where the hoover is!'

She laughs, and even though her cheeks are now covered in a blotchy red blemish and her pure black mascara has smudged, leaving her with panda eyes, she still looks so incredibly beautiful. There's a serenity about Connie, even in the rare moments like this when she's unravelling.

'Sometimes I dream of running away,' she admits. 'Breaking free. Going to Africa and building a school with a community. Pipedreams, I know, but what's the point of being alive if you're barely living?'

I place my hands on my oldest friend's shoulders and look her in the eye, hoping I can convey how wonderful she is. 'You're doing plenty of living. You dance. You're passionate about food, even though none of us like those vegetable crisps you keep trying to foist on us. And you're a wonderful daughter; staying in Sheffield because of your dad proves that. But you know, if you've got a dream, you should go for it. You're young! You're single! You're *free!* Make the most of it. Go to Africa and build that school, if that's what you want.'

'But what about Dad? He'd end up living on mouldy toast and wearing dirty clothes. He's never had to survive on his own. He lived with his parents until he married my mum, and then there's been the two of us for the last fifteen years.'

'There are cleaners and there's internet shopping and all sorts of other services that make life easier. You can pay people to do pretty much anything these days.'

Connie looks wary. 'I'm not sure he'd like having people coming into the house.'

'What'd happen if you met someone? Or if you got a flat in town, a bachelorette pad? He'd have to manage then, wouldn't he? I'm sure he's not expecting you to stay at home forever.'

'He'd have to find a way, I suppose.'

Although the words themselves border on positive there's a dejected air to Connie's tone that leaves me with a sneaky suspicion she'll harbour her dream but do nothing about it. I hope she'll surprise me by being proactive. Sometimes there's justification for being a little bit selfish.

'Just think about it, yeah? Don't give up on your dream too easily. Neither your mum *or* your dad would want that. Nor me.'

Connie pulls at the soggy sleeve of her cardigan. It had swamped her frame to start with and now they're damp, the cuffs hang down way past her knuckles. 'I'll think about it.'

I squeeze Connie's hand, soft as playdough from the expensive hand creams she's devoted to. 'That's all I'm asking.'

Hope and Issy bundle back into the room, their booming voices breaking the serenity. I can't help thinking that maybe it's time we all took some chances. What's that saying, 'a life without risks is a life half lived'?

'Hakuna Matata' begins to play, the jaunty tune sweeping us along until all four of us are singing along at the tops of our voices.

'Isn't it amazing how a song about farts can be so singable?' I giggle. 'I always thought it was hilarious how they got away with it.'

'That's what makes it so funny, it feels naughty.'

'You know you can't sing for toffee, right?' Hope says bluntly.

'Hakuna Matata!' Issy quips back good-naturedly, continuing to sing about Simba and the gangs' problem-free philosophy as he grows before our eyes.

Connie trembles, her shoulders quivering, and somehow I know it's a result of Simba's maturation and independence presented through this song.

'Okay?' I mouth silently, hoping my earlier support is enough to stop her feeling alone.

Connie nods. 'No worries,' she mouths back.

We quietly watch on, moving only to help ourselves to the limited selection of snacks and drinks that remain. It's as Mufasa's spirit sends the message to Simba to 'Remember who you are' that Connie begins to speak.

'I'm going to do it,' she announces, 'I'm going to find out about the volunteer programmes in Africa. It's what I want to do. It's what I've *always* wanted to do. If Mum could see me now she'd be devastated that I'm working in a stuffy office, typing endless numbers into meaningless spreadsheets. I want to make her proud. To remember who *I* really am.'

An excitable buzz fills the room as me, Hope and Issy fire question after question at an eager Connie.

'Do you get to choose where?'

'How much money do you have to raise? Do you need sponsorship?'

'When will you go? And how long will you stay?'

'I don't know!' Connie exclaims with a shrug and a laugh. 'I've only this minute decided to go for it. But tomorrow morning I'm going to start Googling, find out the most reputable charities and how to apply.'

'It'll be amazing,' Issy assures her. 'A once in a lifetime opportunity that'll make a real difference.'

'There's something else, too,' Connie adds. She has a fire in her eyes full of feisty determination that I've not seen in her since our last ballet recital. Naturally she'd had the solo, executing perfect fouette turns and pirouettes that made the kids in the junior classes sigh dreamily. 'I'm not putting off the teaching exams any more.' She looks directly at me, waiting for my reaction.

'No way.' I'm agog. 'You're finally going to bite the bullet and become a dance teacher? At our dance school?' I refer to it as ours, even though we're only pupils. We've been going there so long it feels like we have the right to stake some claim over it.

She shakes her head. 'I'm going to try and get a bank loan and start up on my own. It sounds ludicrous, I know. But there's got to be a disused factory somewhere in Sheffield that I can buy, or at least rent. Line the walls with mirrors, put up a barre, get a sprung floor laid… after that it'll just be upkeep and running costs. And if it doesn't work, then hey ho. At least I'll have tried.'

I can't help it, I have to hug her. In my excitement I go in with a bit more force than I'd planned, almost knocking her right off her feet. It's a good job all those years of ballet have worked on her core stability. She manages, just about, to stay centred and steady.

'I'm thrilled for you, Con, honestly I am. After all those years of nagging at you to do it. Miss Gemma will be too.'

Connie laughs. 'She'll never believe it when I tell her she'll need to get revising the exam syllabus. I think she'd given up hope of me ever putting in for them.'

'We'd *all* given up hope,' I say. Out of the six of us in our class, Connie's the only one who has what it takes to teach dance. The rest of us can hold our own in the showcases, years of practice have ensured that. But there's something in the way Connie moves – something elegant and strong and inspiring – that sets her apart from the rest of us. She was born to dance, no two ways about it.

'Who'd have thought *The Lion King* would be so inspirational, eh?' jokes Hope, a glimmer of a smile passing over her face. 'Maybe you're right, Mon. Maybe it's not just for kids after all.'

Chapter Three

Friday 23rd September
The Sound of Music – Issy's choice*

'So, what's it to be?'

We all look on eagerly as Issy whips a DVD out from behind one of the tatty patchwork cushions that rest along the back of the sofa, straining our eyes to make out the title of the musical we'll be watching.

'*The Sound of Music!*' Issy proclaims, a triumphant smile on her face. 'I love this film. It makes me think of my Gran – she was a huge Julie Andrews fan.'

Connie didn't seem to share Issy's enthusiasm. 'Oh no, it's the one with the nuns, isn't it?' She clutches her head in her hands in a dramatic fashion. 'I've never liked nuns. They scare me.'

'Maybe I should become a nun,' Hope muses. 'My love life's in tatters since Amara decided she didn't want me any more. And at least I wouldn't have to worry about bad-hair days if I had to wear one of those floppy sheet things on my head.'

I raise my eyebrows in despair. 'Floppy sheet things' indeed. 'They're called wimples. And you'd be a terrible nun. You're far too cynical!'

'And an atheist,' Hope adds, deadpan. 'That might be a bit of a problem.'

'This is a real tear-jerker, too, from what I remember,' Connie says, trying to rein us back in. 'I'm going to need tissues, aren't I? *Again.*' She rifles through her patent red over-the-shoulder bag. Folders, notepads and something that looks suspiciously like a Filofax from the 1980s peeps out of the top, and as she pulls a small rectangular packet of tissues out she adds, 'It always gets to me. I don't know why, but it does.'

'Because it's depressing, that's why.' That was Hope.

'It's not depressing, it's *emotive*,' Issy insists. 'And based on a true story too. That poor family… imagine how horrific it must have been.'

'Yeah, imagine having to wear clothes made from floral curtains the colour of wee. It must have been dreadful.' The withering look Issy throws Hope cuts her off before she can rant further about the Von Trapps, which is just as well. If she finds her stride, who knows what she'll belittle next?

'Let's start,' I interject, taking the disc from Issy and inserting it into the DVD player. 'It's not a short film and it's already almost nine. And even if you don't like the storyline, you must admit it's got a classic score. 'Edelweiss'? 'Do Re Mi'? 'My Favourite Things'? They're exactly the kind of songs the Singalong Society was founded for. I think I'm going to get a glass of water to go along with my Riesling because I'm going to need it to hit those high notes.' I hurry to the kitchen, fill a glass with cool tap water and pick up a packet of chocolate digestives for good measure. 'Julie Andrews might make it sound easy, but it's not. Not for us ordinary folk.'

'Be quick, it's starting,' Issy yells, but I'm already back in the room in time to see the long-lens opening shots of the stunning Austrian landscape appear on the screen. Beautiful castles, rolling green hills, clear blue water – and Julie Andrews sporting helmet hair and a shapeless pocketed pinafore.

Before long we're all drawn into the film, laughing at the gentle humour and singing the anthemic songs with all our might. Maria's love song to her favourite things causes us to dissolve into fits of laughter; Hope declaring that anyone who claims doorbells as one of their favourite things deserves to remain in a convent for all eternity.

'What would you sing about, then? What amazing things are there that help you when you feel bad?' Issy asks, although she's been as exposed to Hope's doom and gloom almost as much as me. There doesn't seem to have been much that's raised Hope's spirits since she moved in.

'White wine, most likely,' Hope replies, raising her fourth glass of the evening to the air in a toast.

'Friends,' I add, without missing a beat. 'Friends who accept you as you are, warts and all.'

'Good one,' Issy says approvingly. 'Mine would be weekends. How about you, Con? What fills your heart with gladness and makes your soul sing?'

'My spiraliser.' Connie nods seriously before clocking our disbelieving stares. 'What?' she adds naively.

'We live in a world with marshmallows and blossom trees and mojitos and…' I flounder for something that might be worthy of being Connie's favourite thing, '*Kiehl's hand cream*, and you say a spiraliser? How much have you had to drink?' I tease, knowing full well she's not yet touched a drop. Connie rarely drinks to excess. It's all linked to her desire to be super-healthy and lean.

'What can I say? I've been living off courgetti lately,' Connie says with a shrug. 'But the hand cream is a good shout. I've a feeling I'm going to be really grateful for it come November.'

At the mention of hands, I notice Hope look down and study hers, her knuckles bumpy and red where she's scratched the eczema-inflamed skin. She's not been able to leave it alone lately and when I'd questioned her about it she admitted to liking the uncomfortable sensation of her nails peeling the fine, flaky top layer of skin away. She claimed it felt cathartic, but the red, raw marks looked painful, with even the children in her class noticing the angry scarlet patches in contrast to her creamy skin tone. Hope had always suffered with eczema. It had a nasty habit of flaring up when she was stressed, and since she and Amara had finished, she was incredibly stressed. More than stressed, she was bereft. She wasn't sleeping, was barely eating… she was a mess.

I snap myself out of my distracted thoughts, only just registering the glint of suggestion in Connie's voice. 'Why November?'

There's a theatrical pause where Connie looks like she might physically burst. Her face is shining with unadulterated joy. 'I'm in!' she finally exclaims, clapping her hands together in miniature, yet excited, applause. 'I wanted to tell you straight away, but by the time we'd set up the DVD and got ourselves ready to watch it…' her voice trails off, but the animated glow remains.

'Wait, what?' I do a double-take. I'm at an actual loss for words. 'You mean Africa? The volunteering?'

Connie nods. 'Yes! I spent all of Saturday searching the websites of different charities, and one – well, as soon as I saw the page I knew I was meant to contact them. It was everything I hoped for. They're renovating a school for a community in rural Uganda. *I'm* renovating a school in rural Uganda. Can you believe it?'

She's full of glee, her eyes flaring with passion. She looks so utterly, completely alive, lost in a world of possibility. Not unlike Maria, actually, who's gallivanting with the children on the screen, wielding the ugliest puppets in the history of cinema; although I make a mental note to rewind to this song at the end so we can all yodel along like the Lonely Goatherd. But this is Connie's big moment and although I can't stop my twitching foot from tapping against the lounge floor, I'm desperate to know more.

Hope obviously is too.

'Can anyone offer to go? Or did you have to have an interview? And how much is this costing?' she asks, firing questions at a rate of knots. I silently will my sister not to rain on Connie's parade by making her overthink this decision. I can't remember the last time I saw Connie looking as vibrant, as full of life, as she does right now. I love Hope dearly, I absolutely do, but I can't help but wonder if Hope*less* would have been a more appropriate name for her, given her constant state of negativity.

'Anyone can apply, as long as they're in good health and meet the criteria. And yes, I had an interview over the phone on Wednesday evening. The project leader rang and asked all sorts of questions about why I wanted to do it, if I felt I'd be able to cope with seeing the extreme poverty, any relevant experience I had…' She looks shamefaced. 'I must admit, I didn't have much I could say to that one. Data input hasn't really prepared me for manual labour in temperatures similar to a Yorkshire heatwave. And yes, I have to raise some of the money myself, because they're a charity. The cost of flights and accommodation for a team of volunteers would obviously eat into their funds, when this way it can be put to much better use helping people in need. But that's where the next surprise comes in, and this is even more incredible than me going to Africa in the first place. In fact, you'll never believe me when I tell you.'

A small indent appears in her cheek, a cheeky dimple coming out to play.

'Stop teasing!' I squeal, unable to bear the tension a moment longer. 'Get on with it!'

'Well, I was dreading having to tell Dad. I didn't want him to get upset at the thought of me going away. But I steeled myself up and broached it with him over tea last night, and he said I couldn't have timed it better. Apparently my mum had a life-assurance policy that she'd taken out 'just in case'. And in her will she left it all to me, with strict instructions not to touch it until my twenty-fifth birthday…'

'And that's next week!' I'm aware of my voice squeaking, but my head's whirring at how fast this is moving. Issy's laughing at me, probably because my jaw is literally gaping open in wonderment. I must look so gormless right now. 'I was always jealous of you being the oldest in your class. You'd get the best choice of sweets from the birthday tin in assembly at primary school. By the time it got to my birthday in July there were only ever those fruit lollies left, and they'd always be a bit sticky as they'd been there all year. The year I was six I couldn't even peel the wrapper off.' I remember the disappointment clearly. Inedible sweets as a birthday treat would be hard enough for me to comprehend now, let alone at that age.

'Yes, the policy matures next week, and that's how I'm paying to go. Actually, there's enough there to pay what I need and still have some left over when I get back. Maybe even enough for a deposit on a small dance studio, if I can find a suitable space.'

I shake my head to try and take it all in. Africa? Dance teaching? Where has this newly geed-up Connie come from and what's she done with my best friend?

Connie continues, her voice proud and brimming with positivity. 'No more losing my cool when the spreadsheets don't add up, no more days in a grey boxy office block with an air conditioning system that rattles like a haunted house at a funfair. I'll be in Africa, doing something worthwhile. And then, hopefully, when I get back here I'll be doing what I love.'

'It sounds blissful,' I smile, because it does. It absolutely does. Thanks to her mum's foresight to plan ahead she was going to get the chance to live out her wildest dreams.

'I'm over the moon for you, I really am,' Issy adds, her words full of affection.

'It's going to be a real adventure. You'll come back a woman of the world,' I say with pride. 'And it's brilliant that your dad was so supportive. All that worry for nothing, and I'm sure he'll be just fine. Don't forget to tell him I'm only ten minutes' drive away if he needs a hand with anything. Get him to ring me, promise? I can do a mean beef stew which'll be perfect for those

47

November evenings.' My mouth waters at the thought of the stew, the solidity of the meat and the juicy, chunky winter vegetables an irresistible combination. 'But I don't want to iron,' I say obstinately. 'Anything but ironing!'

I catch Hope scrutinising my dress, a navy cotton number covered in pretty ditsy-print flowers in a variety of shades of pink. Now I look more closely it does have a decidedly crumpled air about it. I probably should have left it hanging on the shower rail a bit longer to ensure all the creases had dropped out.

'Thanks, Mon,' Connie says softly, 'He'll really appreciate that. Me too, of course. And although I can't wait to go away, I know the minute I arrive I'll be thinking of Sheffield, missing our catch-ups over coffee and cake on Ecclesall Road.'

I have to laugh. It's only me that indulges in the creamy cappuccinos and doorstop wedges of Victoria sponge. Connie normally has a sparkling water and a banana.

'But especially this,' she says, gesturing around the room. 'These past few weeks have been so much fun. And life-changing for me, too. Your encouragement was exactly what I needed to spur me on and I don't think I'd have believed I could do it myself without you three believing in me first. So thank you. Thank you, thank you, thank you.'

'You make it sound like you're going forever,' I say worriedly. 'You won't be gone too long, will you?'

I know I'll miss her dreadfully when she's out of the country, even if it is only for a matter of weeks. Although Issy has become my partner in crime, that's mostly through circumstance. She's a wonderful friend, but Connie and I have been a duo since childhood and there's something incredibly special about a friendship that's lasted twenty years. There's no need for pretences between us and we've forged an open honesty that makes for an easy relationship.

The other beauty of a long-term friendship is how there's no need to explain the difficult moments from our pasts. I already know how horrific it was when Connie's mum died. I'd been there with her that September day when Connie had been called to the headmaster's office to receive the news. And Connie had been there for me during my own challenging moments too, not just recently but also during my parents' separation and the subsequent messy divorce, and through Mum's transitions to Mrs King, then Mrs Peto, then Mrs Davies as she'd tried to find true love. What Connie and I have been through together transcends everything else. For all the friends I have, I don't have another friend like her.

'I leave at the end of October and it'll only be for four weeks, so I'll be back in plenty of time for Christmas. You're not getting out of getting me that Kiehl's hand cream that easily,' she jests.

'If you come back safe, sound and happy, it'll be the one year I don't begrudge paying crazy money for your luxury lotions and potions,' I reply with a half-laugh. I've never succumbed to the high-end products Connie swears by, instead bulk buying whatever's on offer when I go to the enormous chemist's in town, but Connie is the epitome of brand loyal. When she finds something she likes, she's with it for the long haul, which I suppose is the biggest personal vote of confidence I could have, considering how long she's been part of my life. From pigtails and scraped knees to lip gloss to jagerbombs, 'Mon and Con', as our dance teacher Miss Gemma always calls us, have come a long, long way.

I grin as Connie blows me a kiss. With her dip-dyed hair and bright red lips she reminds me of a pin-up girl. Not to mention her new-found confidence and self-belief.

'We've got a few more weeks yet before I go,' she says. 'Which is just as well as I have tons of stuff to sort out before then. There's injections for yellow fever and hepatitis A and I need to buy mosquito nets and anti-malaria tablets...' She's counting things off on her fingers as she reels off her list.

'Malaria?' Hope asks with concern. 'Don't people die from that?'

'I've been reading about it online. It spreads quickly out there, but it's easy to protect yourself with a course of tablets. I'm going to make an appointment with the doctor next week and see what else I need to do.' She grins at the thought. 'I can't believe I'm actually going to Africa!'

'You'll have the best time,' Issy says. 'And who knows? Maybe you'll find the love of your life out there too.' She waggles her eyebrows in a way that I presume is supposed to be suggestive but comes off as more pantomime baddie than sex siren. 'I've never really believed that true soulmates would live just a few streets apart.'

A scowl unwittingly creeps up on me. I can feel my jaw tightening in annoyance at the remark. Issy knows that Justin and I lived just around the corner from each other until he left. What's she implying? That he has a better chance of finding someone he wants to spend the rest of his life with now he's on the other side of the world because it'd be too easy if true love was ready and waiting on the same street, or the same estate, or in the same city?

'Stop looking at me like that, Mon,' she says. I feel like a small child being summoned and chastised. I suppose I should be grateful she's using actual words rather than a whistle à la Captain von Trapp. 'You know what I mean. It's a bit *convenient* to fall in love with someone who has the same background as you, lives in the same area, went to the same school… I'm not saying it can't happen, I'm sure it does, but how many people settle for someone just because they're right at hand? There are seven billion people in the world. It's highly unlikely the one true love of your life is even in Britain, let alone Sheffield! If people stretched their wings and searched the world for their partner, maybe there'd be more happy endings. Maybe less divorce, too.'

'And now you bring up divorce,' Hope says drolly, smacking the heel of her hand into her forehead. 'Nice one, Issy. Talk about double whammy.'

'I'm not speculating about specific cases here,' Issy insists, although it still feels as though this is aimed at me. 'I'm making the point that there's something to be said for looking further afield when it comes to romance, that's all. Not every boy next door is worth pursuing.'

'Hmm,' I murmur noncommittally. Issy's trying to dig her way out of this but she's so damn defensive. Why not just come clean and make it blatantly clear that she's referring to me and Justin? Although I come across as confident and perky and uber-positive, I'm a sensitive soul. My friends' opinions matter to me more than they realise, and I hate any form of conflict. It unsettles me, propelling me right back to the loneliness of mine and Hope's childhood bedroom where we'd lie awake as Mum and Dad argued downstairs, their raised voices seeping through the ceiling. They had been painful, lonely nights, and we hadn't had a Frauline Maria to reassure us with chirpy tunes about raindrops on roses. Hope, as the older sister, had allowed me to snuggle into the top bunk with her when the rows got particularly loud and frightening, but the memory was still there, ingrained deep.

One of the things that appealed to me most about Justin was his coolness. He was always on a level, not hot-tempered like my dad. He hadn't ever been the rash, impulsive type – at least, not until he went to live in Chicago with a fortnight's notice.

I miss him. We hardly speak these days, more broken up than on a break. The distance is one issue, the time difference another. It's all well and good having the technology to speak to each other, but we're both working long hours in demanding jobs. With the best will in the world, I don't have the energy to stay up until midnight to talk to him after working with the children all day, and when my alarm goes off in the morning he's tucked up in bed ready to get some well-earned shut-eye. Our lives aren't aligned any more, it's unsettling.

Mother Superior belts out 'Climb Ev'ry Mountain' and I close my eyes, singing it like a hymn or a quiet prayer. I feel as though

I have a hundred mountains to climb myself, because however much I try to kid myself that everything's okay, I'm not over Justin Crowson. Not by a long stretch.

*

The audible snuffles of the four of us ring out through the room as the final credits roll. We sound like a herd of baby hedgehogs.

Issy's the first to pull herself together. 'I think we should be celebrating Connie's bravery. She's going to a whole other continent. We should drinking fizz. I'm going to head down to the corner shop and see if they've got a bottle of something nice. This calls for Prosecco.' She slaps her hands against her thighs as though she means business.

Hope groans, clutching the flat plane of her stomach. 'I've drunk far too much already, and I'm meant to be getting my hair done in the morning. The last thing I want when I'm hung over is someone pulling at my head.'

'Just have a small glass, then, just to make a toast,' Issy replies sensibly, grabbing her jacket from the small brass hook on the back of the door. It's supposed to be specifically for my keys but Issy is forever using it to hang up her coats. She insists it's easier than taking her jacket to her bedroom upstairs and I've given up complaining about it. At least it's marginally tidier than her previous 'coat rack' – when we first moved in together I had to have words with her for constantly leaving her jackets draped over the back of the armchair in the lounge.

'So long, farewell!' Issy calls tunefully. She's in a good mood, if her spritely voice is anything to go by. There's no sign of remorse for her scathing comments.

'Auf wiedersehen, goodnight,' Con and Hope sing in response as the door slams behind Issy. The three of us remain slumped in our seats, even though the DVD has already returned to the menu. We're emotionally exhausted after being squeezed through the musical mangle, but on the screen Julie Andrews has her arms flung apart in wild abandon. I could do with some of that wild abandon in my life right now.

'She didn't mean it, you know,' Hope says, giving me a meaningful look. She's obviously registered my mournful body language and thinks I'm still salty over Issy's earlier comments, when I'm actually battling with my inner heartache. 'Not in the way you thought she did, anyway.'

I look away, unwilling to talk about it and nervously twist a spiral of hair around my index finger. It's a tell-tale sign I'm bothered about something and Hope knows it. I was forever twiddling my curls back in junior school when I was bullied for the gap between my front teeth and I couldn't help but play with my locks when our parents had separated. It soothed me somehow, the texture of my hair against the length of my fingers. When Justin had upped and left, Hope had passed comment that she was surprised my hair hadn't fallen out from being fiddled with so much.

'She's *supposed* to be my friend,' I begin. 'She's *supposed* to support me no matter what, not undermine my feelings. Issy knows exactly how hard this year has been for me, how much it's hurting being apart from Justin. To make out we were never meant to be because of *geography*...' I shake my head in disbelief, the bulky curls dancing raucously. 'It hurts.'

'She wants to protect you, that's all,' Connie says kindly. Lovely Connie, always seeing the good in people, even when they're being as bitchy as can be. Although maybe Connie was right about Issy wanting to stop me from being hurt by Justin for a moment longer. She'd made it clear that in her opinion it'd make more sense to cut all ties. 'And you know it too, if you're being honest with yourself. She wanted to rip Justin apart limb from limb when you told her he'd run off to America with just a few days' warning. It was a good job he was already on another continent because I'd have had serious fears for his wellbeing otherwise.'

I chuckle despite myself and Connie and Hope do too. No one would choose to get on the wrong side of Isadora Jackson. She has no qualms about sticking up for what she believes in. And I'll say this about Issy – she definitely believes in being loyal to her friends.

She'd been in Edinburgh last Christmas to visit her brother when everything had blown up with Justin, only returning to Cardigan Close on the morning of the first day of term to collect a tote bag of resources and a gorgeous old hardback copy of *The Secret Garden* that she planned to read to her class at home time. I hadn't wanted to tell her what a mess I was in via text – I had Connie and the dance girls rallying around me, and what could Issy have done from Scotland? – so it had to wait until we got home from work that evening for me to fill her in on my new relationship status. Issy had gone through the roof.

'Connie's right,' Hope said. 'Issy's different to you, that's all. She says what she thinks and damn the consequences. But everyone's fighting their own battles, Mon. You know how hard she's finding it watching her sister's bump get bigger each week when all Issy wants is to be a mum. Penny's bump's unavoidable now, I saw her in Tesco the other day. She's bloody huge. Like one of those egg-shaped toys we used to have, the ones you flick and they wibble around a bit but always end up upright.'

'A weeble,' I say with a fond smile. 'We begged Mum to buy them for us from a car boot sale at the leisure centre, remember?'

Hope nods, a nostalgic smile passing across her face. It gives her a softness that's rarely seen. 'We played with them all summer long. What I'm trying to say is don't be too hard on Issy. She wants what's best for you, and she thinks forgetting about Justin and finding someone new is the answer. Maybe she's right. Even you don't seem to know what's going on.' She shakes her head in despair and the corners of her lips curl up, full of pity. 'It's like you're in purgatory, not sure if you're coming or going. It's not right.'

54

'It's not as easy as that, though, is it? Not when you really, truly love someone.'

I catch my sister's eye. We're both familiar with the ultimate pain of rejection, when what was supposed to be forever turns into a cutting and unrequited love. I'm not over Justin. Hope isn't over Amara. And no matter how hard we try, it's impossible to move forward when an overwhelming surge of longing is constantly pulling us back to them.

'No,' Hope replies, with a despondent sigh. 'It's not as easy as that.'

The instantly recognisable sound of Issy's key in the lock snaps us out of our misery and into action; Connie gathering the wine glasses that litter the lounge and putting them on the kitchen worktop, Hope removing the disc from the DVD player and me lighting the floral-scented candle that sits in front of the wood burner. It wouldn't be long until that'd be lit too, although we swore we wouldn't cave until November hits. But there's a definite nip in the air as Issy opens the door, a draught sweeping into the house that causes me to fold my arms over my chest in a self-made hug. Autumn's already making its presence felt, what with the temperature dropping and the first burnished leaves already tumbling from the trees in Endcliffe Park.

'I'm back!' Issy calls cheerfully. 'And I managed to get some fizz. There wasn't much choice so it's only cheapo Cava I'm afraid, but it'll do the job.'

'Thanks, Issy,' Connie replies, obviously moved.

There have been times in the past where the pair of them haven't seen eye to eye. Connie had been jealous of Issy for monopolising so much of my time. Plus, I know she feels that as my longest-standing friend it should have been *her* right to house-share with me, but she'd never felt able to leave her dad, until now. It's taken time (not to mention an effort on both sides) but over the years Issy and Con have learnt to rub along together, and small acts like this go a long way towards turning their acquaintance into a proper friendship.

The cork pops with much merriment and as I raise a toast my earlier wobbles are forgotten. I'm unable to hold back the excitement any longer – things are about to change for my oldest friend.

'To Connie, who's taken the first step on a fantastic adventure!' I bellow loudly.

'To Connie,' everyone echoes as we chink our glasses together.

Remembering my earlier promise to find 'The Lonely Goatherd' again, I scroll through the menu on the DVD. The buttons on the remote don't want to behave and it takes a few minutes to get it set up, but once I do there's a sarcastic cheer from the girls.

Hope moans. 'Not those freaky marionettes again. Please, no.'

'You love it really,' I grin, turning it up. 'And it doesn't matter if you don't know the words because anyone can warble a yodel. Come on, let's sing!'

Despite Hope's protest, she is soon yodelling along with the rest of us, Connie and I linking arms and whirling in a dance that's more Cotton-Eye Joe than an Austrian reel. It's liberating to be spinning, the room passing by in a blur while we make nonsensical noises that we pass off as singing. Most of all, it's fun and we don't stop twirling and yodelling until Julie Andrews herself flops at the end of the song.

'Lay-ee-odl-ee-odl-oo!' sings Connie, determined to get in one last hoorah. The booze has gone to her head, I can tell by the way her strong yet thin legs are wavering. She gives in to the wobble, landing on her bottom with a giggle and a bump. My own head is muzzy with the hazy rush of alcohol and a light-headedness from pushing my burdens to the back of my mind.

'Oh!' Issy exclaims. Her wide eyes are glazed and her hand springs up to her mouth as though in surprise. 'I almost forgot to tell you!'

'Tell us what?' Hope asks. Her words are slurring but that

doesn't stop her topping up her glass with the last of the Cava. 'It sounds exciting.'

'Well,' Issy begins tentatively, 'you've got to promise you won't get mad at me.'

That statement alone makes my stomach lurch. Nothing good can come of anything that starts with 'you've got to promise you won't get mad at me'.

'I thought it'd be fun to get a bigger group of us together,' she continues. 'To spend time with more people like us who want to drink and eat and watch cheesy musicals rather than go into town every Friday night and waste half the evening queuing to get served at the bar and the other half snogging undesirables.'

'Hey!' I retort with mock annoyance, 'Speak for yourself! Snogging is not in my remit.'

'What have you done?' Hope asks. Her abrupt tone suggests her excitement is subsiding and there's a decidedly resigned look on her face.

We all face Issy, who's nervously biting her bottom lip between her teeth, the epitome of remorse. Whatever it is, she knows we're not going to like it. My heart pounds as I fear the worst, although I've no idea what 'the worst' could be.

'When I was at the shop buying Connie's Cava, I bumped into the guys that ran that drama workshop with my class.' My heart's still racing. It might sound innocent enough, but she wouldn't be looking nervous if all that's happened is that she's bumped into a few luvvies buying their Friday night beers. 'So, we got talking and I happened to mention the Singalong Society,' Issy blurts, closing her eyes as if that'll protect her from the onslaught of wrath she knows will follow.

'WHAT!'

'You're kidding me.'

'You mean you openly admitted we spend our Friday nights doing this?'

Issy raises her hand to stop the questions. 'They're really into drama and singing – they did a brilliant job getting the kids engaged in this Egyptian-inspired role-play. Ray and Leon they're called, I think. Maybe it's Leo. Or Liam. Definitely Ray, anyway.' Her cheeks flushed pink. 'I thought they might want to join us, because of their theatrical background and all, so I invited them to join us next week. After all, it does feel good to sing and they were really nice guys. I wouldn't have invited them if they weren't. And we're friendly, and the house is easily big enough for a few more people.'

'You didn't,' I groan. 'Please tell me you didn't.'

I'm sure Ray and Leon/Leo/Liam are fine once you get to know them so it's not like I have a personal vendetta against them, but The Singalong Society for Singletons works because we all trust each other. We know each other inside out, warts and all. I don't like the idea of people rolling up willy-nilly.

'I only mentioned it in passing!' Issy replied indignantly, taking in my weary look. 'But they seemed really keen to join us. And the older one, Ray, he's a total dreamboat.'

Ah, so now we're getting to the crux of it. Issy's got a crush.

'Basically you invited them because you fancy them,' Hope said drily, taking a large gulp of the Cava she'd said she really didn't want.

'One of them, not both of them!' Issy huffed defensively. 'Don't make me sound like a hussy.'

'I can't believe you told people about The Singalong Society,' I say, shaking my head. I'm surprised by the feelings I'm harbouring – a glut of shame and a pinch of betrayal. 'And the other week you were all 'oh, let's keep it small, I don't want a house full on a Friday night.' What's changed?'

'I thought it'd spice things up a bit,' Issy replies. 'A bit of fresh meat to enjoy.' She must be tipsy, that isn't a phrase I ever thought I'd hear Issy utter. 'Plus,' she adds as an afterthought, 'I did check and they're both single. They meet the criteria, so where's the problem? Plus, it'll be a way for you to meet someone new, to take your mind off Justin.'

'I thought you fancied one of them,' I say, rolling my eyes at her gall. 'What's actually happening is you're setting me up on a blind date with the one you don't fancy so the three of you can laugh yourself silly at how inept I am with the opposite sex. Great. That's just great.'

'It's more than great, it's inspired,' Issy assures me, totally missing my sarcasm. 'They're decent guys. At worst they'll be a laugh to have around and at best you could find the love of your life.'

I sigh, resigning myself to the fact that there's nothing I can do but accept it. I have no idea who these men are or what they look like, let alone how to contact them. I'm literally at Issy's mercy.

'You've done some things in your time, Issy, but this one really takes the biscuit.'

Wrapping my favourite baggy cardigan tightly across my body and slipping my feet into my well-worn ballet pumps, I step into the dark shared passageway that runs between our house and the next in the terrace. I need some air. My head's swimming, both from the bubbles and the thought of being set up.

Considering how cold it is in the house, out here it's a surprisingly mild and clear night. I lean against the gate post, staring up at the stars. There are so many of them, vibrant against the pitch-black nothingness of the sky. It looks like the floor at work when we've bitten the bullet and had the glitter out.

And although I'm raging at Issy for making decisions on my behalf – on behalf of the whole Singalong Society for Singletons – I can't deny the butterflies in my stomach, fluttering madly at the prospect of next week's meeting.

Chapter Four

Friday 30th September
Grease – Hope's choice

'They've got to be gay. *Got to be.* How many straight guys do you know that are into musicals, hmmm?' Hope was adamant about this, and, as usual, once she got a bee in her bonnet she was unlikely to change her mind. 'And don't look at me like that. Don't forget, I'm the lesbian around here. Some of my best friends genuinely *are gay.* I'm not being judgy, just stating the facts.'

There's a flicker of my sister's stubborn side in the comment, and the pompous in her assurance that she's right. That's Hope all over. In her mind, she is never wrong.

'So, straight men can't like musicals, is that what you're saying?' I counter, mostly in banter (but partly to get her back up – when she's on her soapbox she's top drawer entertainment). 'What about Andrew Lloyd Webber? He's been married to three different women and he's devoted his whole life to musicals. Done pretty well out of them too, or so I'm led to believe.'

I wink, secretly proud to have usurped her.

'Ah yes, but he's still got that camp aura, hasn't he? He's all *over-the-top-theatrical,* like a bad guy in a Bond film. Even his

smile looks sinister.' Hope gurns by way of an unflattering imper-
sonation, but ends up looking more like a *Spitting Image* puppet
than 'The Lord'.

'If the wind changes you'll stay like that,' I quip, quoting one
of our mum's favourite sayings before cheekily adding, 'Although
it could be an improvement.'

Hope tuts in my direction, obviously deciding she's going to
be the mature one in this instance and take the higher ground.

'So you're admitting men who like musicals aren't necessarily
gay?' Issy says, joining me in the goading.

'But they are camp,' Hope says defiantly. She juts out her jaw.
'And *most* of them are gay.'

'What about Gary Barlow?' Connie says, looking up from the
magazine she's been idly flicking her way through to join in the
debate. She never normally reads the glossy magazines – after all
they tend to be full of gossip about C-list couples holidaying in
the Bahamas or declaring the latest reality TV star to be too fat,
or too thin, or too *something*. But she'd seen Issy's guilty pleasure
lying on the coffee table and been sucked in by a strapline embla-
zoned on the cover; something about an actor who'd run a
marathon to raise funds to build a hospital in Brazil. That was
much more up Connie's street; that and the health section.

Connie held up a full-page close-up of the Take That singer.
He was smiling out of the magazine, a cheeky twinkle in his
blue-grey eyes.

'He had that show on Broadway based on *Peter Pan* and didn't
he have something to do with the *Calendar Girls* musical too?
He's huge in the world of theatre,' she says triumphantly, ogling
Mr Barlow for just a moment before placing the magazine on
the side table. 'Gary's not remotely camp. And he's got kids!'

'Doesn't mean a thing,' Hope sniffs, although there's a defeatist
tone to her voice that suggests she knows she's fighting a losing
battle. 'When this Ray and Liam arrive, I bet you anything they're
as camp as Christmas.'

'Ray's certainly not camp,' Issy says, almost as though she's insulted at the very suggestion. 'He's got quite a deep voice, actually, one of those friendly Lancashire accents. Like that tall guy that hosts that gameshow on ITV.' She looks distracted at the thought, and I suspect it's more to do with Ray than the guy on the telly.

'We'll see soon enough,' Hope answers, her eyes narrowing to slits as she bobs her head like a wise old sage. 'We'll see soon enough.'

*

Half an hour later, the rat-a-tat-tat of a knock at the door causes all four of us to jump from the sofa as though a shotgun has gone off in the vicinity. To be honest, that's about the only thing that'd normally dislodge our slouched end-of-week bodies from their relaxed position.

I plump the cushions in readiness, keen to make a good first impression. Two unknown men coming to the house had forced us to clean more thoroughly than usual, and I'm amazed at the difference it makes. I didn't want a few squashed cushions spoiling the new streamlined look. Everything seems lighter, brighter, and the fine layer of dust that perpetually coats the mahogany mantelpiece is gone, swept away by a frenzied Hope armed with one of those old-fashioned canary-yellow dusters with bright red blanket-stitch trim. She'd made a trip into town especially to bulk-buy cleaning products from the dodgy woman on the market. She always threw in a tin of air freshener for free, so our lounge now smells of Woodland Glow, which is actually more like a smoky bonfire.

That we're pushed into cleaning at the prospect of guests proves we're not used to opening our home up to people, in fact it tends to be an unwritten rule that the house is our haven, free from unnecessary guests. Other than the four of us in the room, only Issy's dad (who'd been invited purely because he was handy with a screwdriver and could fix the dodgy curtain rail that had been hanging off in my bedroom) and the no-longer-to-be-spoken-about Justin had been in the house in the past year. Oh, and the emergency plumber who came to sort out the pongy smell that had emanated from drains over bank holiday weekend.

At least these guests were invited through choice, sort of, and there's a safety in numbers – four of us and only two of them. If they look even the slightest bit shifty they're not getting over the threshold and we'd made a promise to kick them out sharpish at the merest hint of any sleazy comments, despite Issy's assurances that they weren't the sort to try their luck. But the rest of us had stood firm and made a pact we weren't going to stand for any nonsense.

'I'll get it!' Connie says, jumping nimbly over the back of the settee. She manages to look effortless and graceful, like an Olympic hurdler.

'It's not even your bloody house,' I hear Hope grumble quietly under her breath.

'It's not yours either,' mutters Issy tersely, with considerably less subtlety.

I'm torn between the two of them. I know Issy genuinely feels for Hope, sympathising for how cut up she is over Amara, but the pair continually rub each other up the wrong way. Issy finds Hope's mood swings draining and Hope can't bear that someone else wants to have the final word. Put bluntly, they're not a house share partnership made in heaven.

'Sssh,' I hiss, glaring in a way that I hope encourages the two of them to behave. 'They're here.'

We turn to face the door, eager to see Ray and Leon/Leo/Liam. Issy's neck strains until she resembles an over-alert meerkat keeping a watchful eye out for potential predators. Or prey. Hope's trying, and failing, not to stare at the doorway – probably desperate to see if they're as camp as she predicted. And I'm not going to lie, I'm curious too.

The tension in the room lifts as a beaming Connie leads the guests through. Her dark eyes are wide and wild, her huge grin infectious. This is a good sign. Connie's an excellent judge of character and if she's smiling then it's unlikely we've unwittingly let two axe-wielding nutters into the house.

I literally step backwards as they enter, a feeble attempt to make more space in the lounge so it's not wall-to-wall bodies, but I bump into the TV cabinet in the process.

Ouch ouch ouch.

Which might be exactly what the men walking in said when they fell from heaven, to paraphrase the cheesy chat-up line, because following behind Connie are two of the best looking specimens Sheffield has to offer. The first has a mischievous half-grin on his face, as though he's an out-and-out rascal. His medium-brown hair's brushed back off his face into a well-coiffured quiff and he looks relaxed in a baggy hoodie and trackie bottoms, as though he knows he looks good and doesn't need to make an effort. If I had to hazard a guess, I'd say he's a similar age to me and Connie, or maybe a bit younger. The second guy's definitely the older of the two, probably closer to thirty. He's well groomed in a less conventional way and has a strong, angular jaw. His dark hair is styled much the same as his friend's, but there are a few wayward wisps of curl around his ears that soften the style. He's sporting a jet-black earring in his left ear lobe and is moulded into a battered black leather jacket that wouldn't look out of place on Danny Zuko himself. Two deep-grooved crinkles crease his forehead as he smiles, and his eyes flicker like fireflies.

My money's on the first one being Ray. He's got the more obvious good looks out of the two and Issy's drawn to pretty boys. Most importantly, they don't look like axe murderers, whatever axe murderers are meant to look like. And they're definitely not camp. Hope'll be gutted.

'Hi,' says Issy, all Bambi eyes and dopey smile as she propels herself forwards. She's leading with her chest, sticking her boobs out until they're impossible to miss. They're hard enough to miss at the best of times – she's all curves. Reaching right past the younger guy who Connie's introducing as Liam – I'd have to find a way to remember that, Issy had insisted he was called *Leon* – she offers her hand to the T-bird clone.

I watch with interest. Having seen my friend in action enough times to know when she has her sights on someone, I recognise the behaviour. It's classic Issy on the prowl. Not only has she flicked her caramel locks so they fall seductively over her shoulder, she's also licking her lips. There are no greater clues than that. She's in flirtation mode, pure and simple.

'Good to see you again, Ray,' Issy practically purrs. She says his name as though it's ten syllables long, drawn out and loaded. I try not to stare, uncomfortable, and notice Hope does the same. It's like we're imposing on a private moment. However, I can't help but watch, there's a tangible spark between them, electricity surging through the room. It's like the science lesson where you put your hand on that big silver machine that sends electricity through you and your hair stands up on end. I was always roped in to 'volunteering' to demonstrate to the class because I looked like a lion with my long curls sticking out at all angles.

'You too, Miss Jackson,' he says politely. He smiles a crooked smile. 'It was good of you to invite us.'

Issy laughs, the tumbling cascade of hair almost down to the small of her back as she tilts her head back. 'Call me Issy,' she says. 'I'm off duty.'

'Issy,' he repeats with a barely there nod.

'I'm Monique,' I say, raising my hand, 'but most people call me Mon.' The teaching assistant in me just won't rest, and when I demand attention I automatically find myself with my arm aloft, mimicking the action I spend all day modelling for the infants. 'And this is my sister Hope, and you've met Connie and

Issy. We've already eaten but there are loads of takeaways around here if you're hungry and a really good chip shop near the round-about at the end of the road. And we've got plenty of nibbles,' I add gesturing to the enormous bowl of popcorn sitting proudly on top of the newly polished table. It's never been so shiny. I quickly reach down to scoop the one rogue kernel that's had the audacity to fall onto the immaculate unblemished surface.

'Popcorn is perfect,' grins Ray. 'And a must-have for film night.'

'Singalong Society,' Connie says automatically. 'Singing is part of the deal. Maybe a bit of dancing, too. But no singing and you're out, I'm afraid.'

'The Singalong Society for *Singletons*,' Issy corrects with a smirk. That was for Ray's benefit, no doubt.

He shrugs out of his jacket, revealing a tight white V-necked t-shirt and, more importantly, tattooed arms. There's nothing Issy likes more than a man with tattoos and I notice her sharp intake of breath as she scans the dark black markings over Ray's fair forearms. She might just as well have melted into a puddle because it's blindingly obvious she fancies the pants off him. Poor guy, if she's set him in her sights he doesn't stand a chance.

'So what is it we're watching? *Grease*?' Liam asks. He's found a space on the settee and already made himself comfortable, sprawling against the arm of the settee with his legs tucked up under him. He's cuddling one of the patchwork cushions to his stomach, like a child with a teddy bear, an act that only makes him seem younger still. Maybe he's closer to twenty…

I'd almost forgotten he was there, what with trying to dissect Issy and Ray's greeting, and in a bid to reduce the guilt I sink into the seat next to him.

'Mon,' I say, offering my hand. My bangles jingle together as he shakes it.

'Liam Holly,' he says. 'Although that's not my actual surname.' I must look perplexed, which quite frankly I am. 'Why would you introduce yourself with a surname that's not your actual surname? It's the sort of thing men in clubs do when they're on the pull.'

I realise too late what I've insinuated and wince at the faux pas, but Liam just laughs.

'I've done that a few times myself,' he says with a relaxed shrug. 'Although I've given false first names too when I've wanted to be anonymous. Mitchell Bowyer's my go-to,' he says with a smirk.

I'm taken aback by both his audacity and his honesty. 'Wow.' I don't know what else to say.

'My actual surname's Raistrick but no one ever remembers it, so I go by my stage name now.' He pulls his hood up, until all I can see of his hair is a small triangular peak at the front. 'That's the one you'll need to remember for when I'm famous.'

I can't tell if he's joking or not, so I offer a smile, which I hope comes across as pleasant and interested. Everyone else is making small talk around us but I'm desperate to start the film. Liam's the polar opposite of me, what with his fake names and self-assured nature.

I cough to get everyone's attention. 'Are we ready to start the film?'

'Always ready for a musical,' Ray says chirpily. 'Especially as Connie said we're watching *Grease*. Proper classic.'

'One of the best,' Connie agrees. 'There's not a bad song in the whole film.'

'And John Travolta looked so *hot*,' Issy says. She fans her face with her hand to prove exactly how smoking she found Danny Zuko, before looking pointedly at Ray and adding, 'I've never been able to resist a man in a leather jacket.'

Ray blushes, obviously flattered. Interesting. There's definitely an attraction between them.

We settle down: Liam, Hope and I squashing onto the small settee, Connie into the stiff-backed armchair, Ray flopping into a cross-legged position on the floor and Issy sinking into the faux-leather beanbag I brought down from my room. Danny and Sandy are fooling about on an otherwise deserted beach and the familiar strains of the *Grease* theme tune start up, accompanied by bubblegum cartoon imagery. Ray immediately joins in with the script, his mock American accent as smooth as melted chocolate. 'This is the main man Vince Fontaine beginning your day in the only way, music, music, music...'

We all look at him dumbstruck but he continues regardless, flawlessly spouting the script.

'What?' he asks innocently after he finishes the spiel. Five pairs of eyes are on him.

'Nothing,' Connie laughs. 'It's just... you know all the words!'

'*Everyone* knows all the words,' Ray replies. 'It's *Grease*!'

Connie shakes her head. 'Normal people don't know the Vince Fontaine bit. They're still swooning over Danny and Sandy in that mega naff intro. Only die-hard *Grease* fans know the Vince Fontaine bit.'

Ray holds up his hands in concession, grimacing just slightly with what I assume is embarrassment. 'What can I say? I'm a fanatic. When I told Issy musicals were my life, I wasn't joking.'

'He's obsessed,' Liam confirms, reaching forward and grabbing a handful of popcorn. His eyes, however, don't leave the TV.

'I wouldn't go as far as to say obsessed. I just take them seriously. But then I have to – it's my job to take them seriously.'

'Oh, do you do other acting besides the workshops for schools?' Issy asks. 'That sounds so glamorous!' Her eyes are large and full of flirtation, as though she's channelling Betty Boop.

'I act a bit,' Ray replies modestly, running the tips of his fingers through his dark hair. Small crinkles appear at the corners of his eyes as he smiles at Issy. 'Amateur mostly, so nothing you're likely to have heard of. I've been involved in a few different local theatre groups and now I've moved onto small independent productions – they organise the visits into local schools. I'm not giving up hope of getting my big break one of these days, though, unless I'm too old, that is. The touring companies are usually only interested in the big-name celebrities – either that or young hunks straight out of drama college. Us old hands say they only get the big roles because they look good on the advertising,' he adds, but with a good-natured air rather than a bitter one.

'You'd look amazing on a billboard,' Issy replies breathily, throwing in a quick flutter of her eyelashes for good measure. I sigh. She's really going all out this time. It's borderline cringe.

'Well, I don't know about that, but I'll take it!' he laughs, his enormous grin flashing two ruler-straight rows of glistening pearly white teeth. I bet he had a brace, I think enviously.

'Honestly, I'm not just saying it,' Issy continues, putting her hand up to her chest as though to convey her trustworthy nature. 'You've got a great look. Really great. The cheeky chappie smile the teeny boppers go wild for mixed with handsome good looks to win over the grannies.' She fingers her necklace and I know she thinks she looks seductive. 'I bet you've melted a fair few hearts when you're treading the boards.'

'Something for everyone, that's me,' Ray smiles jokily. He readjusts his t-shirt, straightening the neckline. A few cheeky chest hairs peep naughtily out of the V. Issy will have clocked them too and probably swooned at the sight.

'You'll get noticed, I'm sure of it,' Issy goes on enthusiastically. 'There are loads of stars out there who didn't get their big break right away. Don't they say rejection is a form of initiation, a way of weeding out the ones with no staying power?'

'Well, I've no intention of giving up,' Ray replies fiercely. 'Even if I never end up on a West End stage I need to know I've given it everything I've got. My mum's always said I'm dead stubborn and never know when to stop, but it's more determination, I think. When it comes to acting, I know what I want and I've got faith I'll get there eventually, even if it takes another ten years.'

'Stop gossiping you two,' Connie shushes, 'it's my favourite bit!'

Suitably chastised, we turn our attention back to the TV, where the T-Birds are lazing over the bleachers, begging for information about how far Danny had gone with the stunner he'd met at the beach. Cut back to the girls, their pink satin bomber jackets and below-the-knee circle skirts totally at odds with each other and yet somehow the ultimate in Rydell High chic, as they grill Sandy for the details on her summer romance; the immediately identifiable riff of 'Summer Nights' playing in the background.

'They're so different, aren't they, the sexes?' Connie ponders with a shake of her head. The electric-blue tips of her chocolate-brown hair shake with her. She's like a rainbow unicorn about to take flight. 'He's acting the big guy, pretending he got in her knickers and she genuinely believes he's a real gentleman who'll treat her well. Males and females are just too different. No wonder my relationships have all been over before they've begun.'

'It's no easier being a lesbian, believe me,' Hope cuts in. 'I don't think it's a gender thing, I think it's a human thing. We like to gossip and brag and make out that everything's rosy even when that's a million miles from the truth. And most of us are crossing our fingers and hoping for true love, even if we don't believe in it.'

I glance over at my sister, hoping to convey the love I feel for her. We've both been hurt badly, given every ounce of our hearts so freely, and now we're paying the price. And although it's not something I'd ever have wished for, in a strange way it's brought us closer together, what with sharing both heartache and a house.

Hope smiles, acknowledging the silent understanding between us, before saying, 'Right, I thought the whole point of tonight is that we're meant to be singing?'

Soon we were not only singing but dancing along to the upbeat tune, us girls warbling along with Rizzo and co and Liam and Ray playing up the machismo. We're all hamming it up, Ray going the extra mile by putting his jacket back on just so he can tug at the collar as he grunts along to the 'well-a well-a well-a uhh's. It's fun and, I have to admit, the boys being there adds something different. Whether it's because we don't know them or more down to their unbridled enthusiasm I don't know, but their showmanship and love of musicals is evident. Even Hope's joining in, her usual dismissive ways brushed under the carpet for the evening.

It is, however, nauseating watching Issy practically drool over Ray every time he thrusts his shoulder in time to the beat. He's a good looking guy, no two ways about it, but Issy's acting as though she's never set eyes on anyone as dishy before. That definitely isn't the case, Issy had shown me the photos of her sixth-form boyfriend Carl – he'd borne more than a slight resemblance to Zac Ephron and was absolutely gorgeous. I'm not convinced she's ever really got over him – she clams up every time she mentions him. And the only one of her many snogs that had progressed into a full-blown one night stand since we'd lived together had been a delicious French restaurateur called Olivier, who had cappuccino skin and eyes like Cadbury's chocolate buttons. Issy has high standards when it comes to looks. We screech our way to the crazily high final notes of *Summer Nights*, arms aloft like a group of shouty Statue of Liberties. At the end of the song Issy motions for us girls to come to the kitchen under the guise of getting more food. She's practically glowing and can barely keep the smile off her face.

'He's even better looking than I remembered!' she gushes, her voice little louder than a whisper. 'Seriously, I've not felt this attracted to anyone ever in my life before. I can't stop looking at him.'

'We'd noticed,' Hope says drolly.

'And he'll have noticed too,' Connie adds. 'You're not exactly subtle with all your talk of 'oh, you'd look great on a billboard' and 'women of all ages would fall at your feet'.' Connie places the back of her hand to her forehead, feigning a swoon.

Hope snorts.

'Am I being too obvious?' Issy looks mortified. 'I can't seem to stop my mouth running away with me. It's like I look at him and my brain turns to mush. My stomach's doing gymnastics and my heart feels like it's about to burst out of my chest. I know it sounds stupid and if one of you was saying this I'd be telling you to stop being so bloody ridiculous, but I've got this feeling about Ray.' I catch her eye. Her pupils are huge dark pools of Ray-fuelled lust. She gives a shy, embarrassed smile. 'I think he's the one.'

Connie, bless her, is full of encouragement. Hope and I, on the other hand, are considerably more wary. We've both become guarded when it comes to matters of love.

'You barely know him.'

'You fancy him, that's all. And that's perfectly okay,' I justify patiently. I don't want to appear embittered. 'But it's been so long since you've had an attraction to anyone. You've forgotten what it feels like. You're making this out to be something much bigger than it actually is.' I lean on the hard kitchen counter, trying to look authoritative, trying to be firm. 'It's lust, end of story. And by all means, have a bit of fun if he's up for it. Sleep with him if that's what floats your boat. But don't fall into the trap of thinking he's the one just because he responds to your flattery. All men love an ego rub.'

Issy looks crushed, the glow that had previously been on her face now fading. She's curling in on herself, a snail retreating into its shell. I've hurt her feelings with my own bluntness, pushed all my fears about love onto her and Ray's relationship, if you can call it a relationship when they've only met twice. But I couldn't bear for her to experience pain like I am right now.

'I thought you'd understand,' Issy says sadly. 'Out of everyone, I thought you'd get it. You always said you knew Justin was the perfect fit for you from the minute you met him. You've always been the one to believe in love at first sight.'

I scoff with forced laughter. 'And look how that turned out!' I sound hostile. Bolshie. I practically hiss the words. 'I was planning to spend the rest of my life with him and he left the country without giving me so much as a second thought. So excuse me if I tell you to be cautious. I don't want you to fall too deep and then end up feeling as shitty as I do now, because to be honest, I'm barely holding it together at the moment.'

Issy, Connie and Hope looked stunned by my sudden outburst, although goodness knows why. They must have noticed I was struggling. It would have been abnormal if I hadn't been after such an abrupt end to a long relationship, surely? It wasn't my fault they found it hard to believe that steady, reliable Mon was capable of falling apart. But I need to vent, just for that split second.

'Ray's not Justin, though, is he?' Issy says, not nastily but steadily. 'And I can't put into words how I feel about him, I just know that I feel it.' She reaches into the fridge, pulling out the carrot cake I spent last night slaving over. The acrid taste in my mouth makes it seem far less appealing than it had then, when I'd been unable to stop myself from licking the creamy leftover mix straight from the spoon. 'I'm scared that if I ignore it or try and hide from it I'll end up with some almighty regrets.'

I look up, my lips pursed tightly together. Who am I to tell Issy what she should do? I'm hardly the oracle when it comes to relationships, if recent experience is anything to go by. 'Then you need to go for it. If you think he's the one then go back into that lounge and find out one way or the other. Because if there's one thing I've learnt, it's that having regrets is the most painful thing in the world.'

By the time we're back in the lounge, the depleted snacks on the table really *are* ready to be topped up. It's just as well Issy's brought the cake through, three red and white barber-pole candles proudly standing tall out of the frosting-covered surface, the lights dancing off the silver foil that covers the cake board.

'It's Connie's birthday tomorrow,' I explain to the boys, as though the candles and 'Happy Birthday Connie' iced on top of the cake weren't enough of a clue. 'I figured a birthday just isn't a birthday without cake.'

'Too right it's not,' says Liam, producing a lighter out of his pocket and taking it upon himself to do the honour of lighting up the candles. 'Have you made this? It looks amazing. Better than one you could buy in a shop.' He looks genuinely impressed and I'm surprised to find I'm pleased to have his approval.

I was proud of my accomplishment – I'd never been much of a baker before. Justin had always been the more natural of the two of us in the kitchen, happy to offer advice on whether I'd be better to stir or fold the mixtures in my bowl, or if the cake tin needed greasing or not. I'd always muddled along, gladly allowing him to take the lead whilst I mooned over his good looks and floppy hair. It was funny how since he'd left I'd sought solace in baking. There was something magical and therapeutic about weighing out the ingredients and watching a sloppy mixture turn into something solid and delicious.

But this cake for Connie was a massive step up from the fairy cakes and chocolate- chip cookies I'd mastered over the last few months. It was much bigger, for starters, plus I'd had to go shopping especially to fetch what was needed for the Mary Berry recipe, which I'd plumped for because it was a reduced sugar option. I knew Connie would appreciate that, even though it was Friday and she'd allow herself to break her healthy-eating regime. I'd piped the cream cheese frosting as carefully as I possibly could and added the sprinkling of chopped walnuts to the sides of the cake with precision, love and care.

'Come on then, let's sing 'Happy Birthday' to the birthday girl,' smiles Ray. The chorus mingles with the *Grease* soundtrack – the film's still playing in the background. It's a mashup that doesn't really work, but no one cares.

As the traditional celebratory song draws to a close, Connie moves to blow out the tiny flickering flames atop the candles. Her brightly coloured hair falls forward as the wax threatens to drip down onto my masterpiece, and Issy reminds Connie to make a wish.

'I don't have anything to wish for this year,' Connie says happily. 'My dreams are about to become reality.'

We all laugh at how sappy that sounds, but as Connie explains to Ray and Liam how she's heading to Africa in a matter of weeks I make a silent wish on Connie's behalf. I wish we'd *all* have our dreams come true. Because Connie might have made her break for freedom, but the rest of us are still bound by our shackles, fearful of hurt and rejection; Hope afraid to contact Amara, Issy too scared to see if Ray feels the same initial attraction as her and me unwilling to pick up the damn phone and ask Justin if this is just a break or if it's the end of our road.

We all need to delve a little deeper and become a little braver – if we don't we'll never move forward from here. And we need to keep moving because standing still does nothing except leave you achy. Achy and alone.

Chapter Five

Friday 7th October
Chicago – Liam's choice*

There's a teetering pile of side plates and cereal bowls stacked up on the draining board. *Again.* I close my eyes and begin counting to ten, my attempt at keeping calm. I get to six before I burst. 'Why is it that I'm the only person in this house who bothers to dry up and put away?'

Hope shrugs dismissively. That annoys me even more. 'We're all busy.'

'Exactly!' I say, my exasperation evident in my tone. '*All* of us, me included. I know I'm only a lowly teaching assistant compared to you and Issy with your Qualified Teacher Status, but I'm knackered when I get home too. It's not like I spend all day looking forward to getting home and tackling the washing up.' I reluctantly reach for the brown and white checked tea towel and begin to wipe a bowl. It's pretty dry already. It's probably been there since breakfast.

'Speaking of Issy, where is she? She's normally back by now.' Hope glances around the kitchen, as though by doing so Issy will magically appear in a puff of smoke, like a genie from a lamp.

'She popped to the supermarket to get some frozen pizzas on the way home. I'm sure she won't be long, but you know what it's like on Friday nights. Half of Sheffield decides to go food shopping. It's bad enough trying to get a parking space, let alone getting to the front of the check-out queue.'

As frustrated as I am, I smile at the thought of Issy. She's been really lovely this past week, washing up excluded. Since my Justin-related outburst last Friday, she'd gone above and beyond to check I was holding it together. She'd bought me some little treats too, like the Ferrero Rocher she'd placed on my bed along with an invite to watch the rerun of *Bugsy Malone* that was playing for one night only at The Showroom, an independent cinema near the train station. It had been just the pick-me-up I'd needed, and she knew that. Musicals made everything a bit less raw, for a few hours at least.

It felt fortuitous that we had each other. We'd started working at Clarke Road Primary on the same day. Back then we'd both been enthusiastic and wet behind the ears, and soon become close friends as well as workmates. It's strange to think that if either of us had got a job elsewhere we'd probably never have met.

We'd only decided to share a house because the leases for our separate flats ran out in the same month. It had been Issy's suggestion that we could save on rent by moving in together, and for the last three years it's worked well. The house might be a bog-standard Northern terrace, but it's just right for our needs; in a middling area with local shops and a nearby park; far enough away from work that we don't bump into our pupils on a regular basis, yet close enough that we can, at a push, walk to school on the few days a year when snow scuppers everyone's plans. Clarke Road is the one school in the area that remains open whatever the weather, much to the dismay of the staff and the delight of the parents.

'I'm sure my stomach understood the word 'pizza'', Hope

says, interrupting my thoughts. 'Did you hear that?!' Her tummy had rumbled like the sound effects on an old-school video game. I'm convinced that not only I but everyone in South Yorkshire and North Derbyshire had heard it too.

'Have you been skipping lunch again?' I ask with a frown.

'I didn't have time to eat,' Hope says apologetically. 'I had a huge pile of comprehension homework to mark and couldn't face the thought of bringing it home, so I worked through dinnertime.'

'That's exactly why I made you a packed lunch in the first place!' I exclaim, exasperated. I'd hoped she might start eating a bit more if I prepared her meals for her, but it didn't look like it was doing one bit of good. 'You always say you're too busy to eat on a Friday and by the time you get home you're on the verge of passing out. What's the point in me making it if you're not going to eat it?' I practically throw the bowl I've been drying into the cupboard and Hope flinches at the clanging noise it makes as it connects with the other crockery.

'It's not like I did it on purpose. I didn't deliberately leave my lunch in the staff room fridge to annoy you. I was just too busy.'

I struggle to keep the frustration and hurt from my face and Hope quickly adds, 'But I did grab a cup of tea at break time,' as though that'll make everything alright.

'That's not enough to get you through the day, though, is it? A banana for breakfast and a cup of tea at lunch? I'm worried about you, Hope. I know you think I'm making a fuss, but you've lost so much weight since you and Amara split up. It can't be good for you.'

My sister looks at me wearily. 'Mon, give it a rest, please. When Issy arrives with the pizza I'll be stuffing my face like the Cookie Monster. I'm hardly going to waste away to nothing, am I?'

That's debatable. Her collarbone is jutting out. She was always slender – it wasn't like she had much weight to lose. I look at

Hope with a critical eye. She's definitely looking thinner, her top is looser than it had been at the start of the term. I know I'm not being fussy. She has sallow skin and dull grey rings around her eyes, and that worries me too. I wonder if that's down to the lack of food or whether she's been having trouble sleeping again. When Hope had first arrived there'd been a continual hum of the TV from the attic bedroom late into the night and each morning it was obvious Hope had been up all night crying. Her eyes had had that tell-tale puffed-up effect that only came from heartbreak. Whereas now she looked worn. Hollow. As though life had knocked the stuffing out of her and there were no tears left to cry. But I don't say any of that, instead saying, 'I worry about you, that's all. You're my only sister. I love you.'

'I know, and I love you too, sis. But you've *got* to stop nagging. It's getting boring.' She rubs her stomach as it grumbles yet again. 'And when Amara gets whatever this…' She pauses, grasping for the right word, '…*thing* is out of her system, everything will be fine. I'll be out of your hair, back at the flat, and everything will be back to the way it should be.'

'Okay,' I concede, knowing that unless Hope chooses to make a change herself things will carry on as they are. She's a stubborn mule. 'Just promise that you'll talk to me, alright? Don't bottle it up.'

'I promise. And the same goes for you, even if I'm not the world's best agony aunt. I'd rather you spoke to me than bottle everything up.'

'Oh, I don't bottle everything up. I bake to relax and stomp out my frustration at tap class every Thursday. Connie's convinced I'm wearing holes in the floor from being so aggressive.' I demonstrate an especially stompy shuffle-ball-change as if to prove my point.

'It's so cute that you two still go to tap class,' Hope smiles. 'All those years in those unflattering turquoise leotards didn't put you off. You still kept going.'

79

'I can't imagine not.'

Hope doesn't understand why dance is as important to me as it is, but the excitement at turning four and being able to start classes at the Eames School of Dance and Theatre Arts is one of my earliest memories. Hope had been having lessons for a whole year before I'd been allowed to join her and I'd spent each Saturday morning kicking up a stink, begging to be left in the studio with the tutu-clad girls rather than dragged around the hardware store with my parents. Hope had endured, rather than enjoyed, dance whereas I'd been eager enough for the both of us, throwing myself into ballet, tap and jazz classes with gusto. Before long Hope had hung up her leotard for good, but I'd kept going to the weekly classes for over twenty years.

'It's the only exercise I get,' I add, 'that and the occasional jog around the park. I'd be a terrible gym bunny. I can't handle all the sweaty muscle men strutting about with their vests and those weird leather gloves for lifting weights. I'm sure they're looking at me and judging.'

'I only ever use the treadmill,' Hope admits sheepishly. 'I could save myself fifty quid a month by cancelling my membership, but I keep hoping I'll bump into Amara there. She's still not answering my calls and I daren't go to the flat. It'd be more natural if we just happened to be in the same place at the same time.'

'Oh, Hope.' I look over pitifully as she places a stack of plates I've dried into the wall cupboards.

'I know she's missing me,' Hope insists. 'You can't give up on something overnight and expect it not to hurt, can you? Even a plaster hurts when you pull it off and that's something that's only been attached to you for a day or two. Me and Amara, we were together for almost four years.'

'I'm not really the authority on relationships, am I? Justin left on a whim after nearly a decade.' I turn away, swallowing down the lump in my throat. I don't want to share my emotions right now.

Hope places a hand on my shoulder. It's familiar – familiar and comforting. 'Have you thought any more about phoning him? It's been a while, hasn't it? Maybe if you came straight out and asked him what he's thinking you'd feel better. Talk it out.'

I shake my head fervently. 'No way. He's over there having the time of his life. He doesn't want me ringing him. We're on a break, and that means cutting back on contact.' I grimace, before curtly adding, 'He knows where I am if he wants to get in touch.'

'But that doesn't mean you can't call him. It's a two-way street. I'm sure he still loves you, Mon. He always has, just like Amara loves me. They're running scared, that's all.'

I turn to face my sister, my face screwed up with doubt. 'I don't think so, at least not Justin. Even his messages have all but stopped. It's hard to talk, with the time difference, but there's no excuse not to text a message when he's free.' I sigh. 'In his mind we're finished. He doesn't need to tell me that. I know it.' Hope raises an eyebrow suspiciously. She doesn't believe me. 'It's too difficult. I can't do long distance, I'm not cut out for it.'

'But what if he finds it difficult *not* being in contact? Have you thought about that?'

'I'm sure he's coping fine,' I say sullenly. 'He's been hanging around with this girl that works in his office; there's pictures on Facebook of them together in some glitzy downtown bar. He's moving on, Hope.' My hands are clenched just thinking about it, angry fists of jealousy and annoyance. It doesn't seem fair that he's out living the high life with his new glamorous girl friend (or should that be girlfriend? I'm not sure) when the closest I get to mingling is chatting to the dance girls as we tie our tap shoes and The Singalong Society, a club I created, which is supposedly to celebrate the singledom that's making me miserable. Great. 'Maybe Issy's right when she says I should be looking for someone else. Liam was telling me about the one night stands he has, he doesn't even tell them his real name half the time. I can't imagine what that's like. Justin's the only boyfriend I've ever had, the only boy I've ever even kissed. Isn't that sad?'

Hope shakes her head. 'It's lovely.'

'It's tragic.'

'It's sweet. And if you're not ready for anyone else, you're not ready. There's no point rushing into something, regretting it and ending up feeling worse than you already do. Take some time for yourself, figure out exactly what you want.'

'Thank you.' I'm moved by this outpouring of uncharacteristic empathy from my sister. What's more, it touches a nerve. I don't *know* what I want any more, everything's become such a frantic blur. I'm forever supporting everyone else – Justin, Connie, Hope, even Issy when she lets me. Perhaps it's time to be a little bit kinder to myself too.

'Come on,' Hope says. 'Let's start the party early and forget about our love lives for a bit. I'll even make you a gin and tonic if you get a glass out of the cupboard,' she adds with a conspiratorial wink.

'I've only just put those away!'

'Then they'll be nice and sparkly, which'll make it even more enjoyable. Get a glass down for Issy too. I'm sure she'll need a drink when she gets back from battling the Friday night shoppers.'

I reach up into the cupboard, grab three tall glasses and place them in front of Hope. Go big or go home, as they say. 'Go on, then,' I say. I'm a lot keener than my voice suggests. That tangy sharp tonic taste would surely help bring me out of my slump and give me back my zing. 'Fill these babies up. And then let's get our jazz hands ready for *Chicago*.'

*

The key jangles in the Yale lock, signalling Issy's homecoming. Hope and I rush anxiously to the door to welcome her, unabashedly scanning our eyes over the carrier bags of shopping for any bottle-shaped items. That gin and tonic certainly whetted our appetite.

'What's with the welcoming committee?' laughs Issy, dropping the bags to the floor as she wriggles out of her short denim jacket. 'Don't get me wrong, it's nice and all, but why do I get the distinct feeling you're more interested in my food shopping than me?'

I feel guilty that she sussed us out that quickly. 'We *are* interested in you. But it's your wine that we're really after,' I joke. 'That and the pizza. You did remember pizza, didn't you? I nearly sent you a text to remind you not to get that one we had last time with the mushrooms.' I motion pushing my fingers into my mouth as though about to vomit. I've never liked mushrooms. They don't taste of anything and the texture reminds me of absentmindedly chewing on one of the erasers that top the multi-pack pencils we have at work. Bleurgh. As far as I'm concerned, mushrooms have no redeeming features. Not one. Oh, except that they look a bit like little men wearing hats.

'You'll be pleased to hear I've gone for a bog-standard marga-rita. Not a hint of fungi. Oh, and I bought a pack of those spicy nacho things you like too. They were on offer.'

I kiss my friend affectionately on the cheek, getting a mouthful of flyaway hair in the process. 'You're an angel. I knew there was a reason we were friends.'

'Anyone'd have to be an angel to live with you,' quipped Hope. 'I think I deserve a medal for sharing a bedroom with you all those years.'

'I'm amazed I don't have a respiratory condition after sharing a room with you and your hairspray,' I retort, but it's only playful bickering. Our earlier heart to heart wouldn't be forgotten that easily.

'Now girls, I've had enough of squabbling kids for one day,' Issy says in her best school-marm voice. 'This new class are always telling tales. 'Miss Jackson, she's stolen my bracelet! Miss Jackson, he's pinging my bra! Miss Jackson, she's calling me a snitch!" Issy's impression of her indignant pupils was spot on. She had the whingey voice down to a tee. 'It's been constant tittle tattle all day. All I want is to sit down on that settee with a glass of red as big as my head and watch something mindless.'

'Well, it's *Chicago* tonight. Liam's choice,' I add. I was surprised when he'd messaged me asking if we had the DVD or whether he needed to bring his own personal copy. I don't know what I'd expected him to suggest, but it wasn't prohibition and murder. 'So nothing mindless, but nothing emotional either. Who knows, we might even get through the evening without anyone having a meltdown.'

'Do you know if Ray's coming too?' Issy asks innocently, unpacking the shopping onto the kitchen side. She's had a faraway look on her face all week and I'm convinced it's because she's fantasising about Ray. She's a lost cause.

'They're both meant to be coming,' I confirm. 'That's what Liam's text said. So as far as I'm aware they'll be here in about half an hour.'

'Right, well I might just go and jump in the shower before they arrive. It's been a loooooong day and I'll feel much more human if I can freshen up a bit. Will you two be alright sorting out the food?'

I look knowingly at Issy, eyebrows raised suspiciously. Primping and preening for the boys' arrival can only mean one thing. She's going all out to snare Ray. 'Sure. You go and get yourself ready to razzle dazzle him.'

Hope groans at my *Chicago*-based pun. 'Can you be a bit less obvious with the flirting tonight though, Is? The whole point is that we're *single*. Friday night film night was never meant to be an opportunity to pull.'

'Ah, yes,' Issy replies, rummaging in one of the carrier bags she's brought back from the supermarket before whipping out a bottle of her favourite coconut shower gel and flipping the

84

cylinder over in her hand. 'But when someone like Ray walks, quite literally, through the door, I'm not going to let him waltz back out again. No way, Jose.'

When she put it like that, I couldn't blame her. Maybe she'd dug deep and found her bravery, like I'd wished.

*

An hour later, the boys have arrived and all six of us are watching Catherine Zeta Jones and Renée Zellweger strut their feisty stuff. It's girl power to the extreme, and kind of inspiring.

'Richard Gere looks like our old stepdad,' I muse. 'Don't you agree, Hope?'

'Which one?' Her brow furrows as she wracks her brain.

'Ian. Definitely the best looking of mum's husbands.' Hope glares, and I quickly add, 'Except Dad, of course,' although, as loyal as I am, even I have to admit Dad's nowhere near as attractive as mum's second husband.

'Ian was nothing like Richard Gere!' she sneers, shaking her head.

I think he is. Not quite as dapper, admittedly, but there's definitely something there. I think it's in the eyes. 'We'll have to agree to disagree.'

'I've always had a bit of a thing for Richard Gere,' confides Connie, an embarrassed giggle escaping her lips at the revelation. 'I think it was *Pretty Woman* that started me falling for him.'

'Maybe Mon can set you up with her mum's ex,' teased Liam.

I poke my tongue out at him. 'Ha-ha. Anyway, we haven't seen him for years. There's been two more husbands since him.'

'And who do they look like? Tom Cruise and Brad Pitt?' winks Ray. He's obviously being sarcastic, but has a charm that means it comes across as funny rather than out and out mean.

Hope snorts. 'They wish! The latest one, Simon, he's about as far removed from Brad as you can get. He's got wire-rimmed specs and buys his trainers from the supermarket, and if that's not bad enough, he's a fishmonger. There's always this lingering whiff on his clothes. It's gross. He smells like death on legs.'

Liam winced. 'That's minging.'

Hope screws up her nose, her distaste obvious. 'Tell me about it. And he's one of those touchy-feely types who always wants to hug…'

'I love this,' I interrupt as the 'Cell Block Tango' starts up on screen – dark, sultry and dangerous. 'All these sassy, scorned women doing their thing. It fires me up.'

'Me too,' Liam adds lasciviously. He's fired up in a different way than I am, no doubt. 'It's like a soft-porn film, bodies writhing, legs everywhere. Stockings are so *hot*. And they're all so flexible.' He raises his eyebrows suggestively, twice in quick succession. 'I slept with a dancer once. She practically tied herself in knots. It was hot as hell.'

'Pervert,' fires Ray at the same time as Issy innocently says, 'Mon and Connie have been dancing all their lives…'

Liam suddenly seems more interested, eyeing up Connie, who's wrapped in her oversized red cardi to keep warm against the chill. If she was Little Red Riding Hood, Liam was definitely the wolf, ready to eat her up. 'Don't even think about it,' she says, her dark eyes flashing. 'You're not my type, nor Mon's either. She's not interested in Casanovas.'

Liam slinks back into his seat, defeated. I've a sneaky suspicion he isn't used to rejection. I'd bet he normally wins over any girl he has his sights on, but not us two. We've got far higher standards.

'I love the way they say 'Lipschitz',' I titter awkwardly, hoping to defuse the atmosphere building between Connie and Liam. 'I always thought they were swearing.'

'I think that's the point,' Issy replies drily. 'Because near nudity and violence isn't enough to be going on in a scene.'

'Have you ever seen this live?' Ray asks her, and only her. The pair of them are in a bubble, oblivious to everything else.

Issy shakes her head in response.

'Oh, you must. It's incredible. The lighting creates this dark, intense mood that hangs over the audience and Fosse's choreography is perfection. I'd go as far as to say the first act of *Chicago* is my favourite act in musical theatre.' He's practically bubbling over.

'Even better than *Grease*?' questions Issy, reaching over to pick a piece of barely-there fluff off Ray's t-shirt. He fleetingly glances down and his eyes stop for a fraction of a second at her chest, where the low-cut black wrap dress she'd worn to fit with the style of the film leaves little to the imagination, before quickly redeeming himself.

'You can't compare the two. They're different beasts.' He glances down again, seemingly captivated by Issy's melonesque breasts jiggling within the tight black Lycra. Ray has the good grace to blush, but Issy's coquettish simpering shows her delight. Her dress was having the desired effect. It definitely made the most of her assets.

'*Chicago* wins, hands down,' Liam says. 'Roxie and Velma ooze sex appeal. I'd pay good money to see a film where the two of them get down and dirty.'

Hope throws a scornful look in Liam's direction. With her lip curling up and her nose wrinkled in disgust, she sneers, 'That's offensive.'

Liam, however, doesn't look remotely phased. 'What can I say? They're both absolutely stunning. I bet every straight man thinks the same as I do, they just wouldn't have the balls to say it outright.' He elbows Ray in the ribs, either unaware or not caring that by doing so he is interrupting the flirtatious moment between him and Issy. 'Don't you agree, Northy? Renée Zellweger and Catherine Zeta Jones make one hell of a sexy pairing?'

Ray inhales through his nose, his nostrils flaring nervously as he bides his time. It's obvious he agrees, but doesn't want to say it aloud for fear of getting slammed.

Issy clocks Ray's twitchiness and jumps on it with glee. 'Oh, you ship it do you?' Issy asks teasingly, raising her hands and curling her fingers into quotation marks. 'That's what the cool kids all say, they 'ship' couples. I've no idea where it comes from, but it's one of the buzz phrases in my classroom.'

'I don't even know what that means.' Ray looks perplexed.

'They want to see them get together, I think… in a sexy way.'

Ray shifts in his seat as Issy smoulders in his direction. His Adam's apple bobs as he swallows before admitting, 'In that case, yes, I ship it.'

Hope shakes her head, her mouth a tight line of infuriation. 'Female partnerships don't exist purely to titillate straight men, you know. When Amara and I were out in town, we'd get all these men coming up to us saying they'd pay to watch us together. Like, seriously? We're not a bloody peep show for people to wank off over. We're a normal couple expressing our love in a natural way. Or rather, we were.' She turns back to the screen, trying and failing to hide the sadness that's seeping out of her every pore.

Connie slides off the armchair, landing with a bump next to Hope on the floor. 'You've still not heard from her?'

'Nuh-huh.'

'Have you thought about going to see her? It's been a month now. Surely she'll realise what she's been missing by now.'

'If she wanted me, she'd have got in touch,' Hope scowls. 'She knows I'm here, she could've rung my mobile… heck, she could have rung me at work if she was that bothered. Her silence speaks volumes.'

Connie speaks calmly, thoughtfully. 'I bet you anything she's missing you as much as you're missing her. We're just too proud, all of us. We hate admitting we've made a mistake. She's probably gagging to pick up the phone and ring you, but is scared she'll look weak if she backs down first.'

'I doubt it.' Hope sounds like a moody adolescent.

'Come on,' I say encouragingly. 'Connie's right. If you love Amara that much, then fight for her! Isn't that what we all want, someone who'll give their all to prove they love us?'

Hope's sarcastic laugh cuts through me like a knife. 'Oh, that's rich! You hardly fought for Justin, did you? He told you he was off and you sat back and watched him go. And you're not fighting now, either.'

'That's different,' I reply, swallowing down the hurt. 'I'm proving I love him by letting him have space. This year in Chicago's important to him, to his job prospects, and I'm not going to be the one holding him back. The situation with you and Amara is totally different. She's probably sat in your apartment right now, a mile down the road. *Your* apartment, with *your* furniture and *your* perfume in the bathroom and *your* pot plants on the kitchen windowsill. For crying out loud, go and see her and talk about this.'

Hope's jumps up, defensive. 'Oh, because it's that easy, is it? I just walk over there and ask if she wants me back? Because she'll still be scared of having to tell her parents about us. So nothing will have changed in the slightest.'

Connie butts in, and I know it's an attempt to keep the peace. She'll be desperate to stop the flying sparks from turning into flames. 'Maybe she'll come to see things your way. Maybe she won't. But you've got to admit, you were happier back at the flat with Amara than you are here, even when you were hiding your relationship from her family. Why make life harder than it needs to be? If being with her is what makes you smile, then go and do it!' It makes so much sense coming from Connie. If anyone can persuade Hope to take action, it's her. 'I know it's hard to be brave. Really, I do. The thought of telling my dad I was leaving him for a month was terrifying, but you know something? It wasn't anywhere near as hard as I'd expected it to be, and his reaction was so much better than I could have ever hoped.' She smiles, warmth and encouragement flooding out of her. 'You never know until you try. People surprise each other every day. Who knows, maybe Amara will surprise you, too.'

Ray nods along wisely, but his puppy-dog enthusiasm is the polar opposite of Connie's considered, well-worded approach. 'Connie's right. Fight for your girl, tell her what you're thinking! Because maybe you'll win her back and maybe you won't, but one thing's for sure – you're not going to get any answers sat here watching *Chicago*.'

*

'I can't believe she actually went,' I say in admiration scooping up the empty dishes and carefully placing them in the bowl of soapy bubbles in the sink. Liam had left not long after the film ended to meet some actor friends at a new cellar bar in town, and Connie made excuses about an early start in the morning and left soon after. With Hope mustering up the courage to go and face Amara, that left just three of us – me, Issy and Ray – to clear up the aftermath of movie night.

'I know, I didn't think she was going to do it until Connie piped up. Do you think she'll be back tonight?'

I shrug as I rinse a bowl under the cold tap. 'Who knows? I just hope we did the right thing by encouraging her to go. I don't think she could handle more rejection. She's like a bear with a sore head as it is.'

Ray puts down the glasses he's been carrying. 'I've got a good feeling about them.' He sneaks a look through the open door that separates the kitchen from the lounge. My eyes follow his to where Issy's brushing crumbs off the arm of the settee into the cupped palm of her hand. She's unaware of Ray's stolen glance, but I'm not. It's tender and true, full of affection and desire. I yearn to be loved like that again. My stomach pangs for it, an out-of-the-blue longing clenching in my gut. I feel like I've been alone for a very long time. 'If it's meant to be, it's meant to be.'

When he's looking at her he changes. He's vibrant, like a switch has been flicked. He's alive. Is that what I'm like when I'm with Justin, I wonder? A brighter version of myself? And if so, what does that make me now, a shadow? A black hole?

'If it's meant to be, it's meant to be,' I repeat.

*

By the time everything's tidy it's gone midnight. I'm flaked out on the settee flicking aimlessly through the music channels looking for something that's got a tune rather than a thumping bassline. It's all just noise until I stumble across a Spice Girls song I haven't heard in ages, part of a '90s party' on one of the retro channels. I don't care what people say, I like them, especially Mel B. Her hair must be even more difficult to control than mine.

Ray pops his head around the door to say he's calling it a night and I say goodbye, quietly glad to be able to vegetate without a house full of people. I've enjoyed the night despite the dramas, even though my cheekbones ache from where I've been sucking them in to perfect my pout. Singing 'All That Jazz' whilst trying to unleash the sex kitten that is hidden deep, deep inside is harder than it looks. Kudos to Catherine Zeta Jones for that one.

But something about watching *Chicago* when it's the very place Justin is left me discombobulated. I didn't want to be reminded of the miles that separated us.

I'm in a world of my own, half asleep, when Issy virtually floats into the room, every inch the cat that got the cream. She's got this blissed-out look on her face.

I eye her curiously.

She bites her bottom lip before breaking out in a humongous grin, a grin of out-and- out pleasure.

'Why do I get the feeling I've missed something big?' I ask, pulling my knees close to my chest.

91

Issy flops into the space beside me, letting out a happy sigh as she does so. 'We kissed,' she says happily. 'And it was amazing.'

She looks at me expectantly but I don't know what to say. Issy and Ray. Kissing. Good on the pair of them.

'His lips are so soft and delicious,' she continues, reaching up to gently touch her own lips, as though that'll somehow revive the sensation of Ray's mouth on hers. 'I'm still tingling. It was all the excitement of the kisses I had as a teen but without the clumsiness or nose-bashing.'

I'm tempted to remind her she's had a bit of practice since then. She's kissed her fair share of frogs. But Issy looks so contented that I don't say a word; I just listen and nod as she relives her moment. I hope I'm smiling in all the right places because I'm only half listening – I'm distracted by Let Loose on the TV singing 'Crazy for You'. My mum loves this song, she always hums along if it comes on the radio, but I don't know if I've ever seen what the band look like before. I can't stop looking at the drummer. He has these beautiful hypnotic sea-glass eyes. Justin's were the same. Translucent. Heavenly.

Issy says my name and I blink, snapping myself back to the present, but it's what follows that makes me sit bolt upright.

'I think I love him, Mon. I think I'm in love with Ray.'

Chapter Six

Friday 14th October
West Side Story – My choice*

'Come on then, spill the beans,' Connie says eagerly. Issy and I heard Hope's news last Saturday morning, but Connie's desperate to hear how Amara reacted to the unexpected visit. 'I want to know what happened.'

We girls had gathered together earlier than usual to catch up on each other's gossip before the boys arrived. It had been an eventful week, all in all.

Hope blushes. 'Well, it didn't seem right to use my key and barge in, even though it's as much my place as Amara's. So I knocked, then I waited – there was no point trying the doorbell because it hasn't worked for months. There was no answer but I knew she was in because I could hear her music playing.'

Hope pauses, flicking tendrils of hair over her shoulder with the back of her hand. She's revelling in being the centre of attention for the right reason, her sparkle radiating out of her. If the heart-eye emoji could come to life, it'd look like Hope looks now. Anyone seeing her would find her unrecognisable from the grey-faced, worn young woman she'd been just a week ago. She still

93

looks thinner than usual, but no longer in a way that makes her appear unhealthy. Now she's glossy, in bloom. Back to her best.

'So,' she continues, clapping her hands together, 'I tried again and knocked a bit harder, and was just about to give up and come back here when the door opened. And there she was, every bit as beautiful as she always has been. I know it sounds super soppy, but I wanted to reach out and touch her to make sure she was really there. Her hair was bundled up under a towel and she was wearing her silk dressing gown, and I could smell the vanilla of her body wash so I knew she must have been in the shower.' She smiled happily at the memory.

'Come on, get to the juicy bit!' Connie urges. 'Tell me what she said!'

Hope willingly carries on regaling us with the tale. She doesn't need encouragement, she's been replaying the whole scene all week to anyone who'll listen. 'I could tell she was surprised to see me but she invited me in. It was weird being back there; nothing had changed since I left. The same photos up on the mantel, the same empty fruit bowl sitting on the sideboard... it was strange. Then she looked right at me and said, 'Why didn't you come back sooner?' and I said, 'you told me to leave, so I left' and she started to cry. I wasn't snappy,' she adds quickly before momentarily glowering at Issy.

When Issy heard the story the first time around she immediately jumped to accuse Hope of being too abrupt. She's first-hand experience of what it's like to be on the receiving end of Hope's sharp tongue.

'But I wanted her to know it wasn't my choice to stay away,' Hope continues. 'I really *was* doing it for her, because she'd told me she needed space, even though I wanted to be with her more than anything else in the world. Anyway, to cut a long story short, I couldn't bear watching her cry so I moved to sit next to her, and once I was that close it was impossible not to hold her – I had to pull her closer. Her body was shaking through the silk of her gown. I didn't even realise I was going to say anything, but I couldn't help it, the words fell out of my mouth. I told her I loved her and missed her more than I could have ever imagined, but that I'm not willing to be a secret any more. I'm worth more than that. *We're* worth more than that. Why should it make a difference if we're both female? We're in love and both of us want what's best for each other, our actions over the past month show that. So I said to her, 'Amara, your parents want you to find a man and settle down because they think that's what'll make you happy. If you tell them that what'd make you happy is being with me, do you think they'd give us their blessing? Once they get past the shock and actually process it? Don't you agree that it's better to be honest?' And do you know what she said?'

Connie shook her head in rapture, enchanted by the romance of the scenario. I can understand why. For all Hope's abrasiveness, there's something both smooth and solid inside, the jewel of a shiny conker inside a prickly, protective casing. My sister doesn't often lay herself bare like this. She's far more likable when she does.

'She said 'okay'.' Hope beams. 'She pulled me closer and whispered it in my ear. And even though my face was damp from the soggy towel and the vanilla scent tickled the inside of my nostrils, all I could focus on was that one word.'

'So what happens next? I mean, you're still living here, so I guess you're taking it slow?'

'We both agreed that when we first got together it had got too intense too quickly. We moved in together within six weeks of meeting,' she reminds Connie. 'We've agreed to take a step back and appreciate each other again. Mon and Issy say I can stay here and me and Amara are going to start dating – actual proper dates. Going to the cinema and into the Peak District for Sunday lunch; all the little things we should have done when we first got together, but never did.'

'That sounds really wise,' says Connie. Reassurance rushes so naturally from her. There's a safety in her words and although there's no reason for it to be so, it feels as though whatever Connie says is going to turn out to be right. 'There's something special about dating. I don't know if it's the anticipation of waiting to see someone or that it's an escape from work and bills and all the grown-up stuff. But yeah, spending quality time together where you're not talking about whose turn it is to buy the milk or change the loo roll sounds a great idea.'

'And we're going to talk to her parents together. They're coming up for Amara's birthday in a few weeks' time. It doesn't feel like the kind of thing to tell someone over the phone, 'Hey? You know you always thought I was going to marry a macho surgeon with a sports car and have a football team's worth of kids? It's not going to happen, because Hope, who you thought was my housemate, is actually my lover".'

Connie smiles as she pulls a plump green grape from the bunch in the fruit bowl. 'I'm sure you'll handle it with a bit more sensitivity than that. But what you said before was true; most parents want their kids to be happy. That's the main barometer of success, knowing that they've found something in their life that brings them comfort. Whether that's singing along to *Frozen*,' she throws me the side eye, 'helping kids reach their potential,' she looks at Issy before smiling kindly at Hope, 'or a headstrong, sarcastic but caring woman. I'm sure all Amara's parents want is for their little girl to be happy.'

Hope bites down nervously, trapping her lower lip between her teeth. 'I hope you're right, because both Amara and I are bloody petrified.'

*

It's not only Issy rejoicing when the boys arrive, it's all of us. Liam and Ray are cradling a large brown paper bag each, the delicious scent of salt and vinegar permeating the air in the lounge and leaving us salivating. Any guests bearing fish and chips are very welcome at 24 Cardigan Close.

'It's my choice tonight,' I say with a smile. 'And I've chosen a film with one of my favourite musical numbers. If you don't know the words then there's no excuse, because you can always join in with the dancing.' I pose in a flamenco-inspired stance, clapping my hands at the side of my face and rhythmically stamping my feet.

My moves don't seem to enlighten the others, who're looking on like I'm talking a foreign language. '*West Side Story*,' I explain before belting out the chorus of 'America' in an unidentifiable (but supposedly Puerto Rican) accent. 'You'll know more of the songs than you think, I promise.'

'*West Side Story*. Good choice,' Ray enthuses, dipping an over-cooked chip in the gravy in one of the stubby polystyrene pots the chip shop uses for sauce. 'It's the show that started off my lifelong love affair with the theatre. I went to see my cousin in a school production and loved everything about it.'

'I love the outfits,' I admit.

'You suit all that vintage stuff,' Liam says, appraising my circle dress. It was an original from the fifties. I'd bought it from a second-hand shop on Division Street after falling in love with the fabric: blue and white gingham. It made me feel like Dorothy every time I wore it. All I needed were some red, glitzy shoes and a couple of plaits and I'd be ready for the yellow brick road. 'Not everyone can carry that stuff off, but it looks good on you.'

'Thanks,' I say shyly.

I'm not used to people complimenting my style. Vintage has always been my favourite; even before it became the fashionable and environmentally friendly thing to do I was scouring the charity shops for something unusual to wear. Justin had thought it amusing, especially when I'd started earning enough to be able to afford the occasional shopping spree at Meadowhall. He'd never understood that the clothes I bought for a fraction of the price were better quality, better made, better full stop. Plus I liked the uniqueness, knowing I wouldn't pass four other girls wearing the exact same outfit as me every time I left the house.

The DVD starts and we're all too stuffed full of carbs to be able to talk, let alone sing or dance. My stomach's rock hard with chips.

By the time we get onto the most well-known songs, 'Maria', 'America', 'I Feel Pretty' and 'Somewhere', we're just about able to move and I make sure I'm leading the choir, even though my voice is one of the weakest of all of us. This is my choice of film, after all. I'm swishing my skirt and joining Maria in an abundance of self-affirmatives. With my friends joining in I realise that for the first time in a very long time I actually *do* feel fizzy and funny and fine. What with their support and Liam's earlier compliment, I'm pretty buoyant, despite knowing the devastating end of the film looming just an hour or so away. It breaks my heart how Maria can be so joyful and full of love when tragedy is around the corner. Romeo and Juliet, or Tony and Maria, or any other pairing of star-crossed lovers, for that matter, have the ability to make my chest tighten in empathy. But right now I'm enjoying basking in contentment. Pretty and witty and bright is a wonderful thing to feel.

*

By the time the film's over my heart's heavy once more. Every last note of the music that accompanied the credits had tugged on my heartstrings with a startling resonance, and goose bumps had unwittingly spread up my arms. It was the same beautiful musical I remembered, the familiar story of forbidden love, but it failed to give me the uplifting feeling I so badly needed, and I silently wished I could go back in time and put *Frozen* on instead for some much-needed comfort.

'When is it you're leaving us?' Liam asks Connie.

I rub my cold arms in a vain attempt to rejuvenate myself. The reminder that Connie's leaving does nothing to warm my spirit.

'Not long now. I leave on the 22nd. I've had my injections – they hurt like hell – and I've started buying things I need to take, some stuff for me and some bits for the charity. They mentioned they're short of pencils and notebooks for the children, so I raided Poundland. I'm actually a bit concerned – my case will probably be well over the weight limit.'

I'd been with her as she'd gone wild in the bargain store, purchasing half the stationery aisle. Then again, it'd seemed silly not to, when everything was such good value. The poor woman at the counter had looked stunned when she'd put down her wire basket of multipack coloured pencils and A5 notepads, but Connie had humbly told her she was taking them to Uganda on a charitable mission. I was surprised by how rewarding it was to hear her say the words out loud. I'd been a very proud friend.

'You're braver than me,' Liam says. 'Don't they have lions and tigers roaming free in Africa? I'd be scared shitless that I'd be eaten alive.'

'Are you serious?' I say. 'Of course there are wild animals in Africa. That's why people go there on safari, to see them in their natural habitat?'

'Yeah, that's what I mean.' Liam's brow furrows as he mulls over the situation. 'Con's gonna have to be careful. I've seen those nature programmes on BBC. Some of those creatures are vicious.'

'I'm not going to get attacked by wild animals,' Connie laughs. 'I'm not going to be in the middle of the plains. It's a large rural community and even if by some chance there *was* any danger, I'm sure the locals would know how to deal with it.'

Liam taps the top of his can with his index finger before pulling back the ring pull with a snap and taking a swig of lager. 'Rather you than me.'

Connie shrugs, unfazed by Liam's comments. I'm loving her new-found confidence, how she no longer seems to worry what people think of her decisions. That's not to say she doesn't care, because I know she does – she's the most thoughtful person I know, internally as well as externally – but she's happy with her choices. This brave new Connie actively pursues happiness rather than hiding away from it.

Issy yawns loudly, stretching her arms out wide. 'I'm so tired I could sleep for a week.' She's echoing the thoughts of everyone in the room. Term's rolling on and yet the half term break still seems eons away. 'I might spend the holidays in hibernation.'

'Like a tortoise?' Ray smiles. He looks up from the slashed material across the knee of his jeans that he'd been picking at all night. It had got gradually wider and wider until his pale skin was shining out of the gap in the black denim.

'I hope I'm a bit less wrinkly than a tortoise!' she retorts. 'And I don't think I'd get away with sleeping all winter either. There'd be a few choice words if I didn't turn up at school again until Easter. But it's been such a hard half term, and it's not getting easier any time soon. It's the class trip on Monday.' She groans at the prospect.

'It could be worse,' Hope offers up light-heartedly. 'At least it's not a residential.'

'That's true,' Issy agrees. 'That's a delight saved for the summer term, four nights in an outdoor pursuits centre near Bakewell. I can hardly wait.' A harrowed look passes over her face, and I know she's thinking of the abseiling wall. Last year she'd started screaming when she made the rookie mistake of looking down halfway through the descent, much to the amusement of her class. She'd insisted it was nothing to do with a fear of heights but that hadn't stopped everyone in the staffroom referring to her as Dizzy Issy for the remainder of the term.

'The one big advantage of early years,' I smile, raising my fisted hands in a mock victory air punch Rocky Balboa would be proud of. 'The furthest we go is the library for story time.'

'It must be fun, working in a school all the time, though,' Ray ponders. He's curled up in the corner of the settee, a fleecy blanket wrapped around him like a superhero's cape. It hadn't taken him long to realise that when we said we weren't putting the heating on until November, we meant it, no matter that the temperature was rapidly dropping. There had been a torrential hail storm on Wednesday, the tiny frozen balls of ice bouncing down a brutal reminder to everyone that the bitter cold of winter was lurking around the corner. 'Everyone talks about the holidays as being the big draw, but I bet it's fun working with the kids too. I always enjoy it when we come in to do workshops.'

Issy rubs her eyes wearily. 'It can be fun. But that's not to say there aren't days when I'm tearing my hair out too.'

Hope nods in agreement. 'It's harder work than people realise. It's not just the lessons and the planning and keeping records on every child's progress. It's exhausting being *in loco parentis* all the time. There's a little ball of panic in the back of your mind all day long, thinking about what'd happen if there was a fire or someone got onto the premises with a gun or whatever. You hope none of these things will ever happen on your watch, but they do, for some poor sods. It's front page of the papers or a bong on the ten o'clock news and everyone's horrified, but for some teacher somewhere that's reality.'

'That's the extreme, though,' I add quickly. 'A possible situation rather than a probable one.'

'It's admirable, the amount you all put into your jobs,' Ray says. 'You're so dedicated. I give acting my all, but at the end of the day it's only myself I'm responsible for. If I don't succeed it's only me I'm letting down. You lot have so much more at stake.'

Issy's aghast face is a picture, as though she's comprehending the importance of her role for the first time. 'Cheers for that. Nothing like reminding me that I'm partially responsible for the future of society.'

'No, no!' he exclaims hurriedly, nervously picking at a loose thread on his jeans. 'It takes a special type of person to be a teacher, and a *really* special type of person to be a good one. And I know you're a good one because you put so much into it.'

'She was up until gone midnight last night getting her resources ready for today,' I confirm.

And even though it's a pie-in-the-sky idea, even though it'll probably never happen, I wonder if I could do what Issy does as well as she does it, if I have what it takes to take the step up and become a fully fledged teacher. I give my all to the kids too and love working in a school. Maybe if I'd pushed myself more I could have had a class of my own. A wave of regret ripples through me, even though I've never seriously considered teaching before. How strange is that?

'No wonder you're a sleepyhead now if you were up half the night,' smiles Ray, creating a nook in his arm for Issy's head to rest in. She willing reclines into the hook of his arm, her hair splayed out around her as her cheek rests on Ray's chest. She nuzzles into the cotton of his t-shirt and he pulls the throw around her shoulder, like a mother bird protecting a baby under its wing. It's such a thoughtful gesture that I think I might cry.

'How many weeks until half term?' Ray asks, stroking the flat palm of his hand across the silky bronze blanket of Issy's hair.

'Two more weeks,' Hope replies. 'Ten working days – not that I'm counting or anything.'

I laugh. We always work out exactly how many more get-ups there are until the next holiday.

'I think I'll be joining Issy in the 'do as little as possible' club during the break,' I say. 'Catch up on all those series on Netflix that I keep promising I'll watch and maybe even do a bit of craft. I haven't done any knitting for ages. Perhaps I'll make something for Penny's baby. And I've got a folder full of recipes I want to try too.'

'Well I'll be out of your hair for most of it,' Hope replies.

'Amara's taking the week off work and we're going to do something together each day. We're planning day trips to Matlock and York and I really want to try that new Italian restaurant on London Road. It had a great review in *The Star*.'

'You two really are going back to the lovey-dovey stage,' I say in admiration. A vision of my sister and Amara sucking on either end of a long string of spaghetti *Lady and the Tramp* style pops into my head. 'It's great that you're back together. Really great.' The words catch in my throat. I mean them, and wish them both happiness, but it's yet another reminder of Justin and what I no longer have.

My heart pangs. Issy and Ray are like an old married couple, a half-smile of contentment on Issy's face as she dozes, Hope and Amara are giving their relationship another shot and Connie's jetting off for a once in a lifetime experience in a couple of weeks' time. Liam? Well, he's harder to read, but even he seems happy with his womanising ways and devil-may-care attitude to what other people think. He's most likely one of those annoying people who float through life, always landing on their feet, and for all his laddish behaviour there's an element of charm behind his good looks, a confidence which most women probably wouldn't be able to resist. I'm sure he's happy with his lot. Everyone around me is living out their dreams, while I'm still aimless. My love life, my career… I don't know what's going on any more.

'I'm going to make a hot drink,' I say, skulking towards the kitchen. No one reacts, they're all too busy listening to Ray sharing a story about Liam flirting with one of the teachers at the school they did a workshop at earlier in the week.

Flicking down the switch on the cream coloured kettle, I lean against the fridge, the magnet Mum brought me back from her recent holiday to Dubai digging into the small of my back. I reach into the pocket of my jeans and pull out my phone. Without thinking I bring up the Facebook app and start typing in Justin's name. His profile pops up immediately, and I'm surprised to see he's changed his profile picture, at last. For as long as I can remember he's had the same one: him holding a bottle of lager at a barbecue at his parents' house with a hapless, drunken grin on his face and a semi-vacant look in his eyes.

I remember that day clearly – the first hot day of the year we sat our A levels. It must've only been May, the sunshine marking the onset of summer, and we'd excitedly got the deckchairs out of the shed as Justin's dad pretended he knew what he was doing with the barbecue. His mum had looked on disapprovingly as we drank, saying we should be revising, but we'd waved away her concerns with the true lack of care of a procrastinating teenager. As it happened, Justin drank way too much, bringing the barbecue to an early end when he violently threw up over his mum's prized pot plants. No matter how many times he claimed it was nothing to do with the alcohol, instead insisting that the burgers couldn't have been cooked through properly, we'd all known the truth.

But that picture wasn't there any more – the one of him smiling goofily against the backdrop of the slatted wooden fence that encircled the Crowson's garden. Instead it's a much more recent picture, one I assume has been taken in the last few weeks or months. There's Justin, standing in front of a large Ferris wheel sporting a strange goatee beard I take an instant dislike to. I don't understand why he's grown it. He's never been one for facial hair and is as far from a hipster as you can get, ordinarily. He's wearing a crisp white shirt and black jeans with shoes that can only be described as loafers. He must be staring into the sun as his eyes are squinting the way they always do when it's too bright and he's not got his sunnies with him.

However, it's the woman in the photo with him that causes my heart to race with panic. It's the woman from work, again. Long blonde hair, poker straight – the complete opposite of my own frizzy locks – and a cutesy navy pinafore over a lemon-yellow t-shirt. She's holding a wispy candyfloss balloon on a long wooden stick. Her bare legs are a biscuity shade of tan, the navy lace-up pumps she's wearing reminding me of a pair I'd once bought for a family holiday in Bridlington. They hadn't lasted the holiday, but my mum said it was because I'd never been light on my feet – one of the reasons I'd excelled at tap rather than ballet. This girl's shoes don't look like they're about to split. She's standing gracefully on her tiptoes, smiling up at Justin as though they don't have a care in the world. But more importantly is her arm, looped loosely around his waist, her thumb hooked into his waistband. That's not the behaviour of an acquaintance. It isn't even the behaviour of a friend. The only conclusion I can come to is the one I don't want to admit to myself – Justin has found someone else.

I gaze blankly at the screen, wondering. Are they out on a date, or is it a trip with friends? Did the person taking the photo later step into the frame too whilst someone else snapped another picture?

The most annoying part of the whole thing is that the woman looks like someone I could be friends with. She doesn't look like a bitch who'd steal someone else's sort-of boyfriend, but then can anyone look like a bitch when they're carrying a candyfloss? I'm not sure it's possible.

My mind races. Are they a couple? Are they exclusive? Of course they're a couple, I think grimly. Look at them together. Have they kissed, or even slept together? Maybe they were at it every night, acting out the Kama Sutra in the bedroom of the luxury studio apartment the bank had found for Justin, the one I'd only seen in pictures.

I feel sick and only the click of the kettle switching itself off pulls me out of my nightmarish daydreams. I slam my phone on the work surface face down, half hoping the screen will crack on impact and shatter Justin's perfect American life.

'Are you okay?'

I spin to face the voice and immediately feel giddy as the blood

105

rushes to my head. It suddenly seems airless in here, the band of my bra too tight around my ribcage. The steam from the kettle spreads over the windowpanes, giving them a ghostly veil.

'Oh, Liam. Yeah, yeah I'm fine.' I fight to regain my composure, putting all my efforts and energy into the task at hand. I'm concentrating much harder than is necessary on reaching for a mug from the cupboard. 'I'm just cold, that's all, so I'm making a hot chocolate. Do you want one?'

'Sure.'

I reach for another mug, mismatched like they all are. Both me and Issy had gained a few over the years, end of year gifts from children with slogans like 'Thank you' and 'Worlds Best Teacher'. The lack of apostrophe on that one made it my particular favourite. I unscrew the cap of the jar of pale brown powder, scooping three teaspoons of it into each mug before pouring the boiling water over the top. The granules dissolve as I stir, leaving a chocolatey liquid in each cup.

'Milk?' I ask, reaching for the large bottle of green-top from the fridge. 'I don't usually bother with it if I'm making instant, but I know some people do.'

'Sure,' he repeats, nodding as I hand him the container. Our fingers brush slightly in the handover. It's the smallest contact imaginable. It's nothing, really. But whether it's the hurt, or the light-headedness, or the outright exhaustion, I don't know, but the milk slips from both of our grasps, landing with a hollow thud on the lino that covers the kitchen floor; and my hands are pushing a startled Liam back against the full-length cupboard. My lips are pressing on his, my hungry tongue easing into his mouth as he responds with fierce, passionate movements. The yeasty aftertaste of his beer is in my mouth. Pressing the length of my body against his I push my hips forward so all my weight is against him, my hands brushing against the hair at the nape of his neck, and along his biceps and under the bottom of his t-shirt until I'm touching the warm bare skin of his back. There's a visceral need, and although I know this man in our kitchen isn't Justin and never will be, I don't care any more. I need to feel attractive and wanted. I don't want to be replaceable.

Liam's panting now as I move faster. My tongue flicks in and out of his mouth like an angry python's, my hands desperately roaming his body. His arousal is impossible to ignore, the hardness forming under his jeans pressing against my hip bone. I reach down to undo the silver button on his jeans, my mouth moving down to the smooth skin of his neck as he lolls back, most likely unable to believe his luck.

We've been in the kitchen three minutes at most. Three frantic, thought-free minutes.

I'm so lost in the moment that I don't hear the footsteps. I don't hear the catch of the door as it opens.

But both Liam and I hear a startled Connie as she struggles to take in the scene – the milk on the floor, the steam on the windows and her best friend's hand on the brink of venturing into the jeans of someone we've joked about as being vacuous and vain.

Her voice is laced with shock. 'What the hell is going on?'

Chapter Seven

Friday 21st October
South Pacific – Connie's choice*

It's been a draining week for us all. Me, Hope and Issy are trudging our way towards the holidays with increasingly dragging heels, Connie's frantically tackling the gigantic to-do list she's made to prepare for Africa and Ray and Liam are wrapped up in a seemingly endless run of rehearsals at the theatre. Add to that the gloomy evenings and the continual downpours that go hand in hand with a British autumn, and perhaps that goes some way to explaining why we're all flagging.

And I'd been worrying about Friday night all week long. After last week's kitchen shenanigans it was bound to be weird seeing Liam, especially as the rest of the group thought it was hilarious that we'd been having a quick fumble like two horny teenagers whilst they flaked out in the lounge sipping wine like proper grownups. It hadn't got any easier as the Singalong Society's meeting drew closer. If anything, it had got worse. My nerves were shot.

'I'm dreading this,' I admit, watching the second hand of the clock moving as though my life depended on it. 'What's he going to think of me?'

Issy laughed. 'Are you worried about upholding your good name?'

I stare her down. 'I don't want him to think I'm the sort of girl who does that kind of thing.'

'It was only a kiss, Mon,' Hope reminded me. 'You weren't having sex on the kitchen floor. Which is just as well, because Connie practically bleached her eyes as it was after seeing the two of you together. If it had been any more explicit who knows what she'd have done.'

'I didn't say that!' Connie exclaims. 'And I don't think he'll judge your morals, Mon. Playing the field is what he does.'

'Ray said Liam went home with a stunning redhead on Saturday night,' Issy chips in. 'Apparently he'd complained about the price of the cocktails she'd been drinking but according to Liam it had been more than worth it,' she added suggestively.

'Oh,' I reply, deflated. The kiss I'd been sweating over all week – the hot, sexy, guilt-ridden kiss – had obviously meant nothing to him if he was out with someone else the very next night. Not that it meant anything to me. It was just a way to take out my anger about Justin and the American woman. Liam was a playboy; I knew that. But when I'd been kissing him, taking the lead in a way I'd never done before, I'd felt strong, beautiful. And although it was only a snog with roving hands, I'd felt desired.

'I'm sure it's all forgotten about,' Connie said kindly. 'Anyway, it's another golden oldie tonight, *South Pacific*. You can't be burdened when watching that, it's not allowed.'

I smile despite myself. I have a feeling this could be a long and embarrassing night.

*

Ray and Issy are sprawled on the settee, their closely knit bodies taking up the full length of the couch. A blanket is draped over them and I have a sneaky suspicion they're holding hands under there, if not more, because every so often they look at each other with gooey eyes, as though they're party to a secret.

'I'm not sure about this film,' I say, wrinkling my nose. I don't care if it makes me look ugly. 'There is Nothing like a Dame' is singing out and I'm not appreciating it one bit. The military men are only wanting to get their leg over and it's making me wonder about Liam and the Saturday night redhead. Did he spend the whole night with her, making love to her until she was blissfully satiated and then spooning her while she slept or was it wham-bam-thankyou-ma'am? I don't know why it matters. I've got no right to even be thinking it. But it bothers me.

I can usually appreciate the jaunty musical offerings as mood-lifting tonics and the tear jerkers as a form of therapy, but tonight I can't concentrate on a thing. I keep stealing glances at Liam, sat with his back against the settee. His grey trackie top is so big on him, his hands pushed into the large pocket across his stomach. He's not singing tonight either, although he says he knows the songs. Maybe this situation is as strange for him as it is for me. After all, he doesn't normally have to face up to his conquests again once he's got his cheap thrills.

'I don't know how anyone as smiley as you can possibly take umbrage with *South Pacific*,' Hope said. 'We all need a bit of sunshine in our lives. I feel warmer just watching it.' The back-drop of every scene was a bright blue sky or a hazy sunset, and I had to agree with her that the beaches did look inviting.

'I wouldn't have had you down as a fan of this one,' I say, surprised. 'Since you and Amara have got back on track you're a different person. A happier person.'

Hope nods her agreement. 'I'm not saying you need to be in a relationship to be happy. If you're in a relationship that's bringing you down, you need to wash that man, or woman, right out of your hair, as Nellie Forbush says. But when you're meant to be together, it's different. Being apart isn't an option. I can't thank you lot enough for encouraging me to take the first step with Amara.' She smiles and pulls the sleeves of her jumper down to cover her hands. It's decidedly nippy now, even if on screen it's tropical. 'We're meeting for coffee and cake in the morning at Cocoa Wonderland,' she says, glowing.

'Oh, I love it there!' Issy says. 'They sell the best chocolate. I bought my mum some amazing Madagascan dark chocolate from there for Mother's Day, do you remember, Mon?'

'I remember we ate it before you gave it her,' I answer, laughing despite my inner grump. 'You had to rush down to Tesco on Mother's Day morning. Those flowers you ended up panic buying were distinctly underwhelming.' I remembered the gaudy chrysanthemums, the clashing orange and pink not what anyone who knew Shirley Jackson would have chosen for her. Every room in Issy's parents' house was painted a neutral shade of magnolia. Even the three-piece suite was a variant of cream. Colour wasn't her thing, so Issy had been crushed when the harassed sales assistant told her all the delicate off-white roses and classic white lilies were sold out and she'd have to hand over the brightly coloured bouquet or nothing at all.

'Anyway,' says Hope, drawing out the word until all five sets of eyes are firmly back on her, 'we're going to go there first thing and then meet Amara's parents for lunch to celebrate her turning thirty.' She pauses, allowing the impact of her words to hit home. 'We're going to tell them we're a couple. I'm absolutely petrified,' she admits.

I reach out and squeeze my sister's hand reassuringly. 'I'm sure it won't be as bad as you expect. And think how much better it'll be to have everything out in the open.'

'Amara's scared they'll disown her,' Hope says. 'Her parents might be Westernised, but they're traditionalists. I doubt they've ever even met a gay person.'

'They've met you,' Connie points out rationally. 'And they *created* Amara. And you've always got on well with them in the past, haven't you?'

'But that's because they think we're just housemates,' Hope reasons. 'It's completely different. It's going to cause such a scandal, not only for her parents but for her grandma too. She's really religious.'

'Isn't her grandma in Beijing?' I reply. I have vague memories of Amara talking about her Chinese grandparents, how they'd been terribly upset when Amara's parents, who'd moved to Britain soon after getting married, had chosen to give her a name that wasn't Chinese.

'She can't do much from there,' Liam says bluntly, 'so I wouldn't worry about her.'

'It's not as easy as that, though. Her family are really tight-knit. I don't want to be the one to cause a rift.'

'You're not going to,' I say firmly. 'It's all going to work out for the best.' On the TV there are cross-cultural relationships blossoming before our very eyes, as though to prove the point that love knows no cultural or racial boundaries.

'I hope you're right,' Hope says, holding up crossed fingers. 'It does put a bit of pressure on the relationship, though, too. What if she tells them and then things don't work out between us? We've only been dating a couple of weeks.'

'Four years and a couple of weeks,' Connie corrects. 'And anyway this announcement is as much about Amara's sexuality as it is about you being a couple. I bet it'll be a weight lifted from her shoulders too when she can be completely honest with her family about who she is.'

'I'll tell you what I am,' Liam grumbles, wrapping his arms cross his stomach. 'Cold. It's always freezing in this house.' He whistles through his teeth as if to prove the point.

'It's always worse when it's raining,' I say, avoiding eye contact. 'Just the sound of the rain hammering against the windows makes me shiver.'

'At least it's only ten more days until we turn the heating on,' Issy said positively, pulling the blanket tighter around her and

Ray. It's alright for her, snuggling up with her new beau. I feel like an ice statue.

'You'll never make it,' Liam says, wriggling on the spot. I can only assume he's trying to keep warm through movement. 'They said on the radio this morning that there might even be snow before October's out.'

'Brrrr,' Connie said with a shiver. 'Hopefully it won't come until after I'm out of the country.'

'Yeah, yeah, we all know you're off to warmer climes,' I say, poking my tongue out cheekily whilst trying to focus on what a wonderful time Connie would have in Uganda rather than dwelling on how much I'll miss her.

'Tonight's your last Singalong meeting for a month,' Ray says. He pulls a sad face, lips pouted theatrically like a silent film star, and draws a line down his cheek with his index finger to mimic crying a solitary tear.

'Exactly,' Connie answers. 'Which means one thing – we need to sing!'

'I don't think I even know one song from *South Pacific*,' admits Issy. 'I always thought it was one of those films grans fall asleep in front of on a Sunday afternoon.'

'You know 'Happy Talk', don't you?' Connie says. 'When we've watched it all we'll rewind it back to that scene and sing it.'

'Or I've got a playlist of songs from the shows on my iPod,' Ray offers.

'Of course you have,' Liam jokes. 'Mr Musicals strikes again.'

'There's nothing wrong with being passionate about some-thing,' Ray banters back, and he and Issy share a glance. They're doing a terrible job of stifling their childish giggles, which makes me even more convinced they're having a fumble under that blanket. 'Speaking of musicals, a mate from work's in an am-dram production of *The Rocky Horror Picture Show* next week. He offered me complementary tickets for next Friday. How about we break with tradition and actually venture out to a real musical for a change?'

My eyes widen. 'That's where everyone wears wild costumes. You're not going to expect me to dress up in stockings and suspenders, are you?'

'Not unless you want to,' Ray replies, laughing. The blanket moves again, but by the 'ouch' that follows I guess Issy's elbowed him in the ribs for his cheek this time rather than something more pleasurable.

'I'm not going to be here,' wails Connie. It finally seems to be sinking in that she's going.

'We know,' everyone choruses in unison, before Ray adds 'Jinx!'

'And you'll be missed,' I say. 'It won't be the same when you're away.'

'*Rocky Horror*'s a good call,' Liam said. 'You can count me in. I'm always up for a bit of cross-dressing.' He winks blatantly at Ray, who gives a knowing smile back. I frown, puzzled by this interaction but don't question it.

'Oh, go on then,' Issy laughs. 'I guess you have to try something new every once in a while.'

'Exactly,' says Ray emphatically. 'So how about you two?' he asks, looking first at Hope, then at me. His eyebrows are high expectant arches and his forehead creases as a result. It makes him look older, but no less handsome. 'Can we persuade you to come and do the 'Time Warp' with us?'

We look at each other, both unsure, until Ray gestures for an answer. 'Oh, what the hell!' says Hope, throwing her hands up in the air. 'Let's give it a go. Can you get a ticket for Amara too?'

'Sure.' Ray rubs his hands together with glee, his beam lighting up the room. 'There's nothing like your first *Rocky Horror* experience. Prepare to be overawed.'

'It'll be a welcome distraction,' I add.

This week has been particularly tough. Although I've avoided

114

Facebook for fear of the temptation of sneaking onto Justin's profile, the image of him and his new squeeze is etched into my mind. I don't need to see the picture again to recall the details, they're already vivid in my imagination, and they hurt. The guilt about Liam on top of that has almost pushed me to my limit.

Being honest, distractions are exactly what I'm looking for. Starting with Liam (otherwise known as the most ill-advised and short-lived distraction possible), I'd also found myself jogging at six am on more than one occasion, cleaning the house from top to bottom and volunteering to run a dance club on Wednesday lunchtimes with a group of sassy Year 5s. Of course, none of it had taken my mind off my predicament. All that had happened was that I'd roll into bed two hours earlier than my usual curfew because I was burning out. I found myself cuddling up to Gomez, the toy cat Justin had given me when we were eighteen, because I'm so shattered and in need of a hug.

Back then Justin had been so desperate to please. When he'd asked what I wanted for my milestone birthday, I'd blurted out that I wanted a kitten. I'd always longed for a pet, but Mum insisted they were too expensive and too tying and too smelly, so Justin bought me a toy cat instead. The black and white plush of his fur was as soft as any real live cats would be, and he had a stomach full of beans that made hugs incredibly pleasing. When he was new I'd slept with Gomez every night, sometimes asking Justin to spray his stomach with the cheapo aftershave he wore so I could sniff it when he went home and feel closer to him. As I'd got older Gomez no longer had pride of place on top of my pillow, instead being relegated to the top of the wardrobe with a random selection of childhood toys that should probably have gone to the charity shop long ago. But where before Gomez had been a comfort, which is why I'd pulled him down in the first place, now he was also a sad reminder of what I'd lost.

*

The film has finished and I'm relieved. I feel antsy and keep stealing glances in Liam's direction to see if he feels as awkward as I do. I don't want the dynamic to change, not the one between us nor the one of the Singalong Society as a whole.

'I could do with a breath of fresh air,' Issy says, fighting a yawn. 'I think I might have dozed off for a moment there.'

'You don't say,' I tease. 'You were actually snoring at one point.' I snort loudly through my nose. I sound, and most likely look, more like a shire horse than an overworked Issy.

She covers her face with her hands. 'I wasn't, was I? Oh, the shame!'

'You were drooling a bit too,' Ray adds, pointing to an irregular-shaped damp patch near the crotch of his jeans. That would've been hard to explain were it not right where Issy had been using his thigh as a pillow. 'See?'

'This gets worse by the minute,' Issy groans, stretching her arms above her body in a bid to wake up. 'Fancy a walk around the block to help my snoring, drooling body wake up a bit?' From the coy glance at Ray, it's obvious this question is directed at him.

'I'll get my coat,' he says, pushing himself up off the sofa.

'You've pulled!' Liam calls after him; just the kind of quip that Ray himself would be proud of.

'He'd pulled from the moment she set eyes on him,' Connie said with a smile.

'Come on then, sleepyhead,' Ray says handing Issy her jacket. 'Let's get going.'

Issy zips up her mid-calf-length leather boots before opening the door, 'Let's get going,' she repeats, before taking Ray's hand and leading him out into the night. The door clicks shut behind them.

'How long do you think it'll be before they're jumping into bed together?' I ask, staring at the closed door. They were probably already having a crafty snog on the other side of it.

116

'It won't be long,' Connie says. 'Did you see that blanket twitching? I'm sure they were copping a feel under it. It certainly wasn't as innocent as they made it out to be.'

'Ray talks about her all the time at work,' admits Liam, butting into our conversation. 'It's always 'Issy this…' or 'Issy that…' And he's texting her all the time.'

'I didn't know that,' I say, slightly shocked. Why hadn't she told me? I'd have thought she'd have shared that with me in a heartbeat. 'She kept that one quiet.'

'Oh yeah, it's been a couple of weeks now, at least. Every time his phone vibrates he's pouncing on it, checking to see if it's her. He's got it bad.'

'Well, Issy's a smitten kitten. Even if she hadn't told me outright she fancies Ray I'd have known, it's blatant. The flirting, the touching – it's all so *obvious*.'

'Maybe they're just meant to be,' Hope suggests.

'Maybe.' I smile half-heartedly, pleased that Issy's so radiant with the first flushes of love (or, at the very least, lust), but also a teensy bit jealous. I want some of that excitement, the can't-keep-your-hands-to-yourself excitement that they have.

Connie pushes herself up from the beanbag with an elegant poise that only years of dancing can teach. 'I'm going to wash these glasses and then I'll have to get moving too. Tomorrow's the big day, after all.'

She makes her way to the kitchen, carrying empty beer cans and as many glasses as she can manage. Hope follows her through with the remainder. For the first time since our kiss, Liam and I are alone.

'You're quiet tonight,' I offer. 'Normally you're singing your heart out.' It's not much of a conversation starter, but it's all I can manage.

'I'm just tired,' he says. 'One too many late nights. You know how it is.'

I force myself to bite my tongue. I really don't want to know any more of the ins and outs of his late nights.

'I'm sorry about last week,' I say. 'Kissing you, I mean.'

He shifts, looking right at me. 'You've nothing to be sorry for.'

'I don't usually do that kind of thing.' Understatement of the century. 'I'm not the kind of girl that desperately throws herself at people.'

'So I gather.' There's an amused look on his face. 'It's fine. I enjoyed it.'

'Oh.' I can feel my skin getting warm. I bet my neck's going blotchy too.

'It's a shame Connie interrupted us just as things were getting going,' he says with a glint in his eye. 'We were getting to the good bit.'

I gulp, unsure what to say, but flattered nonetheless. I hadn't pushed myself onto him – he'd wanted it. He'd wanted more.

'Maybe we'll pick up where we left off one of these days,' he says, placing his hand on mine. His fingers are cold and I remember another one of my mum's proverbs, 'cold hands, warm heart'.

'I don't think so,' I say, trying to keep my voice light as I pull my hand away. 'There's Justin and...'

I don't get to finish the sentence, Connie's calling through to say she's leaving. I've never gone more than a week without seeing Connie, let alone four. It'll be strange and lonely without her. Dragging myself away from Liam, I move to the hall.

Connie launches herself at me, sweeping me up in a bear hug that only serves to let my tears freely flow. My head is one big mess, a picture drawn by a child with no fine-motor skills. 'I'm going to miss you so much.'

I sniff. What a blubbering wreck I am. 'I'll miss you too, Conifer.'

'I'd forgotten you used to call me that,' Connie smiled.

'Connie Jennifer. Conifer.' I laugh through my tears at the happy memories. They're so far away, almost as though they happened to two different girls, not us. Yet at the same time I remember the many hours spent practising pliés at the barre more clearly than I can what I had for tea last night. 'It made sense at the time.'

'I'll never understand girls,' Liam says. 'You're always crying.'

Hope shushes him, throwing him a contemptuous look for good measure to give Connie and I our moment, the chance to say our goodbyes.

'It's a shame I won't get to say bye to Issy and Ray,' Connie says mournfully as she disentangles herself from me.

'Who knows how long it'll be until those lovebirds get back, though,' I say. 'They could be hours yet.'

'How long does it take?' Liam smirks with a suggestive waggle of his eyebrows.

'Hours if it's done well,' I retort automatically, looking straight at him.

His lips part and I realise how suggestive a comment that is. If the intensity of our mind-blowing kiss is anything to go by, I'm sure he can satisfy a woman, however long he takes.

'Erm, I'm going,' Connie says, peering out from behind waving arms as though to remind us she's there. 'Have a great time at *Rocky Horror* next week. Make sure you take a ton of pictures to show me when I get back. Especially of the boys in their corsets,' she adds as an afterthought. 'There's nothing like a hairy chest peeping out over a silky bodice to give me a laugh.'

'Really?' Liam said. 'Good to know.' He winks.

'Stop coming on to Connie!' My nose is out of joint even though I know he's only messing about. That's just the way he is.

'It was a joke,' he says, as though it's nothing.

'Well, sometime it's not funny,' I snap. I don't like the envy I feel; it's an unpleasant sensation.

'It's fine,' Connie insists. Her tone indicates the matter is closed. 'Now remember, I want to see those photos.' She turns to me, adding, 'And if you're able to pop in and see my dad in the next few days, I know he'll be glad of the company. I've stocked the fridge full of fresh fruit and veg but it wouldn't surprise me if it's still in there, rotten and smelly, when I get back. If you can check that he either eats it or chucks it…'

'Sure thing,' I nod, swallowing back the lump in my throat. I purposefully pull my eyes as wide open as I can to stop myself blinking. I'm determined not to cry.

'Have an amazing time,' Hope adds, wrapping her arms around Connie as she squeezes into the doorway. 'Go and change lives.'

'I will,' promises Connie, blowing us a kiss as she steps out into the night. 'Love you,' she adds. For a fleeting moment her breath is visible. Then she and it are gone, the icy air enveloping them both.

'Love you oodles, Conifer!' I shout back, my voice cracking with emotion. As I close the door, determined to keep whatever semblance of warmth I can in the small terraced house, I'm overcome by a need to see Connie. I run up the stairs to my square bedroom at the front of the house, desperately pressing my nose to the window like an excitable child looking for Santa's sleigh on Christmas Eve.

I only catch a momentary glimpse of my oldest friend before she turns the corner, disappearing behind the glowing beacon of the corner shop that would soon be closing for the night.

But I do see Ray and Issy standing next to the lamp post across the street, the grey-white glow it's emitting beaming down on them like a spotlight. Ray's hands are on Issy's face, their lips locked together in a kiss that makes my stomach flip with both voyeurism and envy.

I draw the curtains, not wanting to look and I hear Hope closing the door as Liam leaves too. Then I pull Gomez to my nose and inhale with all my might in the hope I may be able to breathe in a hint of the familiar scent that always managed to keep me calm. But tonight he smells of nothing in particular. There's just a dusty tingle that makes me want to sneeze and leaves me feeling more alone than ever.

Chapter Eight

Friday 28th October
**The Rocky Horror Picture Show* – Ray's choice*

'I don't know how you're not embarrassed. We're weaving our way through the heaving Hallowe'en crowds gathered in town for the annual 'Fright Night' and I'm feeling spectacularly ill at ease. 'Everyone's looking. They probably think we're going to a swingers club or something.'

'Stop being so conservative!' Issy says. 'Lighten up. No one's looking at us, least of all at you.' She casts a disappointed glance over my outfit, which barely qualifies as a costume. I've come as Janet, the character Susan Sarandon made famous in the film version of *Rocky Horror*. In other words, I'm dressed like an old-school librarian in a very ordinary pink dress and white cardi.

'They're looking,' I insist, self-consciously.

'It's Hallowe'en,' Amara says. 'Half the city's in fancy dress. I don't think anyone's that bothered by what we're wearing.'

It was true, the town centre was buzzing with miniature witches and ghouls hyped up by jelly sweets and brightly coloured fizzy drinks. Fairground rides that spread the length of Fargate, the city's main shopping area, had drawn people out, that along with the surprisingly mild weather; and any song with a tenuous Hallowe'en link was being blared out over the loudspeakers. There was a party atmosphere, that was for sure. But nothing would have got me wearing a wilder costume, I felt too conspicuous. Dressing up for performances was one thing – I'd been a fairy, a mouse, the obligatory tree in dance shows – but making a fool of myself in the town centre was something else entirely.

The rest of the group has gone all out, with Liam taking the Frank n Furter costume exceptionally seriously. He's shoehorned into a glitzy black sequined vest top and matching knickers, PVC elbow-length gloves and stockings and suspenders adding to the look. His lips are coated in Issy's best Mac lipstick, the one even I'm not allowed to use, and his eyelids are swathed in pale blue sparkly eyeshadow that hasn't been in fashion since the 1980s. The pièce de résistance is the pair of shoes he's conjured up from somewhere, patent leather peep toes with heels at least four inches high. It's just a shame he's struggling to walk in them and has to link arms with me as we head across Tudor Square towards the theatre.

'People'll think we're a couple,' I say. Anyone looking on must think we're the most mismatched duo on the planet.

Hope and Amara are walking on ahead, their hips swaying like runway models as they sashay along. Their fevered giggles carry on the wind, as joyful as those belonging to the children landing with a bump at the bottom of the tall helter skelter that stood in front of M&S. Amara's parents had been relieved more than shocked by the revelation about their daughter's relationship and both Hope and Amara seemed far more relaxed now there was nothing to hide. Apparently Mr and Mrs Lin had had their suspicions for a while, so it wasn't as big a bomb to drop as Hope and Amara had feared. Amara's mum revealed she'd only been pressing Amara about settling down to try and get her to open up because they'd thought she was hiding something, and they weren't at all surprised when that something turned out to be

Hope. They were in no rush to tell Grandma, though – everyone agreed that what she didn't know couldn't hurt her.

Ray and Issy are dawdling, hanging back so they can steal a private moment. It's just me and Liam right now. Although we're fine, there are no issues between us, it still feels wrong. But that could just be the Justin-related guilt gnawing away inside me, causing my stomach to ache.

Justin and I had had a brief conversation during the week – a rarity in itself these days – and I'd made no mention of Liam or the tonsil tennis, nor asked any questions about candyfloss girl. Instead we'd stuck to the 'safe' topics – the weather and what he'd had for tea. Small talk really, the kind you'd make with a stranger, not a lover. Perhaps I too am prescribing to Hope and Amara's theory that what we don't know can't hurt us, burying my fears behind the mundane.

I glance back towards the slowcoaches bringing up the rear, willing them to up their pace. Issy had hired a French maid costume, much to everyone else's amusement, and with her hair first crimped then backcombed she made a rather wonderful Magenta. With Ray alongside in a cheap synthetic wig and a charity shop suit as Riff Raff they looked pretty incredible. They were openly holding hands with the tenderness of any new couple, undeterred by the outlandish costumes and ghoulish make-up. If anything they were all over each other more than usual.

There's been no announcement about their change in relationship status either in real life or online but it's obvious that they've taken their romance to the next level. Ray had even visited during the week, which was a first as far as I was aware. The two of them had hidden out in Issy's room all night under the guise of watching Netflix, although I have my doubts that that was all they'd been getting up to. What had started off as Friday flirting was without doubt developing into something more serious.

'We were a couple,' Liam teases, wobbling on his stilettos for the umpteenth time. 'For about five minutes.'

My jaw drops, horrified at the thought of someone who knows Justin overhearing and it somehow getting back to him. 'Never say that again, please! Even if you *are* only joking. Someone might think you're serious.'

'Am I really that bad?' Liam asks seriously, tightening his grip on my arm as he turns to face me. I can't take my eyes off his lips; I'm mesmerised by their vivid colour.

There's a sharp tugging on my arm as Liam goes over on his ankle, yet again. He obviously needs to focus on where his feet are going if he's going to make it to the theatre in one piece. With a jolt of my elbow I hoik him back into an upright position. 'You're not *bad*, Liam. You're just a floozy.'

Liam laughs. He takes my comment in the way it was intended – not as an insult. It wasn't meant to be one. I'm only stating the facts. He likes women. He likes sex. 'I'm young and single.' His expression says it all. He thinks I'm a prude.

'Exactly.'

'So I should be able to flirt with, or snog, or sleep with, whoever I want without having to answer to anyone except the person I'm with at that moment. It's fun, that's all.' He lowers his voice. 'There's no shame in admitting a good shag is enjoyable, you know.'

Blood rushes to my face, my elbow stiffens. I'm thrown back to that night, to my hand reaching down towards his crotch, and I can't help but wonder what it would have been like to have taken things further. With all the experience he's got I bet he knows all the right moves.

'Sometimes I wish I was more like you. You don't need an emotional attachment. You have a different woman every week. No-strings nookie and a confidence boost into the bargain.' I smile at him, hoping he can see I'm not being unkind. 'You're living the life of Riley, whoever he was.'

'I'm sure Riley had a blast,' Liam says, moving his lipstick-stained mouth closer to my ear. When he continues speaking his voice is low, confiding. 'But I bet even he had moments where all he wanted was to hear someone say those three little words we're all longing to hear.'

I'm flummoxed. I wouldn't have Liam pegged down as someone in need of any kind of emotional attachment, let alone l-o-v-e. He always comes across as strong and independent, as though he revels in his freedom. Maybe that's the actor in him, pretending he's satisfied, when in truth he's crying out for something more meaningful than a quick orgasm and a wet patch.

My voice cracks as I speak. 'There's more to you than meets the eye.'

'I should hope so,' he replies lightly, tightening his vice-like grip on my arm as we cross the uneven paving and move towards the bright lights of the theatre, 'because if people judged me on how I look right now, they'd be sorely disappointed by what my life really is.'

*

From the minute we enter the auditorium I feel decidedly out of place. Most of the audience are in full-on *Rocky Horror* regalia – long, scarlet-painted nails that could take someone's eye out, waist-cinching corsets squeezing flesh like instruments of torture and ghastly make-up that looks even more freakish en masse. I've a sneaky suspicion there aren't many *Rocky Horror* virgins in the crowd tonight. They look far too comfortable to be first-timers. Unlike me. I'm a rabbit in the headlights.

I gawk at the collection of costumes around me. Some of the ever-growing crowd have obviously taken hours getting themselves prepped for their big night out. I wouldn't be surprised if their costumes are better than those worn by the actors in the low-budget show – Ray had gone to great pains to ensure we knew it was an amateur production. But even with the best efforts of the aficionados, Liam's costume was up there with the best, plus he actually managed to pull it off. He had the swag necessary for it to be believable. And although I hate to admit it, his chiselled cheekbones and pouty lips add something strangely alluring to the overall effect.

'I've never been here before,' Issy says, drinking in the theatre's unusual layout. 'I know that's dreadful when I've lived in Sheffield for so long. I've seen it on TV when the snooker's on, but it never looks as pretty as this on screen.' Hundreds of tiny lights were sunken into the Crucible theatre's ceiling, their brightness shining out against the stark black backdrop like crystal-drop stars against a midnight sky.

'It's a beautiful theatre,' Liam agrees, hitching up his black sequined corset. It slid straight back down, the 'nipslip' revealing wiry brown chest hairs that reminded me of coconut shell and small, chocolate nipples. I release a breath I didn't realise I'd been holding as he covers them again with the basque. For a split second I'd allowed my mind to wander again, my teeth clamping down on the protruding nut-like spheres. What the heck's wrong with me tonight? I'd have to remember to ring Justin when I got home. 'And it's a special place to perform, what with it being 'in the round',' he continues. 'There's something about knowing you're being seen from all angles that brings a new dimension to acting.'

'You've performed here before?' I ask, genuinely interested to know.

Liam nods. 'A few times, actually. The first time I met Ray was in this room. It was a production of *Joseph and the Amazing Technicolor Dreamcoat* a few years ago, we were playing the parts of two of the brothers. The Sheffield acting scene's pretty small, really, and our paths seemed to keep on crossing after that.'

'To my dismay,' Ray says jovially. He offers round his sweets, and we all gladly take one.

'You love me really,' Liam retorts sweetly, a twinkle in his eye.

'Hmmm. I suppose,' Ray says, although the bond between

them is clear to see. They're quite different people, yet their shared love of acting has made them exceptionally close. 'You're like a brother. Annoying, but for some reason I keep letting you tag along behind me.'

'More like a sister than a brother, surely?' Liam replies, innocently fluttering the false eyelashes Issy had stuck on for him. He made the most fascinating transvestite.

'Because of your get-up, you mean?' Amara asks, gesturing to his stockings with her hand. My eyes automatically follow them, passing the large bulge in his small, tight PVC hot-pants and I quickly and deliberately look at the floor, hoping no one has caught me looking. Honestly, I don't know what's up with me. For some unknown reason I'm totally and utterly transfixed.

'The outfit tonight is part of it, I suppose,' Liam says cryptically, before teasingly adding, 'Amongst other things.'

Hope looks puzzled by his elusive answer. 'What d'you mean?'

Liam smirks, loving being the centre of attention. 'Let's just say I'll be dressing as a woman more regularly come January.'

Hope's eyebrows raise skywards whilst I look on in quizzical confusion. 'Do you mean…' Hope stumbles as she searches for the right words. There's a pause, the muffled background noise of the people around us hanging in the air until she finally blurts it out. 'Were you born in the wrong body?'

Ray splutters, spraying the Sprite he'd been drinking everywhere as Issy frantically pats his back.

'Ray'll be doing the same,' Liam continues, his tone steady and serious. His hands are clamped together over his crossed legs. It's all very *Basic Instinct*. 'We're both aware it's going to be an almighty challenge getting people to accept us as women, but sometimes these things have to be done.' He nods gravely as he awaits our reaction.

There's a moment of stunned silence until Ray bursts out laughing, the straw-yellow acrylic locks of his wig shaking along with the rest of him. We all turn to look at him, then back at a chuckling Liam, whose eyes are twinkling almost as much as his eyeshadow. 'He's having you on,' Ray says as he laughs himself silly. He's actually wheezing with laughter.

'No, it's the truth,' Liam says, his hazel eyes wide with exaggerated innocence. 'We *will* be dressing as women regularly. For a time.'

Issy tuts and rolls her eyes as though a penny is dropping for her. 'Is this something to do with the top-secret job you've been working on?'

'Rumbled,' Ray says with a smile, holding his palms up in defeat.

'You could've dragged that out a bit, Ray,' Liam grumbles good-naturedly. 'Hope's face! She could have caught flies, her mouth was open that wide.'

'It's nothing to be ashamed of, being true to yourself,' Hope says defensively. 'There are plenty of women out there who came into this world 'male'. Not to mention those who choose to dress in clothes designed for 'males'.'

'I agree wholeheartedly,' Liam says. 'But I'm very happy being a man. It's fun getting the opportunity to play a woman for a while, though. It's nice to push and try something new.' I'm sure he looks at me as he says that, although maybe that's my overactive imagination running away with me again.

'Oh, it's for a show,' Amara drawls, slapping her hand against her forehead as she finally catches up with the rest of us. 'Is it a Shakespeare one? We studied *Twelfth Night* at school,' she recalls. 'The main character in that is a girl who pretends to be a boy. I can't remember why, though. It seems a long time ago.'

'It's not Shakespeare, it's more a… traditional performance,' Liam explains patiently. 'Men take on the role of women for comic effect. You've probably seen some form of this type of theatre art before. It's incredibly popular.' He winks slyly at Ray and the rest of us silently try to decode the riddle. Me, Issy, Hope and Amara look at each other in confusion. After a long and thoughtful pause we're still none the wiser.

'We're doing panto,' Ray finally reveals. We groan, dismayed Liam's hints went over our heads. 'It's *Cinderella* and us two are the Ugly Sisters. It's on over there in the Lyceum.' He gestures in the general direction of Sheffield's other main theatre, just across the square from the one we're sat in. 'It's a big gig. It's even got Claudette Watson playing the lead role,' he says, naming a singer that had caused controversy in a national talent show by flashing her skimpy thong live on prime-time Saturday night TV. Even the show's head judge, well known for his cutting comments and no-nonsense approach, had been at a loss for words and the press had had a field day on the Sunday. She might not have gone through to the final rounds, but she'd still done well out of her experience. In fact, she'd had more exposure than the winner.

'Now this I have to see,' I say, rubbing my hands together gleefully, 'it'll be comedy gold.' The boys were experts at hamming it up – I knew that from the Singalong Society's meeting. I could only imagine that when they were on stage they were absolutely hilarious.

'You two,' Amara says, shaking her head at Ray and Liam.

'They're terrible! Like two naughty little boys seeing how far they can push a joke,' Hope adds. 'Do either of you ever take anything seriously?'

Issy playfully hits Ray's upper arm, asking how on earth he's managed to keep his role a secret from her for the past weeks.

Ray's head cocks slightly before he answers Hope's question. 'I do,' he answered softly, his arm curling protectively around Issy's shoulder, 'sometimes.'

*

When people describe *The Rocky Horror Picture Show* as an experience, they're not wrong. My experience of getting high is limited to say the least – one puff on a spliff at a party when

I was eighteen left me sick to my stomach and swearing I'd never touch drugs again – but what's been acted out before me for the last two hours is probably pretty damn close to what I'd expect my mind to conjure up when under the influence. From the loopy plot to the annoyingly catchy tunes, losing my *Rocky Horror* virginity has left me feeling, quite frankly, a bit bewildered.

'That was awesome,' Liam says, an appreciative grin taking over his face. His lipstick has smeared slightly on one side, leaving a smudge that makes him look like The Joker. It kind of spoils the look. 'Good call on coming, Raymondo.'

'Ash sorted us out a place on the guest list,' Ray replies casually. 'I just thought it'd be a good laugh.'

'And it was,' Amara agrees. 'Not the sort of thing I usually choose to do on a Friday night, but I enjoyed it more than I expected to.' She looks less flustered than I feel. Maybe I'm closer to the middle-of-the-road than I think.

'You'll be one of the addicts who goes along to every performance before long,' Ray teases, his eyebrows rising jauntily. 'People obsess over this musical. Some go and see it every night it's in their hometown, or even follow the tour. It's a cult classic.'

'I didn't know much about it before,' Issy admits, holding her hand out to Ray. I watch as his fingers curl effortlessly around hers. It's as if there's a gravitational pull between them. Like magnets, they don't seem able to stay apart for long. 'I mean, I knew people dressed up and I knew the 'Time Warp', but I'd never really thought about it beyond that. As a rule, if it's not an all-out romance, I'm not interested.'

'It's unique,' Liam says with a nod, 'but that's why it's stood the test of time.'

'I don't think I'd go and see it again.' The look on Hope's face is less than impressed. 'There's too much audience participation. I've never been keen on organised fun.'

'You've never been keen on fun, full stop,' I jest. 'But I know what you mean. I'm glad I've experienced it, and going to the theatre on a Friday night feels very civilised. Much better than going to a pub and having some bloke with octopus hands grabbing me, anyway. I just think I'd have preferred a different show. Maybe I'll try and get tickets for *Dirty Dancing* next time,' I say, spying a poster promising a theatrical experience that'll 'give you The Time of Your Life'.

'The next time we go to the theatre will be to see these two in drag,' Issy says with a playful tut, waggling her finger at Liam and Ray, as though they're naughty boys who deserve to be reprimanded. 'I still can't believe you kept that one quiet.'

'If you sit near the front on opening night I'll be sure to throw you the best sweeties to make up for it,' Ray promises, a mischievous glint in his eyes.

'Now you're talking,' Issy smiles. 'Save me the Black Jacks.'

Issy seems so relaxed; unusually so. She's always working so hard, determined to give every aspect of her life her all, but now she seems calmer, more chilled out. The frenetic energy she usually exudes is gone, replaced by a mellow aura. In fact recently, in many ways, she seems more like Connie.

Connie. I'd promised her a photo!

'We need to take a picture,' I say, reaching into the side pocket of my bag for my phone. 'I promised Connie we'd take photos so she doesn't miss out on seeing everyone in costume.'

We pose in front of the curved wooden arch of the roof of the Winter Gardens, a smattering of small, multi-coloured lights flashing in the pavement beneath our feet. A fellow theatre-goer, a stranger dressed head to toe in leather, offers to take a shot of us all together and I happily nestle in between Liam and Hope, pouting as we all strike our sexiest poses.

I have to say it's been fun. For a few hours, I completely forgot about Justin Crowson and about the girl in the photo. *The Rocky Horror Picture Show* had been wacky and crazy, and kind of terrifying, but more than that I'd enjoyed letting my hair down for once.

We make our way past the darkened shops and closed cafés towards the taxi rank, Ray serenading us with 'Sweet Transvestite', his strong voice echoing around the almost- empty streets. He's a born performer. The straggling crowds left over from the earlier event are drawn to the clarity of his voice and I can see why. He has a God-given talent. How he's never made more of a success of his career is beyond me. I could listen to him sing for hours on end. Maybe he's right, maybe there is a shelf life for actors. But then who'll play the older characters if the emphasis is always on the young?

'Back at Cardigan Close for a regular get-together next week?' asks Hope, as Liam joins her and Amara in the dome-roofed black cab Amara has enthusiastically flagged down. He looks relieved to take the weight off his feet despite taking off his heels long ago, choosing to walk barefoot, much to my horror. The ground hadn't looked that clean, as I'd told him numerous times. He'd brushed off my concern until he'd trodden on a sticky pink piece of spat-out gum. All I'd heard was a squelch from under- foot and an 'oh shit' from Liam. He'd tried in vain to wipe his foot along the curb, but ended up using his fingers to peel off the goo, retching at the texture as the gum stretched seemingly forever between the ball of his foot and his pincher grip, and at the thought that it had been in someone's mouth. Even that hadn't been enough to convince him to put the shoes back on though. They must have been crippling him.

'Yep,' Issy confirms, calling into the taxi from her position on the pavement, 'back to normal next week. Liam, you can choose the film. Any ideas?'

'It's a surprise,' he shouts, popping his head out of the wound- down window. I giggle at the state of him. His hair's sticking out like he's been plugged into an electrical socket and the make-up Issy had painstakingly applied now looks like the handiwork of an over-zealous toddler. 'See you next week!' He waves regally as the cab pulls away, the motion all in his wrist.

Only as the cab disappears around the corner do I realise Hope's gone home with Amara. So much for taking it slow, I think with a wry smile.

Me, Issy and Ray loiter on the corner as we wait for another cab, and if I've ever felt more of a spare part, I can't think when. Ray's arm is leisurely draped over Issy's shoulder and she's looking up at him with a rosy glow. It's subtle, but enough to remind me I'm the third wheel. Then they're canoodling, whispering sweet nothings into each other's ears, no doubt, as they stare lovingly into each other's eyes. It's official. I'm a gooseberry.

With Connie out of the country and both Ray and Issy and Amara and Hope loved-up, me and Liam are the only two members of the Singalong Society for Singletons that actually *are* single. And Liam'll probably be off out to a club once he's gone home and got changed, hoping to pull some reckless girl or other who's up for a night of strings-free fun.

I shiver, crossing my arms across my body and rubbing my fingertips along the fleshy muscles covered just by the thin wool-mix cardi. I'm sure I'm goosepimply underneath it. It's considerably cooler now, or maybe it's more than that.

I'm alone.

For a fraction of a millisecond I consider ringing Liam and inviting him home with me. Some of the comments he made tonight have me thinking he's not a bad guy under all that bravado, and he's funny and available and had hinted last week that he'd be interested in keeping me warm for the night.

But a nagging feeling stops me; a guilt that it should be Justin I'm calling, not Liam. That thought plagues me on the bumpy journey home and loiters in my mind as I climb, weary and disheartened, into bed.

I should call Justin but I don't. I can't. Instead I lie awake, staring at the ceiling through the darkness.

Issy's headboard knocks rhythmically against the partition wall until two in the morning, punctuated only by the squeak of bedsprings and her and Ray's bliss-filled moans.

Chapter Nine

Friday 4th November
Les Misérables – Liam's choice*

'I hold my hands up. It's a bit more sobering than last week's musical,' Liam admits, presenting the familiar dark case. It was certainly less colourful than *The Rocky Horror Picture Show*. And there's no arguments about it being a sober choice. A sombre choice, even. 'But I had to choose *Les Mis*. It's the musical with the one role I most want to play.'

'Marius?' Hope guesses. I try to imagine Liam in the role. He has a touch of the Eddie Redmayne's if I squint. I think it's the pretty face. 'But isn't he the hopeless romantic?' she adds, a critical afterthought. 'That's a far cry from your reality.'

Liam rolls his eyes at my sister's comment. 'It's acting. It doesn't have to be based on a reality. And maybe I've got hidden depths you don't know about. It's not Marius that I want to play, anyhow.'

'Jean Valjean,' I offer, my voice assured. Enigmatic. Not what he appears to be. Yep, that sounds like the Liam I'm beginning to discover. 'That's quite the musical role.'

'I know,' Liam says, his jaw tight. I wonder if he's disgruntled that the rest of the group are disputing his ability to portray a tortured soul. 'That's why playing him one day is my dream.'

'You dream a dream,' Ray says, pleased as punch of his pun/misquote. 'But with all seriousness, you'd do a fantastic job, mate. You're so good at the character stuff.' He pats Liam on the back, a dull thwack sounding out from the contact. 'And it's a great choice too. It's got grit.'

'Exactly. So many musicals are all-out froth. They bury their issues in humour because that's what they think an audience wants. But *Les Mis*? That goes against the grain. It's rooted in real-life events, set out as drama, told through song, and it's been running for over thirty-five years.' This is a new side to Liam, bubbling up with an excitement he's struggling to contain. 'It might not be everyone's cup of tea, but it brought the novel to a whole new generation. Before it was just a doorstop of a book that no one actually read.'

'I've read the book.' It probably sounds like I'm showing off, but I'm not ashamed of being bookish. I enjoy the classics and I'm bloody proud to have read them. People are dismissive of them because they're scared to try something heavy, but most of them are still relevant to today's society. Everyone can relate to issues of friendship, the class divide, matters of the heart. They're part of what it is to be alive.

'Of course you've read it,' Hope says pithily. 'If it's big enough to take up half a shelf and published before 1900, you've read it.'

'Fair do's,' I concur, tilting my head in agreement. 'I'd never watch an adaptation without reading the book first, it wouldn't even cross my mind. That's why I've still not seen *The Curious Case of Benjamin Button*.'

'*Benjamin Button* was based on a book?' Liam looks incredulous, as though I've revealed some big state secret. 'Seriously?' He shakes his head in disbelief. 'Well, I never knew that.'

'Duh.'

'Excuse me! I don't get much time for reading,' Liam counters. 'Although I always buy the most recent Stephen King when I go on holiday.'

'He's alright,' I say glibly. 'But I'm sure even Mr. King himself would agree he's no match for Victor Hugo.'

'That's the beauty of creativity though, isn't it? Books, plays, music… they're to be enjoyed in their own right, not compared to one another. That doesn't benefit anyone.'

'Here here,' Issy agrees as she enters the room. She's balancing a bowl of nachos smothered in guacamole and melted cheese against her hip. The rich aroma fills the room and a stirring starts in my stomach. I expect it'll turn into a growl before long. 'I'm always saying that. Read what you enjoy, watch what you enjoy… if you like it, you like it – that's the point.'

Ray smiles at her as she places the plate on the table with a clatter. 'It'd be dull if we all liked the same thing, that's for sure.'

'I'll remind you of that next time you complain about watching reruns of *Friends*,' Issy laughs, dropping into the space beside him. It's become their spot now, as though the sofa's exclusively for them. It doesn't particularly bother me – it's not like I'm desperate to sit there or anything – I'm just intrigued by how quickly the two of them have merged into one entity. It's becoming increasingly hard to imagine them apart. Ray had spent every night of the last week at the house, passing me with a shy smile when we crossed on the landing as he made his way to the bathroom, or nodding in greeting as he purposefully put his cereal bowl back in the cupboard after it had been washed and dried.

It feels weirdly normal having him here, which surprises me. In some ways having him in the house seems more natural than having Hope up in the attic, and his effect on Issy is indescribable. She literally watches the clock of an evening, waiting for the moment Ray walks in through the door. They're like two giggly schoolkids kissing behind the bike sheds, coy one minute and unable to keep their hands off each other the next. If they weren't so damn cute they'd be nauseating.

'All set?' Issy asks, reaching for the remote control. 'No one needs more drinks or anything? Because this is a long one,' she adds.

Ray leans down, whispering something inaudible in her ear. Issy guffaws, playfully swatting his arm in amusement. Hope and I tut at each other as they continue laughing at their private joke. I'd hazard a guess at it being innuendo, most likely relating to Ray's 'long one'. That's something I'd rather not dwell on, to be honest.

'Lights off for the cinema effect,' Hope says, bouncing up to flick the switch on the standard lamp in the corner of the room. 'It always makes it more of an event.'

'We know your game. You just don't want anyone to see you cry.'

'I hold my hands up,' Hope said with a smile, literally holding her hands up to emphasise the point. 'I always cry with Fantine. But that's normal. It'd be weirder *not* to cry. That poor woman goes through the mill.'

'Tissues at the ready,' I say, moving the box towards the centre of the table before grabbing a handful of loaded tortilla chips. I'll probably be blubbing myself before too long. I'm so incredibly lonely right now. It's not just that I'm unhappy, but I'm crying out for some physical touch and every time I see Liam I'm reminded of his comment about picking up where we left off, which only leaves me even more frustrated. I wouldn't say I'm highly sexed but ten months is a long time and cuddling up to Gomez every night isn't cutting it any more. I wish Justin were here.

I bite down on the crisp, batting away all thoughts of sex. The crunch rings louder, or so it seems to me, in the newly darkened room.

'Come on,' Issy says, clapping her hands together in true

139

teacher fashion before pressing the play button, 'Let's roll. Because it's Friday night and the end of the week, and Hugh Jackman in tight trousers is a pretty good way to start the weekend with a bang.'

*

Although much of the plot puts us through the mill, the bawdy pub scenes have us joining in with 'Master of the House'. The lyrics are convoluted and only Liam's confident he knows which verse comes where, but we all sing along with the bits we know. I'm nowhere near as drunk as the punters on screen, but my wine's going down very easily and I'm heading towards the deluded state where I think I can actually sing.

Ray's up on his feet, sprietlier than ever as he takes on the role of the unscrupulous Thénardier. He's strutting about the lounge with his legs akimbo, acting like cock of the town and we're all chuckling at the faces he's pulling as he sings. He's got the comedy down pat and does a surprisingly good job at muddling along with the words. If he'd been performing this on stage and messed it up I doubt anyone would have noticed anyway because he's remarkably convincing as a hapless crook. It gives me an insight into how he'll be in the panto, doing anything to raise a laugh. He's got a devilish sense of humour at the best of times but it's the facial expressions that make his representation come alive and have us all cheering him on as he mimics stumbling around, swigging beer straight from the bottle.

The song draws to a close and he takes a bow, a perfect opportunity to give him the plaudits he deserves.

'Thanking you kindly,' he says, reverting to Regency gentleman.

Issy pulls him onto the settee and we all settle down as the darker plot unravels. For all the confidence Ray had shown as he strutted his stuff, he looks more at ease with her by his side. Justin used to make me feel like that; more comfortable in my own skin. Now my head's crawling with doubts. Everything I thought I was happy with isn't enough for me any more. Waiting for Justin's return, my role at school – I'm plodding through life without any fulfilment. Something has to change. I can't live in limbo forever.

*

'That film never fails to get me blubbing,' I say, brushing away the warm tears that are streaming down my cheeks. 'It's so moving.' I don't add that the tears are as much for myself as they are for the characters.

It's not like I'm the only person in the room suffering with leaky eyes. Even Hope's had a misty layer over their surface. Fantine's plight obviously *has* softened her, or maybe her renewed faith in love is giving her the ability to feel more deeply than she has in the past.

'It was Issy's singing that brought tears to my eyes,' Ray kids, ever looking to raise a laugh. 'Anne Hathaway has nothing to worry about on that front.' He places a balled-up fist on his chest and warbles 'I Dreamed a Dream' in an off-key vocal. It's not a flattering impression of Issy's choral ability, but it's undeniably accurate and I can't stifle my giggles.

Issy gasps in mock horror. 'What are you trying to say? That my singing isn't up to your high standards?'

'Your dulcet tones are delightful,' he says, a lively gleam in his blue-grey eyes. They smiled. I'd always thought that was a ridiculous thing to say, that eyes can smile, but Ray's really do. 'But I wouldn't put your vocal ability in your top twenty talents.'

'Really?' Issy laughs, unoffended by the gentle banter. 'I'd ask what you *would* put in my top twenty talents, but I think I can guess…' Her voice trails off as she winks a saucy wink.

'Well, if that's not my cue to change the subject rapidly, I don't know what is,' Liam butts in. 'Jeez.' He shakes his head, then carefully combs his hair back off his forehead with the tips of his fingers. 'I meant to ask, Mon, have you been to see Connie's dad since she's been away? I know you were going to try and get over there to make sure he was managing on his okay,' Liam asks.

I'm surprised by the question, surprised Liam has even considered Mr Williams. It's not like he knows him – they've never even met – and Liam and Connie hadn't been especially close.

'I went round last weekend, just to make sure he was doing alright.'

I giggle at the memory. He obviously hadn't been expecting visitors. The way he'd peeped cautiously around the latched chain on the door before letting me over the threshold had shown his wariness.

Once inside, however, I'd been pleasantly surprised. The house had been tidy but for a small amount of day-to-day clutter on the kitchen table – a box of cornflakes and a carton of milk alongside a creased copy of the *Daily Express* and an empty mug. The faux-tile lino flooring had looked clean and the house itself was warm. The whole place smelt strongly of an apple-scented air freshener, which smelt nothing like real apples.

When I'd snuck a look in the fridge there was a neat stack of upmarket ready meals, the plastic trays wrapped in paper sleeves showing pictures of chilli con carnes and lasagnes that looked far more appealing than any microwave meal I'd ever eaten. Nothing was rotting, and there were signs he'd been to the supermarket recently, half a broccoli and a small tray of button mushrooms that were still a passable colour. Connie had underestimated her dad's ability to care for himself. It seemed he was doing a pretty good job.

He'd offered me a cup of tea, popping the teabag into the large white mug before I'd even had time to respond. He bought Yorkshire tea, the good stuff, and made it just how I liked it, not too milky. I hadn't expected him to remember, although now I think about it, that's how Connie has her tea too, so maybe making a second cup at that strength is so ingrained in his routine that he did it on autopilot. We'd had a lovely chat; he'd told me all about a cowboy film he'd watched earlier in the week and asked about tap class. I hadn't the heart to tell him it was far less fun without my partner in crime alongside me, instead directing the conversation back to the livewire Year 5s I'd been teaching the Macarena. Having sole responsibility for the group of dance-mad girls was surprisingly becoming one of the highlights of my week.

Liam's looking at me expectantly, his mussed-up hair still falling forwards over his eyes and I realise I've fallen foul to daydreams yet again. It's bordering on the ridiculous how often I'm getting distracted by my thoughts lately. 'He's missing Connie, obviously, but it doesn't seem to be eating away at him. We had a cup of tea and a chat before he ushered me out of the house. I think he wanted to watch the rugby in peace.'

'And has he heard from her?' Hope asks. 'In fact, have you? I know she said she might not be in touch as much as she'd like, but I thought we'd have had *some* sort of update by now.'

I nod. 'I had an email yesterday, actually. She has to travel to a nearby town to get internet access, and from what I can tell it's not exactly high tech. But it sounds like she's having a whale of a time. She's made friends with some of the other people out there: a girl called Daisy from Norwich who's on a gap year? And she was eulogising about the guy that works for the charity. I'm not sure if she's got a bit of a thing for him or what, but every other sentence was 'Theo says this' or 'Theo does that'.' I pull a face.

'There's nothing wrong with that,' Ray says. 'A bit of romance does no harm.'

'I don't want her to lose sight of the reason she wanted to go in the first place,' I explain. 'She's been putting everyone else first for so long. I want this trip to be perfect and for Connie to get out of it what she needs.'

'Perhaps that's the point, though,' Ray said. His voice is solid, but not sharp. It makes me want to listen. 'It's not about what *you* want to get out of it, or what you think Connie wants out of it. You can't know what's meant to come out of this trip. You can't plan life down to the nth degree – it's just not possible. And sometimes the best things come out of the wild moments that haven't been planned. Maybe that's what'll happen for Connie in Uganda too. Renovating the school is an experience, and living in Africa for a month when she's never been out of Britain before – well, that's a brave decision to start with. I guarantee she'll come back with even more ambition than she went away with.'

Issy looks on with something akin to awe before reaching out her hand, placing it over Ray's and squeezing. Her lips are tight together, as though she's fighting back tears. 'That's so beautiful.'

'It's the truth,' he says. 'If you let life lead you rather than fighting against it, you find your own path.'

'And do you think you've found your path?' Issy asks, her eyes wide and expectant.

'Absolutely,' Ray says, his face open and sincere.

Just looking into their little bubble of contentment makes me wish for that for myself. They look so, so happy.

I steal a glance at Liam. He's looking at them too; a covert look where his eyes are raised, though his head is not. I'd love to know what he's thinking.

'Anyway,' I say, breaking up the love-in, 'Connie says she'll email some photos next time. It sounds like the school's taking shape and she says the kids are great – really appreciative of the work the charity are doing out there.' A lump sticks in my throat as I speak, a lump full of pride, and my voice cracks despite all my best efforts.

'You miss her, don't you?' Hope says, recognising the giveaway croak in my voice.

'Of course I do.' There's no point denying it. It's strange and surreal to think of Connie so far away, surrounded by people I've never met. Stranger still is how, because of the lack of reception, I can't reach out for my phone, text her and get an instant reply. It's the same as the Justin situation, as though there's a whacking great impenetrable barricade between us. I miss our immediate friendship, and with Issy so immersed in her new relationship with Ray, Connie's absence is even more noticeable.

I miss it all; the laughter and the dancing and talking about nothing for hours on end. Heck, I even miss the kale crisps and the delicate waft from her expensive lotions and potions.

'I suppose that's what happens when you grow up. One way or another, things change.' I smile sadly before adding, 'I guess things haven't changed for the better for me yet.'

'*Yet*,' Issy emphasises. 'There's still time. Figure out what you want and go for it. That's what you've got to do. Take a chance.'

'What if I know what I want and I'm too scared to go for it?' I ask, even though I know the answer to the question before Issy speaks another word.

'Then you need to find the strength from somewhere and take that risk. If you don't even try, you've no one to blame but yourself.' She obviously thinks I'm referring only to Justin, not Liam and the work situation and the craving for more in every aspect of my life, because she adds, 'Just ask him, Mon. Phone him up and ask him. Find out what he wants, once and for all.'

I inhale, breathing in deeply through my nose until the oxygen fills my head with a blissful rush of escape. I know she's right. One way or another, I *do* need to know for sure what's happening with Justin, whether I'm putting life on hold for someone who's already moved on, shouldering the weight of guilt I needn't be carrying.

But I'm not defined purely by my feelings for someone else. The past few weeks have reminded me of that. The other things I love – my job, the kids, the dancing – I need more of that in my life, with Justin or without him. I want to push forward in my career. I'm not willing to settle any more.

Issy's words cause a shift inside me and I know in my heart what I need to do. I'm fired up and raring to go. I'm going to do what I should have done years ago. I'm going to train to be a teacher.

Chapter Ten

Friday 11th November
Singing in the Rain – My choice*

The rain hammers against the window, the old-fashioned wooden frames rattling in the wind. The howling that accompanies it makes me shudder. I'm incredibly grateful the bad weather waited until November to start in earnest despite the forecast threatening a chilly October. Had it been like this a fortnight ago during our heating amnesty, I'd have been frozen solid. As it is I'm wearing a vest, two t-shirts and a hoodie and that's with the radiators on at full whack. My girl-guiding years have obviously prepared me well for all eventualities.

'I'm sick of this weather,' Hope says grumpily. 'It's been chucking it down all week. Every bloody day!'

'You make your own sunshine,' Ray quips, all easy-breezy.

Hope throws him a tired look. In her bedraggled state, it's kind of funny.

'Ha-ha. I'm just trying to keep positive,' he says, unfazed by Hope's lack of enthusiasm. 'Life's what you make it, and all that jazz. And things are pretty amazing in my life right now.'

Issy's face flushes with love. 'And in mine,' she says.

'That's easy for you to say,' I say, sipping my wine and allowing the sweet warmth to take over. It helps. 'You two are joined at the hip. It's easy to be positive when you're love's young dream. It's a bit harder for the rest of us. All I've got to get out of bed for is work.'

Actually, things are pretty exciting in that department right now, but I don't say that to my friends, I'm keeping my teaching dreams to myself for a little while longer. I'd toughened myself up and spoken to the reception teacher about applying for school-based teacher training and she'd been all for it, full of gushing praise that had given me a much needed confidence boost. She'd offered to help me with my application and to put in a good word with the management team when the time was right. She believed in me, thinking my skills and experience would make me stand out from the other applicants. It felt good to be praised and even better to be proactive.

I'd sworn her to secrecy, begging her to keep it to herself for now. Hope and Issy were bound to try and talk me out of it with their usual complaints about how teaching's all planning and target-setting these days. Even if that is the case, I need to find out for myself. I can't go on living a life filled with an endless array of 'what if's' and taking the first step towards a teaching career is a damn sight less frightening than talking to Justin about what the future holds for our relationship.

'I think you need to just do it,' Issy says. For a second I think my confidence has been broken and she's referring to my application and it's only as she continues that I realise she's not talking about that at all. She's still in the dark over that particular plan. 'You can't go on like this, Mon. You and Justin are going to have to talk things over. Sort out your relationship once and for all.'

'I don't know if I can,' I answer sadly. It frightens me to know we need to discuss our future when he seems so distant, in both mind and body.

I'd been on the internet again at lunchtime and there was a

new picture of him with the same girl, the pair of them sat in a booth in a dark bar. Her head was thrown back, as though Justin had told the world's funniest joke and his eyes were crinkled at the corners, scrunched up, as though he too had been laughing. They looked uncomfortably close and it left me uneasy.

'I'm scared.'

'Well, of course you are,' Issy says. Her tone implies that much is obvious. 'And that's natural, but you need closure now, whether that's a yes or a no, or whatever else. You can't carry on like this indefinitely, it's not doing you any good.'

'I know, I know. But I'm not sure I'm ready to hear him say what he's got to say if it's a final no. This is a decade of my life we're talking about here, not a holiday romance.'

'Exactly. And you've been waiting almost a year already. Do you really want to put your life on hold any more? Justin doesn't seem to be hanging about waiting for you.'

That hits me where it hurts and I feel a sudden urge to curl up in a foetal position and hide away from the world. All the earlier joy of the support from my work colleague is sapped out of me by love, or the antithesis of it. Being an adult sucks. It's a constant barrage of problems that require solutions, and solutions aren't something I've readily got.

'I'm not meaning to be harsh, but I've got to be honest,' Issy says. 'You'd be saying the same to me if the roles were reversed.'

'Maybe I need to woman up,' I say dejectedly.

'You do.' That's Liam. He's giving me a loaded look, his head tilted, his eyebrows raised in a challenge.

I exhale loudly. It sounds so easy, so why is everything always so hard? 'In the next week I'll make a decision one way or another about having a proper conversation with Justin, I promise.' The thought of telling him about Liam and the kiss brings me out in a cold sweat, let alone hearing about any of his own conquests, but it'll all come out sooner or later and I'd rather he heard it from me than someone else. 'But don't rush me on this,' I warn.

'You've had a year,' Issy reminds me. 'It's hardly rushing.'

And I know she's right.

The rain tapping incessantly against the window is the backing track to our chatter. It's particularly fitting, seeing as our film tonight is *Singing in the Rain*.

'Come on, let's watch this film,' Liam says when we've cleared every last morsel of food from the table. 'The downpour here is nothing compared to what poor Gene Kelly endures. And even he manages to muster up the enthusiasm to dance.'

*

By the time the film is in full swing, I'm feeling a bit perkier. There's something uplifting about *Singing in the Rain*. It's an old-fashioned feel-good movie and the perfect pick-me-up. I even grab the brolly from the hallway and jig around with it, ignoring all warnings from Issy that it's terribly bad luck to put up an umbrella in the house. It's a lot of fun, swinging it around the room without a care in the world, even though, with every turn, I threaten to knock over either our best wine glasses or her scented candles (lit scented candles, at that). There isn't room to swing a kitten in our lounge, let alone a cat, especially when there are already five people in it. A golf umbrella is pushing it.

We all join in, tap dancing along to the title track with varying degrees of success, Hope groaning as I perform perfectly executed wings and shuffle the buffalo with vigour. 'Serves you right,' I say cheekily, 'if you'd kept going to classes, you'd be able to do them too.' That probably wasn't the case; she'd never had the most natural rhythm.

Both Ray and Liam could move, though. I can tell they've undergone some dance training in their time. I'd seen them messing about before, moonwalking and breakdancing and that sort of thing, but I didn't realise they had as much experience of theatre craft as their technique suggests. Liam's arm lines are exquisite, his taut biceps rippling as he swings himself around the standard lamp, which has been moved into the middle of the room. If he had a trilby and a raincoat he'd really have looked the part; a perfect Don Lockwood.

Issy doesn't join in as the rest of us sing along, staying firmly seated on the sofa. Her pale skin is almost luminous in the flickering light. Since her words of wisdom before the film started, she's been noticeably quieter and she looks peaky too; slightly off colour. I hope this isn't a sign she's coming down with the sickness bug that's currently rampaging through the school. More than a quarter of the reception class have been off with diarrhoea and vomiting over the course of the week. I've been practically bathing in anti-bacterial hand wash, full of fear that I'll be next to be struck down by the nasty virus. I don't need that on top of everything else.

'I remember me and Connie doing a dance routine to this when we were kids,' I reminisce. It had been for a dance exam; one of the first ones we'd done. The routine had been a simple pattern of stamping and clapping to the beat. 'We had these bright yellow rain macs and hats on. I thought I was a right Debbie Reynolds.'

'You're prettier than her,' Liam says.

I try to catch his eye, surprised by the unexpected compliment, but he's already looking away.

My heart's racing wildly, flattered by his words, but then they probably come easy to him. He's got the patter of a used car salesman desperate for a sale. He's full of charm; he oozes it, but I hope his compliment is more than empty words.

Damn Justin and his stupid American girl for turning me into one of those women who needs reassurance from men. I've never been that girl before, although maybe that's because I've always had Justin. The thought that maybe I do rely on male approval, or approval full stop, has me bristling with annoyance.

'Maybe you two'll be the Singalong Society's next couple?' Issy offers light-heartedly.

I scowl. I haven't told her how Liam's been encroaching on my thoughts more and more over the past few weeks. She'd only use it against me, to undermine my and Justin's relationship and make out that what she thought was right – that I *do* need someone else.

'I don't think so,' I say, at the same time that Liam says, 'I doubt it.'

We're on the same page. That should feel reassuring, but it doesn't.

'Monique's too hung up on her ex to even think about getting with anyone else,' Liam continues, running his hand through the peak of his hair. It sounds like a challenge, and I naturally bite.

'I am not!' I argue. 'Anyway,' I add, my voice laden in defiance, 'he's not my ex. We're on a break, that's all, and I'm phoning him later. We've got important couple business to discuss.' The words escape before I've even processed them, and I clasp my hand over my mouth as I realise I've said them aloud and not just inside my head.

Issy's beaming at me with pride, oblivious to the wide-eyed horror I'm feeling, and Hope congratulates me on finally regaining control. It's frightening, their expectation. Pressure's bearing down on me already, as though I've made a promise I might not be able to keep.

'Couple business?' asks Liam, his voice thick and visceral. He swallows, the solid round bulge of his Adam's apple bobbing beneath the fine layer of stubble that's spread scruffily down his neck. 'You mean you're finally willing to stop being a doormat and waiting around for that idiot?'

'You don't even know him,' I reply with a glare. 'So you've got no right to pass judgement. And it's difficult, with the distance and everything... but that doesn't mean we don't love one another.'

I'm quietly hoping everyone keeps drinking at their current rate. Hopefully they're already steaming drunk and will have forgotten this conversation by morning, so I won't have to follow up anything I say I'm going to do. Although damn Issy and her bug. She's sober as a judge.

'Of course not,' he replies steadily. He's looking at me differently now, studying my face, trying to read it. I wonder if he senses how scared I am about making this phone call. That night at the *Rocky Horror Show* Liam had said he longed for love. Maybe he does appreciate how big a deal this is for me after all. 'I hope it all works out,' he adds and whether it's the simplicity of the statement or that it's come from the only person besides Justin that I've ever had feelings for I don't know, but his words send my mind spinning into overdrive.

And I do have feelings for Liam. It's hard to admit and even harder to fathom why, but being around him is driving me slowly mad.

What if Justin tells me that it is actually all over? What if he doesn't even plan to come back to Britain at all now that he's got a new love interest? I don't think I could handle more rejection. And if there's no future for me and Justin, where does that leave me and Liam? I can't think straight. My head's all of a muddle thinking of every possible outcome. I can't begin to second-guess what the heart to heart with Justin will uncover. The whole situation's so blurry and unclear.

I pick up my wine glass, gulping down the remaining red liquid without even tasting it. I feel instantly calmer as it hits my stomach. No one can force me to do anything until I'm ready. One thing's for sure, I'm going to need more wine.

'If you want me to be with you when you ring, I can be,' Issy says, her close-lipped smile peaceful and reassuring. 'For moral support, you know.'

I nod my thanks, grateful for her offer. Because if I'm actually going to do this, I have a sneaky suspicion I'm going to need all the moral support I can get.

I can't sleep.

The conversation about Justin had thrown me off my stride and I'd made my excuses and retreated upstairs soon after. I figured if I hid under the duvet forever I might be able to bury my promise, my heart, myself. But my mind's racing and everyone else is still downstairs; their boisterous laughter and bursts of 'good morning' irritatingly chipper against the bleak thoughts running riot in my head. I'm ready for sunbeams to smile through *now*, please, not soon.

Why had I let my bravado get the better of me? I'm tempted to go back down there. I could say I made a terrible mistake – that actually I'm happy to go along with things the way they've been for the past ten months – but I know if I do that I'll have to face their pity. People think I'm a doormat; that's what Liam said. I don't want to be one, I really don't. It's exhausting listening to the constant 'what if' in my head, like a record spinning round and round on a turntable for all eternity.

My friends are right, I need to put an end to all the doubt once and for all; draw a line under everything that's happened. Because even if Justin does say it's over for good, things won't be any different to how they are already, will they? I'm already alone, already unhappy, and although I'm no expert on love, I know one thing – true love doesn't make you miserable. Whatever Justin says, I can survive it. I've survived all my worst days so far, so there's no reason I can't survive this one too.

Buoyed by something from deep within, I push back the thick duvet and swing my legs over the edge of the bed until my bare soles land on the soft purple plush of my bedside rug. I walk to the landing, lean over the white-glossed banister and call down to Issy. There's a rush of blood to my head that leaves me woozy as I peer over expectantly. When she comes into view her pale, round face looks up at me with concern.

'Are you okay, Mon?' she asks.

'Can you come up a minute?' My hands grip the gloss-painted banister more tightly now. It's smooth and cold against my palms. 'I'm going to ring Justin.'

Her eyes widen. 'Now?' she asks, already halfway up the stairs.

'Now,' I affirm, batting away the nagging doubt inside me. 'It's got to be now, before I chicken out.'

*

My hands are clammy, my palms sticking to my phone case in a way that reminds me of sticky seaside days. But it's not melted ice cream or the tacky gloop of sun cream that's making this hard. It's fear.

'Are you sure you want to do this?' Issy asks. 'I know we've pushed you, but this has to be your decision. It's not up to us to make it for you.' She looks paler still and her cheeks have lost their plumpness along with their colour. I'm unsure if it's a fever or if it's a strange manifestation of guilt on her part for encouraging me to take this step.

'It's time,' I say, pressing the green call button. My friends may have nudged me, but I'm jumping of my own accord. I put the phone to my ear, the long, unfamiliar tone reminding me how far away Justin is. With the six-hour time difference it's almost midnight here but only early evening in Chicago. He might even still be at work. A flicker of doubt creeps up on me and I almost lose my nerve. I squash it down. If I hang up now, I might never muster up the courage to have this conversation again.

'Hello?'

My stomach flips like I'm on a rollercoaster at the familiarity of his voice. His accent's as strong as ever, I can tell that just from one word. That pleases me. It gives me the hope that he hasn't moved on and away from Yorkshire for good, as though

155

that hint of an accent ties him to Sheffield, and to me.

'Erm…' I stumble awkwardly, 'it's me. Mon.' Surely he recognises my voice from one beat in the same way I'd know his anywhere, after hearing it so frequently for so long? But for a reason I can't explain, I feel the need to justify myself. Just so he's perfectly clear who he's talking to.

'Mon!' He sounds surprised, almost flustered. 'I didn't expect you to ring tonight. It's good to hear your voice.'

I smile, placated by his words. That's not what you'd say to someone you have no feelings for, is it? But I steel myself, pulling myself back to the purpose of the call. 'We need to talk, Justin. There are things you need to know. Things *I* need to know.'

There's a pause.

The raindrops pelt down against the window. It's still raining, then, I think. I wonder if it's raining in Chicago too, where it's probably not quite dark yet.

'Okay,' he says slowly, probably wondering what on earth I'm going to say next.

'I don't know where I stand,' I say, using every ounce of bravery I can muster. 'Do you have any idea how hard that it? You're over there living the high life with your new, important role and your snazzy flat and you're doing new things all the time. You've got this whole life I know nothing about, whereas I'm still here in the same old routine. I don't know where I'm going and it doesn't help that we're 'on a break'. What does that even mean? I don't know if you're seeing other people or what.' I'm on a roll now, so I keep going. 'And I kissed someone, and I don't know if that's okay or if I've done something wrong. It was only the once, but I'm eaten up with guilt. I can't do this, Justin. I need to know where I stand.'

There's another pause, and I can hear the rain again, harder now. I wonder if it's another hailstorm. It certainly feels cold enough in the house for Arctic conditions, even with the heating on. I wish I'd put my thick bed socks on to warm the ice blocks that double as my toes. An unsettling knot forms in my chest and I squeeze my eyes shut to block out everything around me as I wait for Justin to speak. I'm scared that if I don't actively focus on breathing, I might forget how to do it altogether.

'You kissed someone?' There's a hurt in his voice.

'Yes.'

'Who?' he asks, his voice wavering. 'Someone I know?'

I shake my head, even though he can't see me. 'No one you know. No one important.' It's not the whole truth. Liam is important, but it feels like the right thing to say. 'I bet you have plenty of girls throwing themselves at you over there,' I say, making a conscious effort to sound light. 'It's like that scene in *Love Actually* where they all fall for that guy's cute British accent. The American's love a Brit, don't they?' I hint. This is his opportunity to be honest about the girl in the photo. I'm convinced she's more than a friend.

He laughs. 'Mostly I get asked to repeat myself. I think they expect proper BBC English, not my northern drawl.'

'So there aren't any girlfriends, then? No one keeping you warm at night in my absence?' I'm more forthright now. I'm feeling courageous. And although my voice is soft and lilting there's a Sheffield steel in there too. Whatever he says, I'm tough enough to take it. 'Because I happened to notice a few photos of you on Facebook with someone, and wondered if it was anything serious, you know?'

He laughs again. He actually has the audacity to laugh. 'Oh, the one in my profile picture? That's Lucinda. She's my boss.'

My body jolts. He's seeing his boss? I know she's young, but still that's got to be a conflict of interests, especially for someone who's always made a point of being professional.

'Your boss?' I repeat. I sound like a parrot.

'Yeah, we had a team-building day down on Navy Pier and I liked the picture. That other one had been up for so long it didn't even look like me.'

'She's pretty,' I say through gritted teeth. My jaw's set so tight it hurts.

'I hadn't noticed.' I can hear the smile in his voice. It riles me.

'Are you teasing me?' I accuse.

'What? No!' He blusters. 'I just hadn't really thought about it. A few of the other guys in my team talk about how stunning she is, but I don't see it. Why would I when I'm not looking?'

My heart slows; the knot in my chest loosens. He's saying all the right things and I trust that he's being honest with me. It's hard to process, that's all. There's been so much unsaid for so long. 'So you're not looking for anyone right now?'

'I've not been looking for anyone the whole time I've been here, Mon. Why on earth would I, when I'm madly in love with you? I meant it when I said that me coming out here needn't impact on us as a couple. I didn't come here to be away from you, I just needed time to do something for me before we settle down. I've always thought we'd be together forever, growing old and getting grey and gummy. I still do.'

I smile at the thought of grey and gummy. It's something we've always said, that we'll still be together when our hair is wiry and our teeth are false. But Justin had been wrong to believe him leaving wouldn't change our relationship; of course it had. You can't spend a year away from the person you profess to love and expect them to put their whole life on hold whilst you're off gallivanting. That's not how love works. Love is compromise.

'I kissed someone else because I can't bear being apart from you. I'm so lonely, Jus. It's difficult loving someone and not being able to be with them and I've been doing that for the best part of a year now.'

'I know,' he says, his words quiet, soft. The gentle tone of his voice washes over me. It makes me want to cry. 'I have too.'

I take a deep breath as I absorb what he's saying. He means me. He's finding it hard being away from me.

'You miss me?' I say finally, the words catching in my throat.

It's unattractive and unbecoming to beg for compliments, but it's the only way to find out if he's actually saying what I think he's saying. I've come this far. There's no way I'm ending this call without some solid answers.

'Yes,' he says, 'I do.' His voice is low, barely there, and although I should be reassured, I'm not. Not completely.

'Things have changed, Justin.' I sigh. 'Did you know that Connie's gone to Africa to volunteer? And Issy's seeing someone now too. They've reminded me that life is short. Everyone else, you included, seemed to realise that life's for reaching out and grabbing dreams with both hands. I've never done that. It's time I did something for me for a change.'

I want him to know that I've come to the conclusion there's more than this, whatever 'this' is. I have to explore what the world has to offer. And I didn't mean travelling, crossing my legs and saying 'ooohhhhhmmmmm' on a beach in Bali in an attempt to find myself – not that I'd ever want to go to Bali, with my fear of flying. It's simpler than that. I don't want to get to eighty and have regrets. I need to do things for myself, for the Monique Brown that no one else sees.

'I'm going to go on one of those cupcake workshops, where they teach you how to pipe properly. And maybe when Connie does her teaching exams for tap I'll do mine too – it'll open up extra doors. She's planning on opening a dance school, you know? If it's popular, maybe I could teach a few classes for her. I've been running a dance group at school and it's reminded me how important dance was to me. *Is* to me.' I'm excited now, realising life is full of infinite possibilities. 'And I want to go to Paris, but it'd have to be on the Eurostar because I don't like flying.'

I can hear his smile down the phone and it warms me. The rain's no longer beating against the window in anger either. 'I know.' His voice sparkles with encouragement and I pull myself taller. 'The world's your oyster. And if I can help you do all these things you want, I will. You've been so supportive of me. I can't

159

thank you enough. Knowing I've got you… it's been a real boost when I've been struggling. Being able to have this time away and knowing when I get back to Sheffield we'll be able to pick up where we left off – it's really allowed me to do my best out here.'

The comment grates on me. 'I'm some sort of long-distance safety net, you mean?'

'More like a guardian angel,' he says. 'My beautiful angel with a curly blonde halo and petal pink bee-stung lips.'

'There's something else,' I interrupt, dismissing his kind words. I'm proving a point, showing he's not the only one with drive and ambition. 'I'm applying to do teacher training.'

Issy gapes at me with eyes like saucers. I turn my back on her, knowing what she's thinking. I like being able to spend my days doing the fun stuff – finger painting and bark wood rubbings and pulling my fingers through cornflour leaving trails that slowly vanish. Living with Issy, I'm under no illusions about how hard teachers work and the pressure they're under. Hope had said it was getting continually worse, even in the time since she'd qualified. But I'll answer their questions later. Right now this is between me and Justin.

'That's brilliant,' Justin enthuses down the line, the joy in his words at complete odds to the horror on Issy's face. 'You'll be a wonderful teacher; I've always thought you would be. You're so good with the kids, so patient and loving. You'll still work in the early years though, right?'

'Probably.' I hadn't really thought about it, but some of the training and experience from my first degree had to be transferable. All the theories I'd learned, names like Bowlby and Piaget, were still filed away somewhere in my brain. They just need dusting off.

'It's really exciting, good on you. So you'll be going back to university?'

'I can train on the job, I think,' I say, hoping that's the case. I've no idea whether or not I'll be considered a suitable candidate for the highly competitive teacher-training programme at Clarke Road. I'll have to go and speak to Mrs Thomas on Monday. She always offers snippets of praise for my displays and she loved the nursery rhyme nativity I'd made the costumes for last year, but will she think I'm worth investing in? I hope so. Right now becoming a fully fledged teacher is a goal I needed to strive for. 'I'll look at other options if I need to, but I'm hoping I'll be able to do it through work. That way I can get paid as I train, too.'

Issy was still looking at me horrified – the last hint of colour draining out of her face with every word I say. I might be tired, but she's exhausted, the pressure on her with the threat of Ofsted looming and additional Christmas activities such as carol concerts and the PTA craft fayre fundraiser pushing her to the limit.

'When I get back it'll be you chasing your dream,' he says, proudly. 'And I'll be supporting you in the best way I can.'

'*If* you come back' I say. 'Life over there seems far more exciting than anything going on here right now.'

He chuckles. 'Of course I'm coming back! It was only ever going to be a year-long placement. I'll be home in January.'

I can't hide my disappointment. 'I thought you'd be home for Christmas,' I say with a pout. My voice is whiney too, but I don't care.

'The project's taking a bit longer than they originally thought. Lucinda says it's more likely to be wrapped up during the second week in January, so I won't be home till after that. Mum, Dad and Benji did mention me coming back for Christmas, but I'm going to be up to my eyes until late on Christmas Eve, then back in again the day after Boxing Day. It's not feasible for me to fly home. I think they're going to come out here instead: have a proper American Christmas. It'll fit in nicely with Benji's school term dates and as they didn't get a summer break this year it'll be their holiday.'

'Oh.' There's nothing more I can say. Even in my most down-hearted moments I'd thought he'd be home for Christmas. And whether we were together or not had almost been irrelevant. I just needed him here to override the negative memories from last Christmas. I'd had plans for us to go to the carol service at St Agatha's, to shop for gifts at Meadowhall the Saturday before Christmas, even though the queues would be ridiculous and full of stressed out shoppers unable to get the presents they'd promised their loved ones. I'd planned to gorge on mince pies with him, even though he was one of those freaky people who preferred them cold and plain rather than warmed up in the microwave and then drowned in double cream.

'Don't be like that, Mon. You know I'd be back if I could, but it's not going to be possible. It'll make it even better when I do get home.'

'I'll be up to my eyes in work in January,' I say tartly. 'I was really looking forward to spending the holidays with you after all this time apart.'

'We've barely spoken in months,' he sighs, obviously frustrated by my snappiness. 'So you can't be missing me that much.'

'You didn't ring me either,' I blast back. 'Don't lay all the blame on me when you're the one who decided to go away for a year. I didn't want to phone because it upsets me to think of you so far away. I know nothing about your life now. Do you know how strange that is? For all I know, you could be with a different girl every night.'

'I told you, I haven't even thought about anyone else. I don't want to sleep with someone who's not you. I don't even want to *kiss* anyone else. The thought repulses me. I want you, Mon. Only you.'

My cheeks burn up as I think of Liam sat downstairs. I remember his eager erection pushing readily against me through the stiff denim of his jeans. I remember wanting to tear his clothes off, because even with my body pressed hard up to his he hadn't felt close enough.

'I know it seems like January is a long way away, but it'll be here before you know it,' Justin assures me, turning my thoughts back to him. 'And with your application and Christmas to keep you busy, you'll be glad not to have me under your feet.'

'I'd never be glad of that.' My voice is thick and raspy, and to my ears laden with guilt.

'It's good to talk to you, Mon, properly talk. We'll speak again in a few days, yeah? You should get some shuteye though, or you'll feel crap tomorrow. You've never been good at coping with lack of sleep.'

That's the truth. One of the few things that turns me into Grumpy McGrump is a lack of sleep. 'Speak soon,' I say quietly. 'Night night.'

'Sweet dreams,' he says. 'I love you.'

And although I love him too, something holds me back. I can't formulate the words.

I swallow down my sadness and pull the now-silent phone away from my ear.

'So?' Issy asks. She's impatient, her gaze full of questions. 'What's going on? Are you and Justin together or not? And what the hell do you mean when you say you want to teach? Have you completely lost your mind?'

I raise my shoulders dismissively, things barely more clear in my mind than they were before. 'I don't know. He says he loves me and that as far as he's concerned we're still together. But I'm not sure, Issy. He didn't really say anything about the fact that I kissed Liam.'

'What would you have preferred? That he called you every name under the sun or that he takes it for the mistake it was?'

I'd expected ructions. I'd almost hoped for them, as though Justin's jealousy would prove our love was worth fighting for. I should feel like a winner for having got away with it, but instead I feel as unsure as ever.

Issy stands up, staring me down. She looks tall, standing over me like that. 'You have to take responsibility for your own life,

Mon. For someone so insistent about being in love you're hardly overjoyed that he's forgiven you so easily.'

'Because it's not that simple!' My blood's boiling with rage. She can't understand, with her precious shiny relationship with Ray all blot-free and perfect.

'You've got to learn to be more resilient. You overthink every little thing, making dramas out of nothing. It must be bloody exhausting in your head, replaying every little thing.'

'I am resilient,' I reply, as much to convince myself as to convince her.

'You're fragile,' she says pointedly. 'You're like an egg with a hairline crack just waiting to split. We all worry about you so much because you rely on us. I'm sure you're as much a part of the reason that Connie didn't go to Africa sooner as her dad was. She didn't think you'd cope without her.'

The words cut through me until I let out a strangled sob. Is that really true? No, it can't be. I'm not holding people back. And I'm not weak; I'm independent. Aren't I?

'And I've seen the way you look at me and Ray, like you're jealous because we're together.' She looks hurt, her already-hollowed cheeks sucked in. 'It's not a nice way to be, Mon. Don't you think I found it hard, being the third wheel to you and Justin for all those years? Those nights when you two were holed up in here watching box sets of *Game of Thrones* and I was in my room, alone except for a pile of marking and my planning folder? But I didn't complain, because you were happy. Can't you be happy for me now it's my turn? Please?'

'I *am* happy for you,' I say. 'I'm just sad for me.'

'And I get that it's hard with Justin being in America, I do. But that's the way things are for now and you either like it or you lump it.'

Issy looks decidedly peaky now, her face a ghostly shade of white and rather than thinking about how to put an end to the argument I make my way towards her, placing my hand on her arm. She never normally looks anything less than perfect, but right now she's a million miles from immaculate. I feel bad for drawing her into a pointless argument when she looks as though she could keel over at any minute.

'You don't look well. Come on, sit down.' I guide her towards my bed to encourage her to perch on its edge, scared that if I don't she'll fall. Her cheeks are pinched, her face gaunt. She resembles 'The Scream' – Munch's famous painting.

She lurches forward as she sits, only managing three feeble words as she clutches her stomach. 'I feel sick.'

With a sorrowful moan Issy retches, the sudden gush of vomit spilling out onto my beautiful purple rug. I instinctively hold her long hair away from her face, because that's what friends are for.

Chapter Eleven

Friday 18th November
Fame/Rent – Issy's choice/Liam's choice

'You've got to be kidding me.' Hope's face is a picture as she takes in the iconic red *Fame* logo. 'I didn't even like that film as a kid, let alone as an adult.'

'It might be my choice, but it's for Mon,' Issy says. 'Ray and Liam too, I suppose. It's only me and you who aren't into dance.'

'It's all legwarmers and high kicks,' she grumbles. 'And that bloody annoying song.'

Naturally that starts us all off singing it, just to rile her all the more, each of us shooting our hands in the air in a statement pose as we give the chorus our all.

'This should be my theme song,' grins Liam. 'I wanna live forever and for people all over the world to remember the name Liam Holly.'

'You've got youth on your side,' Ray says with a laugh. 'The time for me to make my mark is running out fast.'

Issy shushes him. 'So *Fame* is the first film of the night, just for an injection of leotards and ginormous hair.'

'Sounds like my life in a nutshell,' I joke, poofing out my hair to make it as wild as possible. It doesn't need much encouragement.

'And my choice is...' Liam pauses, keeping us all on tenterhooks. He produces a DVD case from behind his back. '*Rent.*'

'Yet another surprising choice from Mr Holly,' I observe. 'A musical with serious issues at its core once again.'

'I don't know it,' Hope says dismissively. Issy says the same.

'You're in for a treat,' Liam promises. 'Life, love, how creative souls are undervalued... I think you'll relate.'

'But we're starting with *Fame*, yeah?'

Issy nods, 'And we'll phone for take-away so it arrives between the two films. The Singalong Society's first double-header.' She sounds genuinely excited. For someone who's ambivalent about musicals, she's pretty animated at the prospect of two back to back.

'That's a whole lot of musical to get through in one night,' Hope says weakly. She's not as easy to win round.

'I know,' I say happily, rubbing my hands together. 'I can't wait.'

'Let's crack on,' Ray says keenly. 'The sooner we start the sooner we can be tucking into our chicken kormas.'

Liam scoffs. 'Korma? It's not worth having curry if you're having a Korma. Madras all the way.'

'Now now boys,' I interrupt, 'let's not get into an argument over the take-away. We're here to sing, remember.' I'm desperate to get started. I could really do with a good old singalong and Issy's choice was perfect for getting up and moving. She and Hope might laugh at the dated dance moves, but I knew it'd be fun for me and the boys; an opportunity to really show off. 'Are you ready?'

'Ready.'

'Ready.'

'Ready.'

And then came Hope. 'Let's get this over with.'

'Look at the determination on their faces,' said Ray as the hopeful auditionees pirouetted their way across the dance studio on screen.

'Desperation, more like,' Liam retorted with a laugh. 'That dread that takes over when you really want a role. It drives you insane.'

I'm transported back to school, back to the audition for the end of year show. Yep, I'd been both determined and desperate. I can't begin to imagine how it must be for Liam and Ray going through that process as a matter of course for every job they went for. Opening yourself up to criticism and judgement from total strangers – it must take a thick skin.

'Does the rejection ever get easier?' Hope wonders aloud.

Ray shakes his head. 'Not really. It's like they say on here, for every fifty thousand people calling themselves actors, there are only five hundred making any money out of it. The competition's fierce for every role, and it can be pretty damning. But that's the nature of the business; the casting people know what they're looking for and if you're the wrong height or your hair's too short or you have a 'mare on the day…'

'You get a lot of knockbacks in theatre. But it's all worth it when you find someone who believes in you,' Liam added. 'And you go into show business on the understanding that the pay's crap and there's no stability. It's not a steady nine-to-five job and unless you're a household name you have to take whatever roles you can to make ends meet. There's no room for pride when you're a jobbing thespian.'

'I bet you've never been a tree,' I say, remembering the fetching brown catsuit I'd worn for one dance show, complete with natty green pompoms that doubled as leaves. 'That wasn't my finest moment on stage.'

'Never a tree,' Liam confirms. 'But I did get paid to dress up as a Teletubby once for a family fun day.'

I chuckle. 'Now that I'd pay good money to see. Were you Tinky Winky? Or Dipsy?'

'Po,' he laughed.

'Ah, the cute one,' I say, before blushing as I realise what I've insinuated and immediately trying to dig myself out of the hole. 'At least you know you weren't typecast.'

'Ha bloody ha,' he replies, sticking out his tongue. 'You're so funny.'

'When's there going to be a song we actually know?' Hope moans. 'The legwarmers and hideous perms are wearing a bit thin already.'

''Fame' isn't until about halfway through,' I tell her, and she sighs in frustration.

'This musical needs more music,' she says fiercely. 'Seeing as it's set in a theatre school.'

'Now there's something I never thought I'd hear you say,' Issy butts in. 'I think you're secretly a fan of musicals since we started The Singalong Society.' Her eyes are alight, teasingly sparking.

'I'm most certainly not!' Hope answers defiantly. But she's fooling no one. We can all see her twitching, desperately trying not to click her fingers in time to 'Hot Lunch' as the kids from Fame shimmy around Shady Sadie's cafeteria. She's not quite at Ray's level of musical fandom, but she's converted, in spite of what she says. Things aren't always clear-cut, and you can say something until you're blue in the face and it might not be the whole truth. There are secrets hidden in all of us; things we're reluctant to reveal. I know all about only revealing part of the story. My smile's been plastered on for the past year, even when smiling was the last thing I felt like doing. Now I'm in a quandary, unsure of my next step. Part of me is convinced I should drop everything to go and visit Justin, because there's been such a strain on our relationship. If it's going to work, we need to work at it. The ocean between us feels insurmountable.

But I can't just drop everything here, however much I'd like to. They rely on me at school and with my plans for next year at the forefront of my mind I can't run the risk of pissing anyone off on a whim. Plus, I'm scared of flying. Irene Cara got that one all wrong when she was flinging her lithe body over bright yellow New York taxi cabs in the middle of a Manhattan street. The last thing I want to do is learn how to fly, but 'I wanna learn how to teleport' doesn't have the same ring, I suppose.

Hope continues to insist it's one big masquerade and the whole Singalong Society is a drag that she tolerates. 'Isn't it over yet?' she asks, dramatically hiding her head behind a cushion.

'Another quarter of an hour,' Liam confirms as on screen a stoned Doris joins the cast of *Rocky Horror* on stage. 'You know you love it,' he adds as he waggles jazz hands at her.

Hope waggles her own back, but with derision.

'Well, *I* love it,' Issy says, undeterred by Hope's feigned disinterest. 'And it's my choice, so you'll have to grin and bear it.'

'Grimace and bear it, more like,' chunters Hope, although for someone who's disinterested her eyes are glued to the screen. 'I'm going to text Amara and see if she can come over. Moral support is necessary if I'm going to make it through this in one piece.'

'Think of the food,' suggests Ray, throwing a pile of take-away menus in Hope's direction.

'Trust you to be thinking with your stomach,' Issy says, but there's an affection in her words.

'What can I say?' Ray grins. 'Food's the way to my heart.'

'And here was I thinking it was my little black dress that caught your eye,' she says with a flirtatious flutter of her eyelashes.

'Oh, it did,' Ray agrees. 'But if you want my heart as well then curry and poppadums are the way forward.'

'Good to know,' she replies. 'Decide what you're having and I'll ring the order through.'

'Ah, so you *do* want my heart?' he says, a flattered smile on his face.

'Ray North, I want every part of you,' she says softly. 'And well you know it.'

*

I'm still humming the theme song during our much-needed break as Ray's sings Doris' audition number 'The Way We Were' and compares her lack of musicality to Issy's off-key warbling. It's a chance to top up our glasses, stretch our legs, nip to the loo and stuff our faces with curry. The song's a total earworm and absolute cheese. Cheese on toast. Cheese on toast with tomato ketchup.

A series of almighty thuds come from the stairwell, whipping me out of my food-related bubble. Panic floods through me when they're followed by a deep and mournful wailing like an animal crying out in the throes of a long and painful labour. What on earth's going on?

As I swing the door open, I almost fall over Liam. He's curled in a ball on the small square of carpet at the bottom of the stairs, writhing, as much as it's possible to writhe when you're all hunched up. The dreadful noise is louder here as it echoes menacingly around the stairwell, and I notice he's clutching his ankle in desperation.

'Are you okay?' It's a stupid question. I can see he's not and if the sound he's making's anything to go by he's in complete and utter agony.

'I fell,' he says simply. His speaking voice, unlike the keening that had been emanating from him just moments before, is unusually high-pitched and full of fear. His hand hasn't moved from his ankle and I wrack my brain, trying to decide whether I should attempt to move him. My first-aid training should be coming in useful, but I'm terrible in a crisis. Something about the recovery position flickers, but I can't recall the correct protocol for a possible break. Do I call for paramedics immediately? Or should I slowly try to move him, if he feels he's up to

171

it? I know if it's broken moving him could do more harm than good, but Liam really can't be comfortable lying there in a heap. He's over six foot tall, for starters, and coiled up in a space just a couple of feet square. With one small twist of his neck he stares up at me, his harrowed eyes connecting with mine. He winces as he speaks. 'It hurts so bad, Mon. It's my ankle. I think it might be broken.'

His words propel me; that and a hot rush of adrenalin. This must be what people mean when they talk about 'fight or flight'. My first-aid certificate counts for diddly-squat right now and there's nothing I've learned from cleaning a child's scraped knee that I can apply to help in this situation, but I know I need to act fast.

'Do you think you could move if I help you?' I ask, although I'm not sure I'll be able to support his weight alone. Most likely I'll need to one of the others to help me. Liam's a big guy, tall and muscular. He's lean, but solid.

'Maybe,' he says, grimacing. He's an eerie shade of white, like a vampire. He'd probably stand a great chance of getting a role in a remake of *Twilight* if a casting director happened to be in our house right now looking for an Edward. Exquisite bone structure, a tortured look and deathly pallor worked a treat for Robert Pattinson, so Liam would be a shoo-in.

'Is it just your ankle that hurts?' I ask, immediately wishing I could retract the 'just'. There was no 'just' about it if Liam thought it might be broken.

He nods. 'The right one.'

Cautiously, I lift the rough denim of his jeans. My fingers brush the coarse hair on his legs, the tangle of medium-brown fuzz at the bottom of his calves. I'm taken back to when he was dolled up to the nines at *The Rocky Horror Show*, where a similar mass of wiry chest hair had been on display. That was the night he first opened up to me, when I'd started to see him as some-thing more than a womanising playboy. When I'd wondered what it would be like to be with someone like him.

I care about him so much and it's upsetting to see him battling such severe pain. For all his machismo and bravado he's as vulnerable and needy as the rest of us. Right now he looks it, too, and it reminds me we're multifaceted, every one of us. Complex creatures, who stubbornly crave independence, when the truth is we can't survive alone. The Singalong Society has confirmed that, the support we all offer each other constantly giving us the courage to step outside our comfort zones.

With great care I roll down the thick-ribbed band at the top of his chunky black socks. I'm petrified of doing more harm than good. As I peel back the fabric I have to clamp my mouth closed to stop myself gasping. It doesn't take a medic to see there's damage. Liam's ankle is already swollen up like a balloon; the whole area an angry shade of purple that a pickled beetroot would be proud of.

'Do you think you could shuffle to sit on the bottom step if I help you? Or Ray might be able to help,' I say, thinking out loud. 'Then maybe Issy could drive you to A&E, she's not had a drink…' Talking through the options helps me realise maybe this isn't a hopeless situation. Perhaps I should try this in other parts of my life too. Vocalise, rather than let my thoughts run away wildly. Be a bit more methodical.

'Well, I can't stay here all night,' he says through clenched teeth. His face is a similar shade to his ankle. He's embarrassed, I realise.

'Ray!' I call loudly, deciding assistance is necessary. He's there straight away, confused as to why his mate's lying helplessly in a heap. 'Did you hear that colossal bang? It was Liam falling down the stairs,' I explain.

'From top to bottom,' Liam added wryly, 'and I bounced on every step.' It's reassuring to hear him attempting humour. If he's got the energy to crack jokes, maybe things aren't as bad as they look.

'His ankle's swollen and he's in considerable pain,' I continue, feeling like a paramedic on a TV drama relaying the event to a doctor, 'but the skin's not broken and there's nothing that looks like a break.' Not that I know much about breaks. Basically all I'm saying is it's not one of those freakish injuries where there are right angles in places there shouldn't be. 'Liam thinks he can move to the bottom step with our help. If we take an arm each and support as much of his weight as we can between us, hopefully he'll be a bit more comfortable. Then we can get some ice on it.'

Liam hooks his arm around me, and although I'm not bearing most of the weight – that's down to Ray – I'm surprised by how sturdy he is. I know he works out a lot – not to mention his bedroom athletics, which no doubt help keep him in good shape – but he's heavier than he looks. More manly.

He swivels on his left foot, lowering himself onto the stair, and his fingers dig into my shoulder as he relies on me to get him sat down safely. It hurts, although my discomfort's obviously nothing compared to his right now. He sucks the air sharply through his teeth. Even without putting any weight on the injured ankle, he's finding it hard to move.

Once he's sat, I head to the large chest freezer at the top of the cellar head, rummaging beyond the stack of frozen pizzas and a couple of steaks that I salvaged from the reduced section at the supermarket last week. Ah, there it is, the bag of frozen peas, unopened. It's a cliché to use peas in a situation like this, but surely there's a reason they've earned their place in First Aid 101. I hope so, anyway. We're not the type of household to have one of those squidgy ice packs you keep in the freezer to reduce swelling.

I hurry as fast as I possibly can and hand Liam the peas. He knows which part hurts better than I do. I wouldn't like to guess – the whole bottom half of his leg is now an aubergine colour.

'Ah!' he shouts, flinching as the bag of peas comes into contact with his skin. I assume it's because the ankle is so tender from the fall and applying pressure hurts, but then he adds, 'That's bloody freezing!'

'If you're fussing about it being too cold rather than the pain, it's a good sign,' I say firmly. I'm more like a school matron with every passing minute. 'Hold them there for ten minutes and then if you can manage it, we'll help you to the settee.'

'I think it's only a sprain,' he says, gingerly holding the peas in place and trying to waggle his ankle against all my and Ray's protestations. He looks so young perched on the step, despite his towering height. I can imagine how he looked as a little boy: wary and vulnerable. 'It was such a shock, that's all.'

'Go and get him a whisky,' Ray advises. 'My dad swears by it for shock. When he whacked his thumb with a hammer putting up the garden fence, he drank nearly a whole bottle of Scotch.'

'Are you sure that was all medicinal?' I say, suspiciously. 'That's a lot of Scotch. And I'm not sure we've got any whisky. I think there's still a bottle of Cava in the fridge, though?'

Liam looks at me in disbelief. 'I fall down the stairs like a sack of spuds and you want to crack open the bubbles? I know we've had our differences at times, but that's ridiculous.' As Liam smiles, to show he's only kidding, I reach over and playfully swipe his shoulder. 'And now you're beating up an injured man. Seriously! If I didn't know better I'd think you hated me.'

'I don't hate you, Liam,' I say, and it's the truth. Against the odds he's quickly become one of the people I care about most; one of my closest friends.

Friends. I realise now how crucial they are. Everything's that bit less daunting when people are watching your back. Without my friends my life would be without colour, devoid of song. As much as I want to see Justin, I don't need to go to America. It's been ten and a half months since I last saw him in person, so what difference will another six weeks make? I've got something special here in Sheffield with my friends in The Singalong Society and I'm finally taking action to reach for my dreams – I've spent every lunch hour this week finding out more about the teacher-training qualification. I worked out that even during my training period I'll be better off financially than I am now, and of course there's far more opportunity to progress as a teacher than as an assistant. I love what I do and I value its importance, but it's nice, just for once, to prove that I'm capable of more.

Also, I really, really, *really* hate flying. Even flying to Corfu scared me half to death. The thought of being stuck in a plane for eight hours, or however long it takes to get to Chicago, makes my head spin. I can't do it, not even for Justin.

No, I'm better off staying here, with my feet planted firmly on the ground. It's still a struggle matching up my and Justin's schedules with the time difference determined to scupper our plans, but with Skype and FaceTime it's almost like he's here with me when we do talk. I can't touch him, or smell his skin, or taste his lips, but I can see the corners of his mouth rise into the first hint of a smile when I say something daft and I recognise the puzzled look when I mention something he doesn't understand, the little vertical lines that crease between his eyebrows.

It's not long now until I can hold him in my arms and give him all the love I've saved for him over the last year. I only wish it were sooner; January isn't soon enough. My body is crying out for attention.

I must have a faraway look on my face because Liam's looking at me quizzically. My heart beats faster at the intensity in his gaze and the feelings that stir inside me as a result. His lips slowly separate and I'm taken back to when they connected with mine and how wonderful it had felt. I force myself to drag my eyes off him. I've got to stop thinking about him like this. It isn't right, and it definitely isn't fair on Justin.

My eyes move beyond Liam and up the flight of stairs and I spy Issy staring blankly down at us. Her hand's clutching the wooden handrail that runs the length of the staircase, although she shows no sign of descending the steep stairs typical of all

Sheffield's terraced houses. She looks absolutely petrified.

She's frozen rigid, scared to descend, and I haven't the faintest idea why. Before I can say a word Ray's up there with her, wrapping her up in the safety of an embrace. Issy shudders, judders as though she's crying uncontrollably. Ray strokes her hair and repeatedly murmurs his hushed assurance that everything's going to be okay.

There's something going on here, something I don't understand and seeing Issy so anxious is freaking me out. I don't like it. I don't like it one bit.

*

There's an unsettled air around Cardigan Close as we ready ourselves for the second musical feast of the night. Since Liam's fall something's changed; something tangible and strange and not entirely pleasant. Liam himself seems alright, so long as he doesn't attempt to move from his spot on the sofa and bear weight on his ankle, but Issy and Ray are far more subdued than usual. The normal lighthearted atmosphere is missing and, to be honest, I'm not in the mood for *Rent*.

Ray and Issy are in the armchair, Issy cradled in Ray's arms like a helpless babe. There's no colour in her cheeks, no smile on her face. She looks harrowed, haunted and utterly dependent on Ray. Her hand is clutching fiercely to his shoulder as though she never wants to let go. They're like one being, and I feel like I'm intruding by sharing the same space.

Hope's yawning, as though she's exhausted. She'll never make it through two hours of rock musical. Her eyelids are flickering as it is, and I'm considering suggesting we all call it a night. The only thing stopping me is Liam. I don't want him to go back to his flat yet. He tried to stand earlier and called out in pain, so how would he manage alone? Ray said there was a steep staircase up to Liam's flat, so even getting to the door would be a challenge. Then what if he needed the toilet or a drink? He'd be crawling around the place on his hands and knees. I'd tried to persuade him to go to the walk-in centre, but he'd insisted he'd be fine with a couple of Ibuprofen and rest, promising to go to get checked out tomorrow if things didn't show any improvement.

The cast of *Rent* are standing on stage singing 'Seasons of Love' and my heart pangs with sadness. I've never reflected on the lyrics before, but now they seem so poignant. One year – five-hundred, twenty-five thousand, six hundred minutes. Give or take, that's the same length of time Justin will have been gone. There are many ways I could measure that time. In films I've watched or biscuits I've eaten or days I've come home from work with playdough caked to my trousers. Or lustful thoughts or sleepless nights or kisses with Liam. It's a long time, a year. I glance over at Liam, his foot still propped on the coffee table. He's singing along quietly, his eyes closed, as though in prayer. That's what he'd look like asleep, I think, peaceful and fragile and oh so beautiful.

The reel of New York's streets takes over the TV screen, the primary-coloured lights of Radio City Music Hall contrasting with the gloom of tent city and his eyes spring open.

'I'm pretty tired,' he says, 'although I think Hope's further gone than I am.'

I look at my sister, curled up at the opposite end of the sofa to Liam. She's fast asleep, emitting a thrumming hum as she breathes which is just audible above the scene playing out.

'It's been an eventful night,' I agree.

'I think I'm going to head home. I'll call a taxi,' he says ruefully, 'I don't think I'm up to walking.' He moves his ankle down from its resting place and winces at the movement.

'I'll drive.' I've only had one glass of wine tonight, and although I never normally risk driving after drinking anything at all, I know I won't rest until I see Liam back in his flat safe and sound.

I'm curious, too, interested to know what his private space is like. You can tell a lot about someone by where they live.

'Don't go to any trouble…' he begins.

'It's no trouble. I want to.' I frown. 'I don't think I'll be much help getting you up the steps, though.'

'I'll shuffle up on my bum if I need to,' he says nonchalantly. 'I've done that before when I've been pissed.'

I laugh, despite myself. 'It's a bit different being drunk to being injured!'

'Stop fussing,' he insists. 'I'll manage, but I am exhausted. Can you take me now or shall I get a cab?'

'I'll take you.'

I reach for my car keys and help Liam up. His arm's slung around my shoulder as he hobbles awkwardly across the room. As 'One Song Glory', my favourite song from *Rent* begins, I close the door on Ray, Issy and a snoring Hope and wrap my arm around Liam's waist. Roger's voice sings of time flying, muffled but recognisable through the walls.

This whole musical is about how things decay and regenerate in every part of life. How, in the blink of an eye, the world can change.

Time. It's the strangest, strangest thing.

*

I knew the area he lived in wasn't the best, but I hadn't expected it to be as downbeat as this. The maisonettes have a reputation for being rough and squalid, a favoured haunt of spineless crack dealers and desperate addicts, but it's much worse than I expected. Firstly it's almost pitch black, with every other streetlight broken. It doesn't feel safe, and an angry man is shouting obscenities at his wife/girlfriend/hooker. His vile words echo in the darkness. The bins are overflowing and the bitter stench of urine overwhelms me as I help Liam through the communal walkway and

179

up a dark, curved stairwell. Even with him beside me I feel threatened, and as a crunch comes from beneath my feet, I jump. Looking down, broken glass, jagged and sharp, glints back up at me.

'Home sweet home,' Liam says half-heartedly as we reach an olive-green door with the number 47 written on it in tippex. The paint's peeling off, curling away like it's been attacked by a cheese grater.

I don't know how to respond. He'd often joked about being a hard-up actor, but I hadn't realised he lived in such a dive. It made Cardigan Close look like Buckingham Palace.

'I know it's not much, but it's a roof over my head,' he says defensively, drawing his arm away from me. My heart heaves with shame for being so judgemental and not being able to hide my fear from my face.

He sucks in the air through his teeth as he digs into his pocket, pulling out a single gold key tied to a piece of red wool.

'I didn't know what to expect, that's all,' I say quietly as he unlocks the door. The smell of clean washing wafts out, refreshing and uplifting against the dull, oppressive grime.

Liam flicks the light switch. Nothing happens, not even a blink of light. He cusses in frustration and for one horrified moment I wonder if he's living in total squalor, like Mark and Roger in *Rent*. Maybe the electric's been switched off because he's missed one too many payments.

Liam's shuffling along the hallway wall, leaning his weight against it and I follow as closely as I can, scared to lose his shadowy outline to the darkness.

'Are you okay?' he asks. His voice still holds that gruff defensiveness.

'I'm fine,' I lie. My heart's racing with fear but there's a glimmer of red light shining in through a window; probably one of the shop fronts or restaurant signs from the nearby main road.

'You can light my candle,' he says as we reach a large rectangular living space. I squint, trying to make out what's in the room. There's a large, low shape that I assume is a settee and a waist-high cabinet or chest of drawers pushed against the wall. There's a trunk or table next to the settee, squat and stubby.

'Don't you have electrics?' I ask tentatively. I can still hear shouting, the faraway fight causing my shoulders to tense.

He laughs. 'I'm hardly loaded, but it's not that bad. Someone from the council's meant to be coming to sort the wiring next week. The lights in the hall and lounge haven't worked since I moved in. But I wasn't just going for the *Rent* link when I mentioned lighting a candle. There are a few on the mantelpiece, and a lighter. If you put the kitchen light on it'll shine through, too.'

I make my way to the far wall, stepping through the bright slice of scarlet shining through the window. I understand now what it means to be living on your nerves. Everything's heightened here, in this unfamiliar darkness. I fumble for the lighter, relieved when my hand touches the cool plastic. The fattest part of my thumb presses against the metal cog, causing the spark to burst into life and I touch the flame to the wick of a thick white candle balanced on a saucer.

The light takes the edge off my anxiety. The warm glow lifts the room and although everything is still hazy, I can see the room more clearly. Everything's bathed in a soft-focused amber hue. The settee is old and worn; a dusky pinkish velour like the one my grandparents had when I was small, and what I'd thought was a window behind is actually a door leading to a small balcony area. Against the wall there's a bookcase crammed full of paperbacks, and the rectangular trunk doubles as a table. There's a thick orangey-red carpet, at least it looks orangey-red, although it's hard to be sure in this light. Buttery yellow floral curtains hang wearily from a rail.

'So this is your place.' It's an obvious comment, but it's all I've got.

181

'It is.'

'How long have you lived here?' I can't imagine it's been long; nothing about this room screams 'Liam'. Everything looks as though it's come from a second-hand shop, all jumbled and mismatched, and not from any one particular era.

'Since the spring. I couldn't hack it at home any more.'

'Trouble with your parents?'

Liam inhales. 'My brother.' There's a weighty pause but I don't interrupt. 'He got into drugs. The hard stuff.'

'I'm sorry.'

'Watching him fall apart was too painful and seeing my parents question everything they'd ever done for us… that was the worst of all. They spent every penny of their savings putting Jase into rehab. They were so desperate. We all were.' He looks physically drained as he speaks, as though talking about it hurts.

I recall how awful it had been watching Hope lose control, how difficult it was for Issy to accept Penny's current condition. Siblings had a lot to answer for. 'It must be scary, watching someone you love change.'

Liam inhales again, purposeful and loud, shutting his eyes tightly as he does. 'I wanted to help, but nothing I said or did could stop him looking for the next hit. I had to get out of there, even if it was to a shithole like this. If I'd stayed any longer watching him fade away I'd have driven myself insane.' He shakes his head sadly as he flops back onto the settee. 'I couldn't stay there, waiting for him to kill himself. He had the world at his feet, everything to live for. I don't understand why he did it.'

I sit down next to him, the flickering candles casting freakish shadows against the walls. Placing my hand on his cheek, he turns to look at me. A single tear is trickling down his left cheek.

'I didn't used to be like this, Mon, I wasn't… flighty. I never used to sleep around and party all night, but since everything with Jase…' His voice tailed off. 'It's how I grieve, Mon.' The

182

meaning behind his words hits me like a truck. 'He died in April.'

The sadness etched on his face breaks my heart and as he falls into me, broken and bereft, I wish there was something – anything – I could say to take away his pain.

As my arms become his blanket a line from *Rent* rushes to the forefront of my mind. Quietly, comfortingly I whisper, my lips brushing against the warmth of his ear lobe. 'I'll cover you.'

*

It's the middle of the night yet I can't sleep. What Liam told me is plaguing my thoughts. It explains so much about him, why he's so up and down and hard to read, and I wish he'd felt able to tell me sooner. He'd sobbed into my shoulder for an hour, the weight of his head pressing against me as heavy and life-affirming as it gets. Through strangled cries he'd told me every heartbreaking detail; all the things he wished he'd said and done. I hadn't wanted to leave him alone. I'd wanted to hold him all night long and ward off the nightmares of the past, but he'd insistently told me to leave.

I give up even *trying* to sleep. It's futile. There's no point phoning Liam, although I desperately want to. He'll be out for the count by now, I hope. I can't ring Justin, either, because he's heading out to celebrate a friend's birthday straight from work, but I can't face tossing and turning all night.

Throwing back the covers, I twist myself out of bed. Maybe the warmth from a mug of hot chocolate would be enough to lull me to sleep.

I'm as quiet as I can possibly be on the stairs, not wanting to disturb Hope and Issy, who're probably fast asleep. It's only as I reach the bottom of the stairs, standing on the very same spot where Liam had landed earlier, that I hear the sobbing.

Tentatively, I peep through the gap in the door where it's been left ajar.

Issy's sitting on the edge of the settee, weeping. She looks up and sees me watching her, her whole body shaking as she breaks down.

This is my cue and I'm there like a shot. There's no way I can stand back and watch her struggle.

'Hey, hey,' I say soothingly. 'Whatever's the matter?'

She snuffles noisily and without care. 'It's too much.'

I'm confused. 'What is?'

'The guilt!' She practically screams the words. 'It's eating me alive and I deserve it all.'

'I don't understand…' I want to, but I don't.

Her cheeks are blotchy and wet. I've never seen her so forlorn.

'I can't keep it in any more,' she cries, dragging the back of her hand under her eye to catch a teardrop that's threatening to fall. 'Eight years I've kept quiet, because I blamed myself. Eight years! Do you know how hard that's been? Carrying grief around that long?' She sniffles again. 'I'm scared, Mon.'

I put my arm around her, and for the second time tonight I hope it brings comfort. However, I still don't have a clue what she's trying to tell me. 'You're with me. There's nothing to be scared of, I promise.'

'But I don't want you to hate me,' she stutters.

I look right at her. 'I could never hate you, Is.'

She closes her eyes, breathing in deeply. 'Even though it's something awful?'

My heart's pounding with anticipation. I don't know if I'm prepared to hear this, whatever it is she's going to reveal to me. 'I'm your friend. I'll support you no matter what.'

She opens her eyes but avoids looking at me, instead fixing her gaze on the far wall. She looks terrified, bewildered.

'The reason I'm so desperate for a baby, why I've been so protective of Penny…' She pauses and bats her hands in front of her face, trying to compose herself between the sobs. 'It's because I was pregnant once. When I was her age.'

I'm staggered. Whatever I was expecting her to say, it wasn't that.

'I wasn't as brave as Penny, though,' she laughs bitterly. 'I didn't tell anyone except Carl. And he wasn't exactly thrilled at the prospect of being a dad.'

Carl. The Zac Efron lookalike she'd gone out with during sixth form.

'He told me he wanted nothing to do with the baby, and he'd have nothing to do with me either unless I 'got rid'. Those were his exact words. 'Get rid of it or we're over'. I can see the rise and fall of her chest, rapid and fraught. 'I wanted to keep the baby. I knew it'd be hard being a mum so young and I was scared to death of telling my parents, but there was no way I was going to have an abortion and I told him that. And that's when he took matters into his own hands.'

My blood runs cold. 'What do you mean?' I press, visions of gin and knitting needles and all the other horrific procedures I'd heard were meant to induce miscarriage rushing into my head. I'm woozy at the thought, but I need to stay strong for Issy.

'We were at school, up in the science block. Carl was furious at me because I wouldn't have an abortion, really raging.' She looks more angry now than sad. 'We had a blazing row. He was shouting in my face; he looked so menacing. I remember thinking he wasn't the same Carl, not the one who'd been so gentle with me before. He wouldn't have put pressure on me. That's when I screamed back and that's what made it happen, Mon. I should have shut up and kept quiet and then it would have all been alright.'

'What happened?' I say, gulping down my nerves.

Issy spits out the words, incandescent. 'He pushed me down a flight of stairs. And he was really strong, Mon. He really used his force. I went from the top to the bottom: eighteen stairs and he just stood there and watched me. My baby didn't stand a chance.'

Realisation hits me. *That's* why she freaked out so much when she saw Liam had fallen – it had brought back all the memories she'd tried to forget.

I pull her into my body, wishing I could take away her pain, but nothing I can do will help her. I can only listen; listen and support.

'If only I hadn't argued with Carl,' she curses. Her voice is laced with pain. 'I wound him up. That's what made him do it.'

'No,' I say firmly. 'This was his doing, not yours.' I can't bring myself to say his name. The thought of what he did makes me feel sick.

'I don't think I'll ever get over it,' she says, crying into the curve of my neck. And what she says next breaks my heart. 'I should have a child of my own, but Carl took my baby away from me. He left me on that landing whilst I screamed out in pain, as I bled and ached and thought I was dying. And he never spoke to me again, either. Not one single word.'

Chapter Twelve

Friday 25th November
Oliver! – Hope's choice

We've gathered earlier than normal so Connie can regale us with stories from her time away. Liam, Issy and Ray are listening with interest to her tales of the hospitality of the Ugandan families and the three hour long church services they attended on Sunday mornings. I'm interested, too, but I've already heard all about her trip – I went to her house the very evening she landed, to find her brown as a berry and talking as fast as the Artful Dodger. She was overflowing with exuberance. It's so good to have her back, to know our clique's back to our full capacity, or at least it will be once Hope gets back from the gym. She's being virtuous at the moment, she and Amara both committing to losing a couple of pounds before they put them all back on again with the excesses of Christmas.

When Hope finally arrives, she's less than impressed. 'It's so dark and miserable,' she complains, shaking raindrops off her black brolly as she stands in the doorway. 'I shouldn't have bothered showering after my workout, I'm soaked to the skin.'

She's letting all the cold in, but she either doesn't notice or doesn't care. My teeth are chattering as I silently will her to shut the door quickly. We need to retain what warmth we've got in this house, although at least it's toasty in the lounge now the log burner's back in business. 'I don't think I'm made for British winters,' she adds.

'Maybe you should jet off to Africa like Connie did,' suggests Issy. She's not being serious; a smile is creeping onto her lips. Minx.

Hope shakes her head vehemently. 'Nuh huh. That's not for me. But I could fancy a fortnight in the Maldives or somewhere. Escape to the sunshine for a bit. Maybe when I'm older I'll be one of those people who spends half the year in Australia and half in the UK; chase the good weather.' I just know that in her mind she's stretched out on a sun lounger on an Aussie beach, wine in hand, Amara rubbing sunscreen on her back, not sopping wet in a mid-terraced red-brick house in Sheffield.

'You'd miss the rain if you never saw it,' I say.

'I doubt it,' Hope replies, peeling off her soggy jacket with a frown and placing it on the red-hot radiator. 'I'm soaked through! Look, I'm dripping all over the floor!' Her skinny jeans, usually a deep indigo shade, look almost black now they're so drenched.

'I'll get you a towel,' offers Issy kindly, heading up the stairs, 'hang on.'

Hope sighs, gladly catching the taupe bath towel as Issy throws it down.

'Cheers, dear,' Hope calls up the stairs.

She bends forward from the waist, scrunching her long hair dry between two layers of towel. There's the merest kink in it when it's wet like this. Personally I think it suits her more than the over-straightened style she's been favouring lately.

When she stops leaving puddles in her wake, Hope spies the food on the coffee table, an even more lavish spread than the usual offerings. Admittedly, we always manage to eat our way through whatever's laid out on any given Friday, but this week it's on a whole new level. Perfect triangular samosas, sausage rolls, onion bhajis, Kettle chips, breadsticks and dips, coleslaw and potato salad – and more than enough for us to nibble on all night.

I fold my arms defensively as Hope takes in the veritable buffet and rolls her eyes. I get in first, determined to put my side across before she accuses me of trying to undo all her hard work on the treadmill. 'I know it looks like a lot, but I've not had any tea. I've hardly eaten all week what with the inspection so I did a bit of a trolley dash and shoved in anything that could be heated in the oven in twenty minutes or put straight on the table.'

'It's been one hell of a week,' Issy agrees, rubbing her eyes wearily as she lies back on the settee. She looks snug in her onesie, having already had a long soak in the bath with the last of the bubble bath. Gone were the days of her dressing up to impress Ray. He couldn't care less what she wore so she'd reverted to her comfies. 'I know I'm a good teacher, but as soon as those inspectors come into my classroom I lose all my confidence and become a jibbering wreck.'

I know that. I've seen her anxieties first hand. Issy's literacy lesson had been observed this morning and at lunchtime I'd found her physically rocking herself in a corner of the staffroom, still a bundle of nerves as she awaited feedback. And the truth is, Issy's a fantastic teacher – and not just in the academic sense. Yes, she moans about the ludicrous amounts of planning and prep and the pressure on both children and teachers to achieve targets set by people who've probably not set foot in a school since the day they sat their last exam; but she manages to walk the fine line needed to work in junior schools. She's cool enough, without trying too hard. She's firm, but fair. She has an opinion on the latest must-see film and who's the best looking member of the boyband of the moment without it feeling forced. Young people like her and with her encouragement, they believe they can do whatever they set their mind to. What's more, they want to achieve for her as much as for themselves. Issy's exactly the type of teacher I aspire to be, one day.

'I've never understood what it is that Ofsted actually *does*,' Liam admits. 'All I know is that teachers hate it.'

'It's stressful,' I affirm. 'Even if you know you've done all you can do; even if you've bribed your class with extra break time if they behave when the 'special visitors' are in, it's the most ridiculously stressful experience. It's not natural, being scrutinised like that by strangers. And as soon as they're looking in it's like I'm performing in some low-budget film. I start gurning and emphasising my movements and giving children the thumbs-up every five seconds.' I demonstrate my double thumbs-up and too-enthusiastic smile before grabbing a mini sausage roll. I pop it into my mouth in one go, ravenous.

'At least it's over, for now,' Hope smiles. She's taken the whole inspection in her stride. 'They won't be back for another few years. You'll be a fully qualified teacher with your own class by then, Mon,' she adds, which fills me with both excitement and dread. This week's been hard enough, and I only had to do what I was told. Using my own initiative in those kind of circumstances would be something else entirely; a real test of my ability to perform under pressure.

'I don't want to go through another Ofsted inspection again, ever.' Issy's emphatic. 'I was a wreck. I threw up in the sink in the art corner when I was setting up this morning, just through sheer nerves.'

'Urgh.'

'You can 'urgh' all you like. I was the one who had to clean it up before that miserable-looking inspector came prowling. Like things weren't bad enough.'

'As long as it's not that nasty bug,' I say, holding my arms up in a cross to indicate I most definitely don't want to come down with the lurgy. I hope I look like I'm warding off viruses, but fear I actually look more like a hopeful contestant for *The X*

190

Factor. 'It's still hanging around and people don't seem to be able to shift it; it's a superbug. Jamie Percival's mum's been laid up for over a month now,' I say, referring to the parent of my favourite reception child. I know it's not fair to have favourites, but I do. Jamie's wise beyond his years and a dream pupil: keen and polite. If I can somehow find a classful of Jamies, teacher training will be a breeze.

'You're fine, aren't you love?' Ray says, affectionately kneading Issy's knee. 'Just ready for Friday night and putting your feet up.'

'Too right,' Issy agrees as she stretches her arms above her head. 'There's no place like home at the end of a tough week.'

'We should watch that some time,' I say. All I get back is blank looks, and exasperated I say, '*The Wizard of Oz*? Now that's a musical of epic proportions. 'If I Only Had a Brain', 'We're off to see the Wizard', I smile fondly, 'and 'Somewhere Over the Rainbow', of course. That's just beautiful. It never gets old.'

Ray shakes his head. 'We can't fit in into the schedule yet, not until after Christmas. I sorted through my DVD collection when I was back at my mum and dad's house. I brought back some beauties, including a Christmas classic for the Friday before Christmas.'

I try to shake it, but thoughts of last year's Friday before Christmas rush to the forefront of my mind. It's unsettling, but at least this one should be full of hope and promise, watching a film in the safety of my own home surrounded by some of the people I love most in the world. And the New Year will start on a positive note with Justin's impending homecoming, which has to be preferable to the heartache I carried through this January.

'I'm looking forward to Christmas,' Liam says. His ankle's up on the coffee table, a makeshift prop to take the weight off it. He's taken great delight in showing off his whopper of a bruise – now a purpley-brown with mustard-yellow trim – and was walking with a pronounced limp, which I'm sure he's over-egging to make sure everyone remembers he's a wounded little soldier.

I'd been relieved he'd made the effort to go to the walk-in clinic, where the nurse had confirmed it was a sprain and prescribed painkillers and rest. 'My mum makes the best roast dinner. Turkey, stuffing, pigs in blankets, all the trimmings… and her roasties are better than any top chef's.' He doesn't mention his brother, so I don't bring up last week's conversation, either, but Christmas was bound to be tough for his family this year. An empty seat where Jase should be sitting; fewer presents under the tree. One name less written inside the flurry of cards that would arrive from well-meaning friends, or worse, acquaintances who hadn't heard the dreadful news, writing four names in their card instead of three.

'Everyone thinks their own mum's the best cook in the world,' Ray laughs. 'And I hate to disappoint you, but the award for best Christmas dinner would go to my mum, hands down. She does this amazing potato and swede mash with gallons of cream cheese.' He smacks his lips together at the thought. 'It's mouth-wateringly good.'

'I don't think me or Mon would ever claim our mum's roast worthy of praise,' says Hope mournfully. It's true. The meat's always tough and chewy, the veggies soggy from being left to boil for far longer than necessary and her attempts at gravy are famously unsuccessful – either too runny or too lumpy. The unspoken promise of the shop-bought chocolate log and posh ice cream which inevitably follows is the only thing that keeps us eating our annual Christmas lunches, because there's nothing about the main course that appeals.

'Speaking of 'Food Glorious Food', let's get this show on the road,' Liam says, setting the DVD to play.

Jolly orchestral music of hits from *Oliver!* plays out; a megamix of tunes that it's impossible to resist humming along with. We're bopping our heads like nodding dogs in the back of a Ford Fiesta, eager to be taken back to Dickens' London.

'This should be our anthem,' Hope says, piling her plate high with finger food. So much for watching what she eats. *Oliver!* is in full swing, the workhouse boys lusting after pease pudding and saveloys. Watching this certainly makes me feel grateful: for my job and my home and the array of food we're able to choose from.

'Agreed,' I say, biting down on my fifth cocktail sausage of the night. They're absolutely delicious. 'I love this song.'

Ray obviously loves it too, using a breadstick as a conductor's baton to ensure we all join in. Some of the notes are ridiculously high and by the end we're all giggling because we're squeaking like little mice.

'And now it's the best line in the whole film,' says Hope.

We watch on with baited breath, waiting for Oliver to hold out his bowl for more. We join in with Mr Bumble as he bellows a disbelieving 'MOOOOOORE?', exaggerating the pronouncement and repeating it numerous times with increasing zest. We laugh hysterically at our joke until Connie sensibly reminds us that, actually, it was mildly amusing the first time but downright annoying after that because she can't hear what's happening in the film.

We calm down, although odd chuckles escape, which earn us disapproving glances from Connie.

'It's good to have you back, Con,' I say, enveloping her in a sideways squeeze. 'And it was lovely to hear more about your trip. It sounds so rewarding.'

'It was,' she enthused. 'Those kids' faces – they were so grateful to us all. They don't have much, but they're delighted with everything they're given. I've never seen as many smiles as the day we showed them their finished classroom.'

'You did a good thing.'

She shakes her head, unwilling to accept the praise. 'It's all because of my mum. I couldn't have done it without her money.'

'She'd be so proud of you,' I say. 'Of you and what you did.'

I look over at Liam, checking how he is. We've been in contact more than usual since last week and he's continued to open up to me. All the time I'm learning about his life, understanding what makes him tick. What he shows here in front of everyone else is the tip of the iceberg, the cheeky chappy who plays the field, yet there's so much more to him than that. He's kind and generous and caring, and desperate to do more to help those in need. He's a bit like Nancy in *Oliver!* – a tart with a heart of gold. Although how much of a tart he is under normal circumstances I'm not sure. He's had such a terrible year I can't really judge his behaviour. He smiles warmly at me and I grin back, hoping he knows I'll do anything possible to support him.

The film plays on and we hum along to the well-loved tracks, singing the lyrics we can remember as we go, laughing all the time. There's a tightness between us all, much like there is between the ramshackle community thrown together in the film. Together we're strong, unbeatable.

*

With all the chatter I hadn't noticed Hope had snuck off up to the attic room until she waltzes in, her holdall casually slung over her shoulder and announces, 'Rightio, I'm going to the flat.'

My heart constricts in my chest. 'What do you mean?' I say, although I already know exactly what she means. She's going home – for good. It hits me hard. There have been nights she's stayed with Amara, but for the most part she's still been sleeping here at Cardigan Close; part of their attempt to take things slowly. Although Hope's exhausting and irritating and downright infuriating at times, it won't be the same once she's gone. I'll miss her so very much.

She looks at me, a remorseful look, which makes me feel

terrible for wanting her to stay. What Issy said a few weeks ago about me holding people back plays on my mind.

'I need to be with Amara.' When she says it like that it sounds so simple.

'Good for you,' Ray says heartily. His positive comment gives me a welcome moment of respite to comprehend the change in circumstance, and Hope beams at him for his backing. Ray's genuinely pleased for my sister, I can tell, and not for the first time I think Issy's chosen well. He's one of the good guys.

'I was never meant to be here for more than a few nights,' Hope says. 'It ended up being a bit longer than planned, and I can't thank you two enough,' she adds, looking back and forth between Issy and I. 'You've been fantastic and made me so, so welcome, but I've got to get back to the flat. Something's telling me the time's right for me to be back with my girl. Now our relationship's out in the open and everyone we love knows the truth, we can start to live like a proper couple. Not have to hide. Just *be*.'

Issy smiles; warm and true. 'For what it's worth, I think you're doing the right thing. When you know something's right, there's no point in waiting. Why delay the inevitable?'

'I'm so pleased for you,' I say to my sister, really looking at her for the first time in ages. She looks so much healthier than she did when she first came to Cardigan Close. Her dark hair is now back to its glossy best and falls at least an inch longer, so it skims over her chest like a mermaid's. She's still slender, but rather than being skinny her body has regained the soft curves that she'd always previously had. She's more like her old self in every way – her snarky, snappy comments now come across as confident and forthright, with a smidge of wit; the way it's been my whole life.

She leans forward, sweeping me up in an all-encompassing hug. It takes my breath away with its ferocity. 'Thanks for everything. You're the best sister a girl could wish for. I don't know what I'd have done without you.' She plants a kiss on my cheek. I can feel the greasy residue of her lipstick sitting on my skin, but I don't wipe it off. It's as though it seals our bond, somehow.

'You're always welcome wherever I am,' I say, and I mean it. For all our differences, the house is going to feel much quieter without her in it.

'Hopefully everything will calm down now,' she says with a smile. 'I don't want any more wandering. I don't want any more nights without Amara by my side.'

'And you won't have any,' Issy says considerately. 'Now go! Your girlfriend's waiting and it's already almost eleven. If you don't leave soon you'll run the risk of turning into a pumpkin.'

The excitable buzz reaches its crescendo as Hope sets out, heading back to her rightful home. Warmth bursts through me on her behalf. She's getting a second shot at happiness with her one true love. I just hope and pray that come January, when Justin's back in Sheffield, we too will be delighting in the pleasure that is reignited love.

*

As I change into my striped cotton pyjamas, I can't stop singing 'Consider Yourself'. My cockney accent is well below par, imitations never being my forte, but the song itself is proving to be an earworm I can't escape, no matter how much I want to.

Clambering under the duvet I reach for the novel I've been reading for the past few nights: a thick family saga set in rural Ireland during in the 1940s. I love how books have the power to transport me to a different place and time. Anything's possible between those pages and I live vicariously through the characters. Their happiness, their elation, their total gut-wrenching pain; it's set out before me, reeling me in until it's almost within my body, within my heart.

The light from my bedside lamp emits a silver-grey haze as I turn the pages and before long my eyes are heavy. I doze, hushed to sleep by a lullaby of well-written words and the half-light.

*

The long, shrill sound of my phone's ringtone rudely wakes me, my eyes popping open as though they're spring-loaded. I squint at the glowing blue digits on my radio alarm clock, struggling to adjust my vision to the light – 1.22am. It'll be Justin. I swipe the screen and answer with a sleepy 'Hello?'

'Hi, love, how're you doing? Had a good day?' He sounds bright and cheery, which I expect he is after finishing work for the week. Hearing his voice makes the world seem that much smaller, and him that little bit nearer.

I struggle to stifle my yawn. 'Good, how's yours been?' It's no good. I can't help my own natural reflexes. I give in to the exhaustion, my mouth stretching wide until I'm sure I resemble one of those super-cute lion cubs on a poster. If the lion cubs have yesterday's mascara smudged under their eyes and a pillow crease ingrained down one cheek, that is.

'All the better for the thought of the weekend,' he says, before adding, 'and for speaking to you, of course. That goes without saying.'

'Of course.'

'So how's your evening been? Did you have your film night?'

I pause. It's not that I've kept the Society a secret, it's more that it doesn't feel relevant to share it with Justin. After all, it had started out as a way to celebrate each member's single status. I can't imagine Justin would appreciate the thought that I'd been genuinely wondering about our future when he'd been so assured we'd make it through our time apart unscathed.

'We watched *Oliver!*,' I say, pulling the duvet up over my shoulders. It wasn't a lie, but it wasn't the truth. It doesn't feel like enough. I'm holding back on what's become a major part of my existence. The Singalong Society's helped me keep going when I've been close to giving in, but it'd be impossible to put into words how important it's become to me, and to everyone else. It's something that can only be appreciated from the inside, if you're in our circle.

'I've never seen it,' he says. 'But it's *Oliver Twist* with songs?'

'Right.' I don't feel like elaborating. I'm worn out.

'Are you sure you're okay?' Justin asks. There's concern in every beat. 'You sound a bit…' he waits, struggling to find the word. 'You sound a bit distracted or something.'

'I'm stupidly tired,' I admit. 'I came to bed, planning to read until you rang, but must have dropped off.'

'Oh, love, I didn't mean to wake you.'

'I know.'

'How about I speak to you tomorrow instead, let you get your beauty sleep? Not that you need it,' he adds hastily.

'That'd be good.' I'm more tired than I care to admit.

'Sleep tight, sweet dreams,' he says, the familiarity of the words making me convinced I can feel my heart swell with love under its ribcage casing.

'And to you,' I say, 'For when it's your bedtime.'

'Speak tomorrow,' he adds. 'I'll look forward to it.' I can hear the smile in his voice.

'Me too.' I pull the duvet more tightly around me. The cocoon is comforting, safe. This must be how it feels to be a foetus in the womb, the weird light and the dazed feeling and the humming – like being under water. Although I bet an unborn child's humming isn't from guilt at not being completely honest. They have nothing to feel guilty about, all pure and unblemished and free from sin. Not like me. Not like Liam with his downy-haired legs and his pillow-soft lips taking over the darkest corners of my mind.

'I love you,' I blurt, fast and sleepy. It's the first time I've said it since Justin's been away; the first time since he unwittingly rejected my non-proposal.

'I love you, too.' The buzzing in my ears seems louder now.

We hang up, Justin to start his weekend, and me to delve deeper into the womb that doubles as my bed, and I feel blessed to have Justin, dear, sweet Justin, who loves me with all his heart. Our present's pretty rotten with that whacking great ocean driving a salty wet wedge between us, but we can work on our future once he's home.

But I've got to try harder to stop myself from thinking about Liam and I definitely, absolutely, have to find a way to stop aching to kiss him again. The more time we spend together, the more I like him, but acting on my desire would be a sure-fire recipe for disaster. He's troubled, grieving, and his flirtatious remarks are nothing more than comments he'd offer up to any woman he hung around with. In his eyes, I'm a friend, nothing more and I need to stop acting like there's more between us than there is. Compliments come easy to him, and although it's flattering that he feels able to open up to me I'm going to drive myself potty by reading too much into every word he says to me.

I bury my head deep in my pillow and wrap my arms around Gomez. Clamping shut my eyes, I will myself into a peaceful slumber where the sweet dreams Justin wished for me would be waiting. But in spite of my exhaustion I'm restless and the guilt that riddles in me doesn't feel nice. It doesn't feel nice at all.

Chapter Thirteen

Friday 2nd December

Walking on Sunshine – Ray's choice*

'And now, for tonight's special showing…'

Ray's loving every second of the big reveal. His words are long and languid, his voice belonging in a trailer for the latest block-buster movie. We watch on, waiting to see what treat is in store.

Our reactions when he shows us the box must be a sight to behold, and probably not for the right reasons.

Liam snorts. 'What the fuck is that?' His words are clipped.

'*Walking on Sunshine*,' Ray says, as chipper as ever. The way he flashes the case around reminds me of one of the models that used to show off the prizes on quiz shows when I was a child. 'Featuring the greatest hits of the eighties, or so it says.'

'Come on, mate. It looks awful. What's it even about?'

'It's *Pitch Perfect* meets *Mamma Mia*,' Ray counters, reading directly from the box. He's wielding the plastic case like a weapon. 'And it's the singalong version, loads of catchy music from the decade that taste forgot.'

Liam looks on doubtfully. 'My Aunt Judy loves everything eighties. She had this VHS tape full of repeats of *Top of the Pops* that she'd taped off the telly. She played it until it went all wibbly and got caught up in the video recorder. She actually cried real tears when she realised it was beyond repair. I bet you any money I know these songs word for word, and I wasn't even born until the nineties.'

'It'll be a laugh,' I say. At least it was nothing heavy. 'And there's no excuse for not knowing the songs – they're all the ones that get churned out at every wedding do or Christmas party.'

Connie shrugs. 'I'm willing to give it a go if everyone else is. After coming back to this gloomy weather, I'm glad of a bit of additional sun, even if it is only through the TV.' She bends back the stalk of her banana until the waxed yellow skin splits pleasingly, then breaks the fruit in half before biting down on it.

'How about you, Is? Hope?' Liam looks at them hopefully, obviously willing them to take his side.

'Anything Ray recommends is good enough for me,' Issy says cheesily. She's looked more like her usual self over the past day or two. Maybe the relief of surviving Ofsted had helped her relax, maybe whatever lingering bug she'd had had finally left her alone, or perhaps sharing the burden of what happened to her all those years ago had played a part in her newly rediscovered wellbeing. There's a flush of colour high above her cheekbones and it suits her, especially after the grey pallor she's sported for the past few weeks. I'd not mentioned what she'd shared with me again but I'm sure Issy knows I'm always here to talk, or to listen, whenever she needs me.

Hope concedes, 'I'll go along with the majority vote but I can't promise to know all the songs.'

'It'll be fine,' I say. 'They're basically karaoke when they're the singalong versions, and no one'll judge you if you're out of tune.' I change my mind, thinking of the incessant ribbing Ray gives anyone who doesn't have his natural vocal ability. 'Except maybe Ray. Anyway, you know 'Holiday' word for word – it's

201

one of those songs that's in the jukebox of your mind from the minute you're conceived.'

'Along with what else?' Liam asks, looking entertained for the first time all evening.

I place my finger to the corner of my lip and raise my eyes upwards in the most thoughtful pose I can muster. "Bohemian Rhapsody', 'All You Need is Love', 'Suspicious Minds' and the theme tune to *Coronation Street.*'

'Esteemed company,' Ray replies with a grin, nodding his approval. 'Come on. I want to watch this film. I don't have a clue what it's about, in case my elusive answer hadn't told you that.'

'But it's your choice!' Connie laughs.

'I found it in my mum's collection,' Ray sheepishly confesses. 'Which means it's probably a stinker. But I couldn't pass up the opportunity to watch a new musical and if I'm going down, you lot are coming with me.'

I smile. Of course we are. That's what The Singalong Society is all about.

*

There's no denying it, the film is naff. The eighties hits are the only redeeming feature. We squeal with delight with each new song we recognise, and an especially loud whoop erupts when Human League's number one hit 'Don't You Want Me' starts up. Sheffield music at its best and Issy's throwing herself into it as she sings about waitressing in a cocktail bar. By the rousing chorus we're all on our feet, Liam included. He's obviously on the mend. The on-screen hen and stag do's are in full swing when I'm distracted by a persistent tapping on the window pane. No one else seems bothered so I try and ignore it, putting it down to the rain, which yet again hasn't stopped all day, or a stray branch from the overgrown evergreen that's in dire need of a trim scratching against the glass. I focus on the hunky actor dressed up like Adam Ant, a white stripe painted across his face, but the noise continues. It's only after five minutes, when everyone else is still happily oblivious, but I'm increasingly perturbed that I mention it.

They all look at me like I'm daft.

'It's the wind,' Connie says, offhandedly. 'Nothing more sinister than that.'

I'm still not sure. That doesn't sound like the wind to me.

'I don't think it's anything bad,' Hope says, in a bid to reassure me. I think she's trying to shut me up, because against all the odds she's enjoying herself with this film, the tiniest shimmies of her shoulders giving her away.

'I never said it was anything bad. I'm just curious. I've never heard it before, even when it's been blowing a gale.'

The noise continues, louder than ever. It's more like a tune now, regular and rhythmic.

Liam audibly sighs, knowing I won't allow him to kick back and relax until we find out what's making the noise. 'I'll go and check.'

'My hero,' I say pretending to swoon. There's actually not much pretence involved. He looks particularly attractive tonight, sporting a tracksuit top in a muted shade of green that changes the colour of his eyes. I wonder if he was wearing brown if they'd look darker. Hazel eyes are strange. Alluring, but strange.

He pulls up the hood of his sweater in preparation to brave the storm and moves quickly but awkwardly towards the door. There's still a stutter in his step, his ankle dragging as he walks.

It's only a minute or two later when he's back in the room, his hoodie soaked through despite the short time he was exposed to the elements and there's no knocking from outside now, no scratching. Instead there's a quiet mewling noise coming from the cradle of Liam's arms, and there, nestled amongst the soft yet soggy fabric of his clothes, is a tiny bundle of black and white

203

fluff. 'I think I've found our culprit,' he says, proudly showing off the bedraggled kitten like a first-time father. 'Can someone get a towel to dry him off? He's soaked to the skin, bless him.'

Hope hurries through to the kitchen, returning with the tea towel we call 'the posh one'. It had come from one of the upmarket vintage-style shops on Division Street. Liam takes it from her and vigorously rubs the kitten dry, while it mews its squeaky mew.

'Look at the poor little guy,' he says. 'Imagine being that small and stuck out there in that storm all alone.'

The kitten's no bigger than Liam's hand, and it looks stunned by our cooing faces, his bright blue almond eyes peering out from the fluffy fur in wonder. My fingers tingle as they brush Liam's sodden jumper as I reach for the kitten, and Liam jumps at the contact, his face barely an inch away from my own. It would be so easy kiss him right now. I can see the rise and fall of his chest, the kitten bobbing up and down, up and down with his heaving breath. He wants this too; I'm convinced he does.

I force myself to tear my eyes off him, studying the kitten with all my might. The similarity is uncanny. It's a living, breathing incarnation of Gomez. I pull him to me, so he's resting against my pounding heart, Liam disgruntled to be so easily brushed aside after his gallant rescue efforts. This kitten is my reminder, saving me from wrecking my relationship with Justin, I know it. I'm sure that in some weird way he's a gift from Justin.

'Hey there,' I say, ruffling his fur with the flat of my hand. As his ears prick up and he tilts his head towards me, I know I'm a goner. There's no way I can let this kitten go. 'Aren't you the most gorgeous thing in the whole wide world?' I'm speaking in that patronising voice people use when they talk to babies. I've finally lost the plot.

'Shouldn't we feed it?' Liam says. It's a rational and practical suggestion and might stop the kitten's demanding squeals.

'I don't know what they eat when they're this small,' I admit,

'Can they eat special kitten food? Or are they not ready for solids yet?' I'm clueless about this, what with this little Gomez miniature being the closest thing I've ever had to a pet.

Connie's already pulling on her coat. 'I'll go to the shop and see what I can get. It'll surely say on the packets whether it's suitable for kittens. And I'm going to keep a look out for his mum, too. I can't imagine she'll be far away. She must be worried sick.'

I hadn't even considered that and my heart sinks into the pit of my stomach at the awful thought. There's a poor mumma cat out there somewhere, wondering where her baby is and here I am plotting and planning how I can keep him. It's a brutal reminder that he's not really mine.

I fuss the kitten, taking sole responsibility despite Liam's best efforts to intervene. His breath's on my cheek, that's how close he is, but I won't allow myself to be tempted. This is no time for distractions. The kitten needs me.

Connie returns more quickly than I expect, her face troubled as she runs into the lounge. I know right away something's terribly wrong. She looks completely harrowed.

'What's the matter, Con?' Issy asks with concern.

Connie looks like she might throw up. Her face is drained of all its colour.

'There's been an accident,' she says eventually. She's trembling. 'Out on the road.'

None of us know what she's trying to say and it's only when Hope comes right out and bluntly asks her that we get the full story. Connie had been making her way to the shop, walking as fast as she could. Her head had been focused on the ground to hide her face from the never-ending rain. But when she reached the junction a lifeless lump lay in the middle of the road: a fully grown cat that Connie swore was the absolute image of the kitten we had here.

I feel even more protective of the kitten than I had before.

'Oh, it was terrible.' She's shaking. I instruct Liam to wrap the blanket that's hung over the back of the settee around her quivering shoulders. 'I've never seen a cat that's been hit by a car before. Its eyes were actually out on stalks, like in a cartoon. She must have seen the car that hit her coming towards her and been petrified.'

'What do we do?' Ray asks. 'We can't just leave the mother's body there in the middle of the road.'

'I think you can call a vet,' Issy says, but she doesn't sound too sure. 'They'll be able to look after the body and see if anyone comes forward as the owner.'

'How many vets do you know that are open at this time?' Hope asks. 'They'll all be closed. Is there such a thing as an A&E department for animals?' She whips her phone from her pocket and begins tapping furiously on the keypad. 'I'm going to look,' she said. 'There's got to be somewhere that can help.'

It's a sickening thought that this defenceless kitten is all alone in the great wide world, and I'm silently thankful that it was Connie, not me, who'd found the poor mother, especially if it looked exactly like this little furball. A Gomez lookalike lying destitute in the road would have been an omen rather than a salvation.

The kitten's heart beats in my hand as Issy talks to a staff member at the local cat shelter, giving them our address and phone number. They're going to send someone to collect the body to see if it's microchipped. 'I'll look after you,' I whisper to the mewling orphan. 'Nothing bad will happen to you now. I promise.'

*

It was impossible to regain our party spirit to watch the film's conclusion after the evening's traumatic turn of events. There was something in the air, a sense of funereal mourning and although we're determined to remain upbeat we give up on the DVD. We're not in the right frame of mind.

Connie heads home, keen to check her dad's not eaten the remainder of the Victoria sponge I'd made for the pair of them and Hope wants to meet Amara off the bus after her late work shift. Issy and Ray excuse themselves, heading to the sanctuary of Issy's room.

Liam and I are alone, except for Gomez. That's going to have to be his name (and he's definitely a he, the lady from the cat shelter confirmed it when she came to check him over. She'd left us with everything we'd need to take care of him and a handful of pamphlets to help us with every possible eventuality. She'd seemed harassed, the shelter apparently heaving with unwanted felines. She'd been relieved when I'd said I'd look after the kitten myself rather than have him stretching their resources further. And I'd been relieved I didn't have to let him go).

'Are you okay?' Liam asks, reaching out and stroking Gomez, who's sitting in my lap.

I want to answer no, that having his hand in such close proximity to my already tormented nether regions is tantamount to cruelty. But of course, I don't say that. I squirm a fraction and assume he's talking about the distressing events of the night. 'Sure. It's not the way I thought it'd be, but it looks like I've got the cat I always hoped for.'

'He's a cracker,' Liam replies, smiling at Gomez in wide-eyed wonderment. I wouldn't have had him down as a cat lover, but he's definitely vying for the kitten's attention. 'Give me a ring if you need a hand. I'm not saying I'll have all the answers, but we always had cats at home when I was growing up. And any excuse to make a fuss of this little mite, I feel me and him have a special bond.'

Liam had rescued him; I'd adopted him. We're practically sharing ownership.

'I will,' I promise.

'Do.'

He makes to leave but turns back at the last minute, giving Gomez one last scrumble on the stomach.

'See you soon, Mon,' he says gently, planting a delicate kiss on my forehead. It happens so fast I almost doubt it happened at all, but there's a burning sensation where his lips had touched my skin.

'See you,' I echo. But he's already heading out of the door and into the night.

Chapter Fourteen

Friday 9th December
Mamma Mia – Ray's choice*

I'm slouched in the armchair with a blanket draped over my knees and Gomez (the cat, not the toy) fast asleep in my lap. He's a little hot water bottle, scorching and cosy. He's quietly purring with satisfaction and I can't believe he's only been a part of my life for a week. He's already an integral part of our household.

Each day when I get home from work he's waiting, and as soon as I walk in he's there, following me around like a pull-along toy trailing in a toddler's footprints. He's so expressive, much more so than any other cat I've seen. Every so often he'll yawn with all his might, his mouth opening wide to reveal baby-pink gums with small white teeth that look like the fragments of a plate smashed to smithereens. Or he'll look at me with his bright eyes, young and old all at once, as though he knows exactly what I'm thinking. He trusts me. He relies on me.

Justin couldn't believe it when I'd told him how much he resembled Gomez, even down to the tuxedo markings. 'He's obviously meant to be with you,' he'd said, then 'we'll have to make sure wherever we rent's alright with us having a pet.' I knew it should make me smile, that he's planning our life. But every time he says something like that, something so totally lovely, I feel trapped. By my conscious, by Justin, by my very existence.

I stroke Gomez and calms takes over. It takes over me at least; Gomez starts squawking. For something so small, his voice is incredibly loud.

'How was the nativity?' Hope asks, referring to the simplistic retelling of the Christmas story that the infant classes have been practising for weeks. Today had been the grand showing, with proud parents and grandparents squeezing into the school hall to sit on shrunken plastic chairs whilst they strained to hear their precious offspring's few words in the spotlight.

'Really lovely, actually,' I say, and it had been. Even though I'm not remotely religious, it touches me every time. 'And at the end Mary told me she wants to marry Joseph for real when she's older.'

A chorus of 'aahs' follows. I decide not to add that when we went back to the classroom to get the children changed into their regulation royal blue and black uniform there'd been a large puddle of wee left where Mary had been sitting, slap-bang centre stage. I'd had to clean up the mess as the delighted parents milled around for coffee and Christmas biscuits, the mop bucket and disinfectant looking rather out of place in the makeshift stable. I doubt the innkeeper threw some Dettol around after Jesus' birth to make sure everything was sterile.

'How cute,' Issy says, with a wide smile. 'It seems to be all about babies at the moment.'

She's not wearing that pained look that sometimes haunts her when she speaks about babies, I notice. Instead she looks ethereal, at peace. Maybe the arrival of Penny's little boy, who'd been born in the early hours of Wednesday morning, had mellowed her. Perhaps being an auntie will be enough to satisfy her maternal longing for the time being; a reminder that not all pregnancies have a devastating end.

'We went to see Baby Sam yesterday,' Ray says, reaching out to hold Issy's hand and closing it in a squeeze. 'He's absolutely beautiful.'

'He really is,' Issy agrees. 'He's got this wild fair hair and a chubby red face. He looks like a less bumbling version of Boris Johnson,' she laughs.

'I'm not sure I'd use the word 'beautiful' to describe Boris Johnson. I wouldn't trust him as far as I could throw him,' Liam mutters, loud enough that it's only me that can hear him. It's typical of Liam to dispute the cuteness of Issy's newest relation, speaking without thinking.

'I don't really like babies,' he admits, his voice switching to full volume. 'It's not the crying or the nappies. I just don't see myself as a dad, ever.' Issy looks on in startled disbelief, as though she's unable to process how anyone can not want kids. She's had a similar conversation with Hope before, who's ambivalent either way about having children.

'But you sleep with anything that moves!' Issy says incredulously. 'You've probably got children all over Sheffield that you know nothing about.'

Liam shakes his head adamantly. 'There are no Baby Liams out there, I assure you. Condoms are my friend.'

'Condoms can split,' Connie retorts in a flash and for a brief moment a panicked look shadows Liam's face.

'That's my worst nightmare,' he replies with a judder, before turning to Ray. 'Imagine if that happened? It's frightening to think about the consequences.'

'For you, maybe,' Ray replies elusively. I throw him a suspicious look, convinced that yet again I'm missing something blindingly obvious. 'Sometimes life has a way of dishing up the most incredible surprises.' He places his hand across Issy's stomach and his face fills with love as he rubs circles on her belly.

I gasp as it all becomes clear.

This is momentous.

It's huge.

'No way!' squeals Hope, throwing her arms around a grinning Issy. 'You two are having a baby?'

Issy nods shyly. 'It was a bit of a shock, happening as quickly as it did. We'd spoken about children before we even kissed, because it's something that's so important to both of us, but it wasn't planned. We'd thought it'd be something that'd happen a year or two down the line. So when my period was late and I felt so rubbish…'

Something dawns on me. 'That explains why you've been so ill for weeks,' I say. I look at her stomach differently now. It's difficult not to, knowing the miracle that's hidden away under her cable-knit jumper. 'You've not had that bug at all. You've got a little person growing in there.'

She nods again.

I'm so overwhelmed I think I might cry. Issy motions me to come to her and I hug her tightly, whispering my congratulations through my stifled tears. No wonder she was so scared after Liam's fall. I realise now it hadn't just brought back the horrific memories of her miscarriage. She was scared in case history repeated itself and she lost this baby too.

'I'm over-the-moon happy for you, mate,' Liam says with a grin, patting Ray on the back. 'I know how much this means to you. I can't believe you're gonna be a dad.'

'I can't believe it myself,' Ray says, his eyes twinkling with pure joy. 'Everything's moving so fast, but in the most awesomely incredible way, you know? It's early days – Issy's only nine weeks gone – but we're going to enjoy every moment. Every new life deserves to be celebrated.'

'You're going to make wonderful parents,' I add. 'That little one doesn't know how lucky he or she is having parents like you two.'

'I'm so glad it's out in the open,' Issy gushes with relief, 'It's been awful trying to keep it quiet. Especially when I was so nauseous all the time.'

'Let's celebrate,' I say, throwing my hands into the air. I'm so flustered with all the excitement, it's high time I start pulling myself together. 'I made a big batch of chocolate chip cookies. They're massive. Honestly, they're like dustbin lids. They're well worthy of breaking into to celebrate a baby announcement.'

'And then let's get the film rolling,' Hope says.

Liam agrees. 'I'm going out after this, so don't want to be too late finishing here.'

'On the pull again?' Hope says with a disapproving look and my stomach lurches as I wait for his answer. It's painful thinking of Liam with someone else, even though I have no claim over him whatsoever.

'No, actually,' Liam responds, peeved at being prejudged. 'Some of the lads from the theatre are volunteering at a soup kitchen in town. We're taking soup and bread rolls to the homeless, along with baby wipes and fleecy blankets.'

This revelation shames Hope into a mumbled apology. She looks mortified as she sips the dregs of her tea. I suspect that the mug is empty and she's just miming the action to hide her shame at her misconceptions.

'What a great thing to do,' Connie enthuses. 'Giving your time to help others is so rewarding. Well done, Liam.'

He actually blushes at the praise, especially coming from Connie. After all, she *is* the queen of volunteering – in our group at least. 'Well, we're the lucky ones. It seems only fair to give something back to the community.'

'You're doing a good thing,' I say. I've a sneaky feeling Liam's going to keep on surprising me for as long as I know him. He's the kind of person you think you've got sussed and then they do something so totally out of left field, which makes you reconsider everything you thought you knew about them.

'Thanks.' His voice may be gruff, but I can tell he feels good about what he's doing. He looks away modestly, before turning the conversation to tonight's musical. 'So, what's the musical for tonight, Ray? I hope it's something better than that dross from last week.'

'*Mamma Mia!*,' Ray answers. 'A film which fits in rather nicely with all the baby talk, really, doesn't it? And there are no excuses for anyone not knowing the words to the songs in this one.'

I actually clap with excitement. 'I love Abba!'

'Me too.'

'Get in.'

'Yeah, they're epic.'

'The ultimate.'

Ray looks around startled before breaking out in a lop-sided grin of bemusement. 'I've actually done the impossible. I've found a musical we all agree on.'

'Come on, let's whack it on,' Issy says. 'Although if I cry when it gets to the wedding scene, I'm blaming my hormones!'

*

It's Friday night and the lights are low, but there's no need for us to go anywhere. We're making our own entertainment, especially as this DVD is another singalong edition. It means we're able to give our all without worrying about being the butt of everyone's jokes for the rest of the evening if we make a slip-up. We're well lubricated by the fizz we'd opened to toast Ray and Issy's good news, ready to take on the high notes. When 'Dancing Queen' strikes up I wish I had a hairdryer of my own to sing into or a bed to bounce on, but Ray's already claimed the most suitable makeshift microphone in the room – the remote control – and I have to make do with singing into the now-empty champagne bottle. By the time the song reaches its crescendo all of us are on our feet, mimicking the moves of the women of the island as they dance as though their lives depend on it on the sun-drenched pier. We're practically falling over each other what with the limited floor space, but it's the happiest I've felt in a long time. The feel-good film (along with the bubbles and the celebratory cocktails Hope's rustled up from the remnants of the bottles of spirits in the kitchen cupboards) have lifted my spirits and there's a party atmosphere at Cardigan Close as I hold Gomez aloft and twirl dizzily around.

By the time the film reaches its conclusion we're all in exceptionally high spirits. My voice is hoarse from shouting along to the Abba soundtrack, my body worn from the non-stop dancing.

It's been a perfect night, all in all, and as everyone's drifting their separate ways I appreciate just how much I've enjoyed it. I'm not ready for it to end.

Liam's sitting on the bottom step of the stairs pulling on his trainers. His ankle's recovering well, as his willingness to join in the dancing proved, and I wonder if he's got plans to go on to a club and continue the party after he's done his good deed for the night. The thought of him keeping someone else company sends surges of jealousy around my body. My head might be muzzy but it's clear enough for me to realise I don't want him to leave here and run into someone else's arms. I want him for myself.

'Stay,' I say, my tired voice catching at the word. The word is loaded.

He peers up at me thoughtfully but doesn't reply.

'Spend the night with me, please.'

Saying the words out loud is a relief and I'm floating until Liam's response brings me back down to earth with a startling bump. 'I don't think that's a good idea.'

I swallow, feeling small, hurt, and push past him, stumbling up the stairs to my room as I blink back the tears of rejection.

I hear the front door slam shut. He must have let himself out, to do whatever he pleases with someone else. Someone who's not me.

*

I'm sick of going over it in my mind. I've had too many sleepless nights riddled with anguish, debating how I'm going to word what I need to say. I know it'd be easier to talk to Justin in person, but that'd mean waiting until after Christmas.

I've considered not coming clean at all and just crossing my fingers that my feelings for Liam will disappear, but it doesn't really matter if they do or not. I've been wondering what it'd be like to sleep with someone else when I'm meant to be with Justin. It won't be easy, but it has to be done.

I move the pile of freshly-laundered clothes from the seat of the armchair in my room and sink down into the space I've created.

I take a deep breath.

And I make the call.

*

I don't realise how loudly I've been sobbing into Gomez (the toy, not the cat) until I hear the rat-a-tat of knocking against my bedroom door. It's followed by Issy's voice, calm and cool.

'Are you alright in there, Mon?'

I drag the back of my hand under my nose, leaving an unattractive snail-trail of snot across my skin. 'I'm fine,' I lie, my voice wobbling.

'I don't believe you,' she calls firmly. 'I'm coming in, okay?'

I nod gently, even though it's futile. Issy might be an amazing friend, but she doesn't possess superhuman powers. She can't see through a solid wood door.

The door creaks as it opens, reminding me that I really need to oil the hinges. It's been squeaking for as long as I can remember, but it's only now starting to grate on me. But then I'm in a fragile state right now, all things considered.

Issy sidles up to me warily, perching her bottom on the arm of the chair. She speaks in a voice saved for sympathy. 'Have you been on the phone to Justin?'

The tears return as I recall the hurt in his voice. 'Yes,' I say, between sobs. 'I told him about Liam. Not just about the kiss, but the rest of it too. The thoughts I've had about being with him and how I asked him to stay the night.'

If she's shocked by my revelation she does a good job of hiding it.

'Oh, sweetheart,' she says, sweeping me up in a bear hug that does little to make me feel better. 'Even if it doesn't feel like it now, you've done the right thing by being honest. You couldn't have kept a secret like that forever. It wouldn't be healthy.'

'I know,' I sniffle.

'It must have been dreadful for Justin,' she continues. 'These things are hard to discuss properly over the phone.'

I'm not listening as she continues her a spiel, some mumbo jumbo about everything happening for a reason. She doesn't understand. Instead I watch Gomez (the cat, not the toy) as he creeps under the desk, settling on a pile of old college work that I've not looked at in years. I hope he's not going to wee on it.

It's when Issy wraps her arm around my shoulders that I'm finally able to formulate the words I've been trying to get out.

'I told him everything, the whole story. And he says it's okay, he forgives me.'

That's when the floodgates open fully, the tears stream down my cheeks as though they'll never stop.

'Well, that's a good thing, isn't it?'

I nod, then shake my head, unsure whether it's a good thing or not. Justin knows and he loves me anyway, which should be enough to make my heart soar right out of my chest, but it doesn't. If anything it feels heavier than ever.

'He was shocked,' I admit. 'I don't think he had a clue how messed up my head's been. But we talked it through and I explained what happened only happened because Liam's here and he's there…'

'And is that true?' Issy probes gently. 'Because you and Liam have been getting pretty close. You were running around after him when he was on crutches. I mean, I know you're always kind and thoughtful – they're some of your most positive traits – but some of the things you did for him went above and beyond.'

'I'd have done it for anybody,' I insist, knowing she's referring to how I drove Liam to and from rehearsals each day so he wouldn't have to face the chaos that is rush hour on public transport. The buses are always jammed, standing room only, and the trams aren't much better either. 'If someone had knocked into him he could have done some real damage. I just wanted to help him out.' I don't mention how much I'd enjoyed listening to him practising his lines, repeating terrible, terrible jokes with varying intonation and telling him which was most amusing. How empty I'd felt each time he'd walked away.

'And it's admirable,' Issy says, placing her hand gently on my arm. 'But it seems to me like your relationship with Justin's making you miserable. Love should never make you miserable. It should make you shine like a beacon, want to shout about it from the rooftops. Make you want to be with the person you adore at every possible moment, and it might not be what you want to hear but I wouldn't be a good friend if I wasn't honest. I'm not sure Justin's that person for you any more.' I feel strangely stubborn, protective of the years Justin and I have spent together. 'I don't want you to feel you don't have a choice. You and Justin have been a couple for so long – all your adult life – and if he's what you want, then fine. It's more than fine; it's great. But maybe the reason you kissed Liam in the first place wasn't because you missed Justin and needed to feel wanted; maybe there's something between you two that needs to be explored. Have you considered that?'

'The thing with Liam was nothing,' I say, the finality I'd hoped to convey in my voice wavering as Issy stares me down. 'Well, not nothing. He's a good kisser, I'll admit. Liam was there, you know? And up for it. And it was crazy and stupid, but for those few mad minutes it felt good.' My heart races as I remember how good and that causes my words to tumble out, messy and quick. 'That was all I needed and it fulfilled its purpose. Not every hook-up has to last forever, but that doesn't mean it isn't special in that moment.' I want to laugh at myself. It's exactly the sort of thing Liam would say when defending his flings. I only hope I'm convincing Issy more than I'm convincing myself.

The look Issy gives me back is dubious. It's the same one she gave me in the staff room earlier when I told her I didn't eat the last chocolate digestive out of the biscuit tin at break time. Mind you, she was right to be suspicious on that front. I'd only just brushed the crumbs from my lips when she posed the question.

'It's Justin I love,' I say fiercely, pushing my inner turmoil down to the very bottom of my stomach. 'He's the one; he always has been. When he gets back to Sheffield we're going to enjoy each other again, like Hope and Amara did. Really cherish each other, you know? That's all I want, Is. For him to be back here and for us to get on with the rest of our lives together.' And for all my longing for Liam to disappear into thin air, I think, but I don't say it aloud. I can't. I need to focus on Justin and the future we have together.

I don't want to consider anything else. Justin's been there for me for so long. And he still loves me, even after all this time and my awful recent misdemeanours. Liam's gorgeous and sweet, and there's so much more to him than meets the eye. But he's also acting like a total playboy, enjoying nights out on the pull like a rampant student during freshers' week. Which would be absolutely fine and not bother me at all, if it wasn't for the fact that in spite of what I'm saying, I think I might be falling in love with him.

Issy smiles before squeezing me in towards her ever-expanding chest, which must be a side effect of the pregnancy – unless she's had a boob job on the sly. 'So long as you're happy, Mon, it's good enough for me.'

I smile weakly back. At this moment I'm far from happy.

Chapter Fifteen

Friday 16th December
Mary Poppins – Ray's choice (again)*

It's surprisingly snug in the lounge of 24 Cardigan Close this evening. The heating's cranked up, the wood burner's crackling away and I'm shrugging out of my cardi – something that's pretty much unheard of for this perpetually cold house.

We've decided to order food in tonight – a celebration because we've made it to the end of term. What's more, I'd finally handed in my form for the teacher-training application, which was bloody petrifying. But Mrs Thomas hadn't laughed me out of her office as I'd passed the A4 envelope right into her hand, which I'm taking as a good sign. In fact, she'd said she was impressed by my ambition.

I'm carefully pulling down a stack of dinner plates from the cupboard, so we won't have to do it in a rush when the delivery arrives. The plates are surprisingly heavy, except the melamine one that someone will have to make do with. There's going to be seven of us tonight, and our crockery set only runs to six of everything, except bowls, because Gomez knocked one off the dining table earlier in the week. Bowls run to five. Amara's joining us to celebrate, even though she's still got to work next week. The department store she works at will probably be chock-a-block busy right up until closing time on Christmas Eve, and Ray and Liam have another few days of rehearsals planned – but Hope, Issy and I can finally relax tonight knowing it's the end of a long and stressful term. It's always hard during winter. The dark mornings are an absolute killer and it's freezing cold to boot. But now, with the promise of two weeks' worth of lie-ins in sight and Justin's return next month meaning my life will no longer be on pause, there's a light at the end of the tunnel.

'Did you ring the order through?' I ask Connie as she strolls in from the lounge. She's nibbling a cracker, the dusty crumbs catching on the air. 'And how long is it going to be?'

She screws up her nose and manages to look adorable with it. I don't know how she does it. 'At least an hour, so they said. It's a busy night.'

'I thought everyone'd be out tonight. Don't people have works Christmas do's any more?'

She shrugs. 'You're asking the wrong person. I'm not working at the moment, remember.'

'No, you're volunteering because you're a kind-hearted person willing to give something back,' I remind her as I pull a handful of knives and forks from the cutlery drainer by the sink. Since her trip to Uganda, Connie's definitely got the bug for working with those in need and has been spurred on to look for local projects to support. Twice a week she's sorting through the bags of donations at a charity shop near the Botanical Gardens, as well as working with the same homeless charity Liam had been involved with through the theatre. He'd put her in touch with his contact, Babs, who'd been so enthusiastic about the project that Connie had offered her services at once. I'm in awe of Connie and her selflessness. I couldn't be more proud of her.

'Oh, it's such a pleasure,' she beams, clapping her hands together in front of her in joy. 'Everyone there is so experienced and they're all so friendly and welcoming. It's a really wonderful team. I'm not saying it's all easy, because it isn't.' She sighs dejectedly. 'A man who came to the food bank yesterday had lost his job last month. He's got three children to feed, and a Dalmatian that gets through a ridiculous amount of dog food. He looked so downhearted,' she said sadly. 'He said he might have to take the dog to the dog shelter, even though he doesn't want to. I wish I could do more to help people.'

'You're doing more than most, and that's admirable. There aren't many willing to give up their time so freely.'

'Well, I won't get the chance when I finally find a suitable studio space. I'm looking at a disused factory in the morning if you want to come along and give me your opinion. It's out at the end of the tram route, somewhere near Halfway. I don't think I can stretch to anything in the centre of town, even renting is extortionate.' She crosses her fingers in front of her. 'I'm hoping to get it all sorted – by the time I've done my exams I can start advertising for students.'

I raise my hand with a grin. 'You've got one right here when you're ready to start adult tap classes.'

Connie tuts, embarrassed. 'Come on,' she exclaims humbly. 'You're as good a tap dancer as me. You wouldn't learn anything new in my class.'

'Yeah, but dancing's not half as much fun without you. I found that out when you were in Uganda. Plus, I want to support you in your new venture. These are exciting times for you right now, Con. I want to be part of it.'

'And exciting times for you, too,' she insists. 'Justin will be back after Christmas and you'll be moving out of this place. Not to mention the preparation for teacher training. That's a lot of change all at once.' She places her hand on my arm, comfortingly. 'You could always try a bit of yoga, you know. Keep the stress at bay.'

'I don't feel stressed,' I say, honestly. 'I feel like I'm back in control after drifting.' I'd deliberately distanced myself from Liam over the past week, building up a wall to protect my and Justin's relationship. Spending time with Liam away from the rest of the group was asking for trouble. It had to stop. It's simple, although I miss his company more than anyone would know.

Connie smiles, her big brown eyes twinkling happily in response to my words. 'Good for you. I was worried about you. When I got back from Africa you didn't seem like your usual self.'

'You don't have to waste your time worrying about me,' I scoff.

'Of course I do,' Connie replies, looking me directly in the eye. 'You're my best friend.'

*

'When I was growing up this was my favourite film,' Issy reveals through a mouthful of chicken biryani. 'I must have watched it a hundred times.'

'It's another Julie Andrews' classic,' Liam quips. 'Although I can't watch it and not curl up and die on the spot for Dick Van Dyke's terrible cockney accent.'

'It's bad,' Issy agrees, 'but so bad it's good. A bit like *Made in Chelsea*.'

'That's just bad,' Ray says with a laugh.

'You love it, really,' she replies, poking her tongue out affectionately.

'I actually wanted to fly like Mary Poppins when I was little,' I say, to peals of laughter from everyone. 'Hey, I was only about six! I thought it'd be pretty amazing to have a magic umbrella that made me fly. With a duck-head handle, no less.'

'Impossible is what it'd be,' Hope smiles. 'But I remember that. You used to jump off the settee with your pink brolly up and try to fly. Mum was convinced you were going to hurt yourself. She hit the roof.'

'Which was more than Mon did,' Ray jokes.

'That's awful,' Amara replies, even though she's laughing. 'Anyway, I thought you were scared of flying?'

'That's just aeroplanes,' I reply, snapping a poppadum in half with a satisfying crack. 'I don't think I'd have the same problem with magic umbrellas.'

I press play on the remote control, hopeful that the combination of the film and the Indian food will stop my sister sharing some of the embarrassing stories from my past.

'And I'd still like to do it now,' I say defiantly. 'I reckon it'd be fun to be up there flying over the cars and houses.'

What I don't say is that I wish I could fly over the ocean, over deserted islands and humpback whales, so I can start working on getting things back to normal with Justin. That's the kind of magic that would be supercalifragilisticexpialidocious right now.

*

We're all enjoying singing about sugar helping the medicine go down a bit too much, laughing and joking and singing along as Mary Poppins snaps her fingers and beds make themselves as a result. Issy hopefully clicks her own fingers, looking rather disappointed when the empty bowls don't magically find their way to the kitchen sink and wash themselves.

'You'll be watching this with your little one next year,' Liam says to Ray. 'This film's always on telly at Christmas.'

'I can't wait. There's so much I'm looking forward to sharing with him from my own childhood. Introducing him to *Star Wars*, taking him to the match… going to the pantomime, even, if I'm not sick to death of shouting 'It's behind you' by the time this run's over.'

'Erm… you do realise we could quite easily have a girl? There's a fifty/fifty chance, more or less,' Issy says.

'Then I'll introduce *her* to *Star Wars*, take *her* to the match and we'll go and watch the pantomime every Christmas without fail, so long as I'm not in it because dressing up as a dame's the only job I can get,' he smiles. Is that better?'

'Better,' Issy agrees, smiling warmly in return. 'Because whether this baby's a boy or a girl, our little one is going to be so, so loved.'

The look Ray gives Issy is complete adoration. 'He or she already is.'

*

Bert and Mary are skipping along on their jolly holiday, enjoying one another's company as they're served by attentive penguins.

I look at Liam, taking off Dick Van Dyke with more than a passing likeness. Everyone's laughing, because that's the thing about Liam. He's not as obvious a joker as Ray, but he's funny too, when he pitches it right. And he'd been so kind to Issy, insisting she stay sitting down with her feet up whilst he handed her the dish full of jelly sweets because 'it must be exhausting growing a baby'. He catches my eye as everyone else carries on with their less impressive impersonations and winks at me, as though he's sharing a secret. I wish he wasn't on the opposite side of the room so I could apologise for last week's proposition, but he's either forgotten about it because he was more tipsy than I'd thought or thinks nothing of it. He has women throwing themselves at him all the time – why should I be any different than any of the others inviting him into their beds?

As he turns back to the TV I close my eyes tightly and think of my happiest thoughts in an attempt to find my laughing place. When I open them I'm exactly where I was before.

Chapter Sixteen

Friday 23rd December
White Christmas – Ray's choice (yet again)

Issy and I have made the most of a lazy day on the sofa, working our way through all our favourite Christmas films with a chocolate orange and a large tub of Cadbury's Miniature Heroes for company. We only move when Connie's knock at the door alerts us to the fact that it's pitch black outside and therefore must be time to start baking the mince pies I'd promised to have hot from the oven for our final Singalong Society meeting of the year. Hope and Amara assured me they'll show up early this evening with some ready-to-eat nibbles and Ray and Liam are going to come as soon as they wrap up at the theatre. They're certainly putting the hours in now, with just weeks to go before the opening night.

'I'm so excited about decorating the tree,' Connie says, rubbing her hands together excitedly. Her cheeks are cherry red from the cold, the same colour as the tips of her hair are again now. She certainly looks festive – in fact she reminds me a bit of a Christmas elf. 'Where did these decorations come from anyway? You've got tons.' She fingers a thick length of silver tinsel from the top of the large cardboard box that contains a gaudy mishmash of baubles.

'They were my mum's,' I admit. 'She's bought new ones with each marriage – her tree this year is all red and gold.' I pull a face that I hope shows my distaste. I've never been a fan of themed trees. 'It looks like it should be in a shop window, not a house.'

'Well, there's something of every colour in here,' Connie says cheerily, rummaging through the rainbow of colourful spheres. 'It'll be a proper old-school tree, like the one my dad always has.'

I smile at that. I'd always admired the Williams' family tree. It was an explosion of glitter, a mix of homemade angels and one-off decorations, which grew year on year; and it had always had multi-coloured lights, even when every other house on the block opted for the minimalist white ones. Their tree was warming, like something from a traditional Christmas card, and I had no problem at all if our tree emulated that.

'I strung the lights around it yesterday,' I say, nodding towards the small artificial spruce. 'That's always the fiddly bit, so I thought I'd get it out of the way. Then all that's left to do is the fun stuff.'

I pull a string of tinsel around my neck like a feather boa and shimmy. I'm more excited than I thought I would be. I'm looking forward to spending time with the rest of the gang.

'And I've brought presents!' Connie says excitedly, gesturing towards a large carrier bag filled with packages.

'Trust you to be organised,' Issy calls through from the kitchen. 'I've not even wrapped mine yet.'

'I thought you were getting gift bags instead of paper this year?' I say, my eyes narrowing. Every year Issy threatens to give up on wrapping paper, saying it's one job too many in the Christmas rush, yet every year she's still wrestling with the roll of wrap and a tape dispenser, complaining about how hard it is to get the backing off those weird little metallic bows that get stuck on the top of presents.

Issy looks at me triumphantly. 'I did. It'll only take me a

minute or two to write a name on each label and then 'voila!' I'll be ready for Christmas. At least, the presents will be.'

'When are you going to Ray's parents?' Connie asks. I knew Issy and Ray were leaving tomorrow evening – she'd packed a case with all her essentials before we'd started our movie marathon. I think she was silently praying for a heavy snowfall that would make Snake Pass impassable and mean they'd have Christmas Day in Sheffield rather than Bolton.

'Tomorrow,' she says with a grimace. 'It's not that I don't like Ray's family – his mum and dad are pretty cool as far as parents go, and his sister's really lovely – but it's not relaxing is it, being in someone else's house? I don't feel like I can put my feet up on the couch or lounge around in my pyjamas.'

Connie laughs. 'You're giving them their first grandchild, I should think you'll be able to get away with whatever you want.'

'True,' Issy replies, before bursting into giggles. 'His mum's been knitting for the baby already. She actually asked me on the phone if I preferred pure white or lemon yellow for a receiving blanket.'

Tears spring to my eyes at the thought. Issy being pregnant is one thing, but her actually being a mummy with a real live baby of her own? That's something else entirely. My heartstrings are well and truly tugged. 'What did you say?'

'I told her white. It's timeless and will match anything, so it won't matter what colour we paint the nursery when we move into the new place.'

My heart beats rapidly. I know she and Ray are planning on moving in together, somewhere further away from busy main road with a garden rather than a yard. But I'm still not prepared for it. Suddenly everything feels much more real. Is and I won't be housemates for much longer. There'll be no more nights on the sofa watching Disney films, at least, not unless we're watching them with her son or daughter once they arrive.

Justin's still talking about the two of us finding a place together when he gets back from America. He'd encouraged me to go and look at a flat that had come up for rent in the same block as Hope and Amara's, but I didn't want to go. Just thinking about moving in with him after all the time we've spent apart makes me feel like I've a lead weight pressing on my chest. But I don't know what the alternative is. I can't afford to rent this place alone.

'I'm finally starting to feel festive,' Connie says. 'One of your mince pies will be the perfect finishing touch to get me in the mood,' she says, looking at me greedily.

'Yes, yes, I'm on it,' I say, arranging the necessary ingredients on the work surface. 'But I'll be able to get this pastry made much more quickly if I can have the kitchen to myself,' I add. I work better without distractions.

'Anyone'd think you were trying to get rid of us,' jokes Connie.

'Don't complain about it!' Issy says. 'Come on, let's wait in the lounge. I'm sure I've got that Michael Bublé Christmas album somewhere. Why don't we put that on and start sorting through the decorations. There are way too many to go on the tree, so we're going to have to be selective.'

Connie nods. I can tell she's itching to get her hands on those decorations.

'Shoo,' I say, flicking a tea towel at my two closest friends as they jump away, squealing. 'Let me get on with this or there'll be nothing in the way of mince pies!'

*

I have to say, the tree looks pretty amazing. At four feet tall, it might not be the biggest, but it looks quite impressive now it's balanced on the table in the curve of the bay window. There are all manner of decorations adorning it – one on every artificial branch – so it's a real feast for the eyes.

'It looks like Christmas threw up in here,' Liam says brightly, placing the glittery gold star on the top of the tree.

'Makes a change from Issy throwing up,' I joke. She's still suffering terribly with morning sickness, which had, according to her, started the moment she found out she was pregnant and showed no sign yet of abating.

Issy rests her hand on her stomach. It's still the same shape as ever, the small curve her usual tummy rather than baby bump at the moment. 'Don't mention it, please. It makes my stomach flip over.'

'Quick, change the subject', Hope says. 'We don't want to have to clean up anything other than those strands from the tinsel and the sprinkles of glitter.'

'Have a mince pie,' I offer, the tangy fruity aroma wafting as I wave the plate under her nose. 'If that doesn't settle your stomach, nothing will. Pastry is the answer to every question.' I have to admit they're pretty good. Better than the shop-bought ones, anyway.

'Oh, go on, then,' Issy says, unable to resist the temptation. 'I'm sure I can force one down.'

'Are we ready for the big switch-on?' I ask, gesturing towards the tree. 'It's not quite Oxford Street, but we need to celebrate it. It's the official start of Christmas.'

'Turn the big light off, then,' Liam says, and the room darkens momentarily as Connie flicks the switch.

'After three,' says Ray, his hand poised over the plug, 'One, two, three!'

The lights flicker into action, the tiny bulbs twinkling in the darkness of the room.

I can't hold back my sigh. It's partly the simplistic beauty of the tree, which to me has always been the physical manifestation of Christmas. But it's also a sadness that our time as The Singalong Society is running out. Life's moving on for each of us. We're on the brink of change.

Gomez appears as if from nowhere, batting at a plastic orange bauble hanging from one of the lower branches. The tree quivers and for one terrifying moment I think the whole lot is going to come down.

'Stop it, Gomez,' I scold, scooping his tiny body into my cupped hands. He cricks his neck, nuzzling into me. I lean down to plant a kiss on the top of his soft furry head. His eyes are wide and wild, as though he'd rather be playing with the bauble. He's a scamp through and through.

'Come on,' Ray says. 'Let's get a Christmas drink and then start the film.'

'*White Christmas*,' Connie says. 'This is such an underrated film.'

'It really is,' Ray agrees, as we ensure we've got a drink each and food on our plates. 'You can't go wrong with a golden oldie.'

The boys are in their element shortly after as 'Sisters' starts up, what with it being one of the numbers they've been rehearsing for Cinderella. The two of them are hamming it up, bumping their hipbones against each other as they mock-simper about caring and sharing. They're quite the duo and I know they're going to go down a storm when the panto opens next month. Both Ray and Liam have mentioned that they're hopeful it'll lead them to bigger, more lucrative, projects.

'These old films have always got someone swinging around a lamp post or something,' Hope observes. 'I don't get it. No one does that in real life. I don't get why in musicals it's such a big thing.'

'I've done it before now,' says Ray with a shrug.

'Me too,' says Liam. 'I pretended to pole dance on a lamp post once when I was blind drunk. There's photo evidence too.' He puts his head in his hands.

'There are worse things you could do,' I say.

'You've not seen the pictures,' laughs Ray. 'He was only wearing a pair of tightie whities. Other than that he was stark-bollock naked.'

I imagine the scene and find myself clamping my legs closely together to try and shut down my body's natural response to thoughts of Liam in only skimpy underwear.

He's watching me, a self-satisfied smirk on his face at my reaction, so I make my excuses and head to the bathroom to regain my composure. Keeping my cool around Liam is turning out to be more difficult than I'd anticipated.

*

When the final scenes have played out on the TV screen, Liam makes his excuses and starts bundling himself up ready to face the icy cold; firstly putting on a large puffer jacket and then adding a thick scarf and beanie hat. The forecast has warned snow's a genuine possibility, and Liam had been sure to come prepared for that eventuality. Maybe if there is a snowfall Issy will get her wish of a Yorkshire Christmas after all.

'I'm heading off now,' he says with a wave, his eyes peeping out between the ribbed trim of his hat and the top of his scarf, 'But I'll catch up with you lot after Christmas. 'May your days be merry and bright',' he quips with a laugh. He scans the group and I'm sure his eyes hover on me just a moment longer than on everyone else.

We gather around, offering hugs and Christmas greetings, and I'm reminded how far we've all come in a few short months. It's hard to comprehend that without Issy's moment of madness rashly inviting the boys when she'd bumped into them in the shop, we wouldn't be here together now.

Liam's making his way out of the door and heading into the bitter night air when Connie notices the presents still placed, wrapped, under the tree. 'He's forgotten his presents!' Scooping up a rectangular box which looks suspiciously like chocolates, she chases after him. I can hear her cussing as her bare feet hit the paving slabs, which must be icy-cold.

'I really enjoyed tonight,' I say.

'Me too,' says Hope, taking a bite from the last remaining mince pie. The sticky filling oozes out and she quickly catches it with her free hand to stop it landing on her white top. 'Close call,' she says, spraying crumbs everywhere. Gomez is there immediately, hopeful that it's something he can hoover up – greedy cat. He's growing so rapidly now – the vet had been delighted at his progress when he went for his first injections.

Connie bursts back into the room, the cold air whistling in with her. We all immediately grumble, shouting at her to close the door to keep in the warmth we've spent all day building up. She's grinning inanely, her eyes twinkling more vividly than the lights on the tree. 'Well, I would close the door, but I found someone in the alleyway…'

I expect it to be Liam, coming back for one last beer. He's forever fearful of missing out.

That's when I see him, his silhouette so familiar. He's wearing a navy woollen duffel coat with large wooden toggles, the kind little boys and Paddington Bear wear, and his nose is bright red from the cold. He's shivering as he closes the door behind him and I don't trust that he's really here. I literally can't believe my eyes.

'Justin,' I say. My voice is wheezy and strange. For some reason I'm holding my breath.

'Hi, Mon,' he says shyly, slipping his black canvas rucksack off his back and letting it fall to the floor. 'I told the Chicago office I was coming home for Christmas after all.'

I can't breathe and then I find his arms around me, my cheek crushed against the itchy material of his coat. He buries his nose into my hair and plants the smallest of butterfly kisses on top of my head, whilst Gomez rubs against my ankle, fighting for my attention.

I inhale Justin's scent – that same beautifully familiar scent I'd been straining to smell from my cuddly toy. It's really him; it's really Justin.

234

I want to cry.

I want to be overcome with lust and a need to shout my desire for him from the rooftops the way Issy said was a sure-fire sign of love. But I'm not overcome. It's like being reunited with an old friend rather than the love of my life. Nice, but not magical.

My heart heaves.

This isn't how I'd imagined our reunion would be.

*

When I wake the next morning I'm a different person, a true singleton.

After the initial shock had worn off and I'd stopped clinging to him like a baby monkey holding tight to its mother so my legs didn't buckle under me, Justin and I had taken a walk. We'd needed privacy. It's not easy to get reacquainted after so long apart, especially when you have an audience.

So we'd wrapped up and headed out into the desperately cold night – one of those where your fingers go numb and stiff through your gloves, and we walked and talked our way along Ecclesall Road, stopping every so often to peer into the frosted seasonal windows, which looked so warm and inviting.

We'd gone to a favourite pub, one hidden away on a backstreet with tatty upholstery on the comfy seats and a jukebox full of indie music. And there, in a darkened booth, we'd kissed until our lips were sore, until the bell for final orders at the bar jangled in the distance and Mike, the stocky bald barman who'd worked there forever, apologetically tapped Justin on the shoulder and told us he needed to lock up.

I'd yearned for a fireworks kiss, the kind where colours flash on the inside of your closed eyelids. The kind where your whole body melts and fizzes and smoulders. The kind I'd shared with Liam. But it turned out kissing Justin wasn't like that any more, no matter how hard I tried to make it so it was. It was pleasant;

perfunctory. And it had suddenly dawned on me that maybe our relationship *was* built on habit rather than something more substantial, and although he's a sweet man, that isn't enough for a future, and certainly not a forever. It wasn't meant to be.

A painful conversation had followed, with tears on both sides – the final page of our decade-long story. We'd reminisced and we'd laughed, all the while knowing that it was the end. It was strange and new and scary and exciting, but most of all it was right.

There was no bitterness, no argument. Just a quiet sadness that our time was up and the same promise that comes with every ending. The promise that something else is about to begin.

*

We'd planned to meet up at the pub again this afternoon, the whole Singalong Society, plus Justin, because there was a Christmas singsong organised. Ray and Issy wouldn't be able to stay long, needing to reach Ray's family in Bolton before teatime, but I was looking forward to extending the Singalong Society's festive celebrations. Singing is what we do best. Mike had had an idea he could make it like an old-time London pub knees-up with all the punters joining in as they raised their pint glasses in the air, but had mentioned it at least four times in the two minutes it had taken to usher Justin and I out of the door. We'd promised to show our faces and he'd seemed happy to know he had at least a few people coming to his event. We'd laughed at his worries. It wasn't likely he'd have an empty pub the Saturday before Christmas.

It might not be normal to spend my first night with singleton status out with my ex-boyfriend, but I don't want to be normal any longer. I want to try new things, take risks, be daring. I want to do everything I've ever dreamed of.

*

'It looks alright in here when it's all trimmed up.' Hope sounds surprised. To be fair, she's not wrong. What's normally a rather dark and dingy backstreet pub (although that's part of its charm) is looking far more welcoming, with the flickering amber flames dancing in the fireplace and the irregularly shaped tree bedecked in gold stars in the corner. There are a few of those tasteless seventies decorations that look like slinkies strung out across the ceiling, too, but we can ignore those.

'It does,' I agree, shuffling along the bench to make room for Justin, who's just walked in. I thought it'd be strange seeing him now, but it isn't – not really. The only thing that's awkward is being around a table with Liam and Justin together. Part of me feels like a floozy having my only-just-ex and the person who confirmed our relationship was over sitting either side of me, but Justin and I haven't had a standard relationship for such a long time. It doesn't feel raw and painful having him here with the rest of the group – just a bit surreal. But he is frowning at Liam, who's totally oblivious as he chats away to Ray and Issy. Oh well, Justin either likes it or lumps it, that's the thing about sharing a friendship group. He can always find other people to hang out with. On the bright side, at least Justin's a singleton, so he meets the criteria for membership in our gang, which is more than some of the members currently do…

'What's it like being in a pub and not being able to have a drink?' Liam asks Issy. He sips at the creamy head on his Guinness, gaining a momentary moustache in the process. His tongue's the same vivid pink as Gomez's as he licks the froth from his upper lip. He looks different tonight, sexier. Maybe that's all in my head, though, maybe because there's the hope that now I'm single too he really could be mine. 'I can't imagine it,' he continues. 'There was this one time a couple of years back when I was on antibiotics and the doctor said I shouldn't really drink on them. It was hell. Everyone I knew had a birthday that week and they all wanted to go out on the lash. In the end I gave in and had a few pints.'

'Well, I certainly won't be drinking,' Issy says, taking a martyr-like sip from her orange juice. 'There are so many things that can go wrong during pregnancy, without taking unnecessary chances. I'm worrying myself sick over it, aren't I?' she says, looking at Ray.

He nods, 'I keep telling her to step away from Google, but she won't listen. Nothing but worry can come from looking at medical stuff online.'

Hope choked on her drink. 'Like that time you were convinced you had E. coli because you had diarrhoea, Mon. Remember?'

Justin smiles fondly. 'I remember. It was after that biology school trip, where we'd been looking for creatures in that pond. You were convinced you were going to die.'

I pull myself tall in my seat, indignant. 'The symptoms matched up. Even Dr Gordon said so.'

Liam shuffles forward in his chair, resting his elbows on the polished mahogany surface of the large, round table we've managed to snag. That was the advantage of getting here early and setting up stall for the night – we'd had our pick of the seats. It was getting decidedly busier now. 'So, what was it?' he asks curiously. 'I take it from their reaction it wasn't E. coli.'

Justin and Hope crease up in laughter.

'It was a stomach bug,' I admit shame-faced. 'But the doctor said it was better to be vigilant, so I don't know why you all think it's so funny,' I say, although I doubt they can hear me over their laughter. For some reason they think this is hilarious. 'Anyway, we weren't talking about me, we were talking about Issy making the wise decision to avoid alcohol for the next nine months.'

Issy groans mournfully. 'It sounds so long when you put it like that. Although it's not another nine months, it's only seven.' She places a protective hand over her non-existent bump, and Ray's hand automatically joins it. I swallow down the lump in my throat at the beauty of the gesture.

'Haven't you got a scan soon?' Connie asks. 'Don't they do it at twelve weeks?'

'Yes,' Issy confirms, 'we've just had our appointment letter through. Nine o'clock on New Year's Day! Isn't that a crazy time for a hospital appointment?'

'Hospitals are like that, though, they work all kinds of funny hours. It's not like they get regular holidays.' I feel a pang of pity for the hospital staff. I can't imagine not having the seven-weekly breaks to count down to, not to mention how they have weekends and night shifts to work too. Suddenly the rigidity of school hours seems appealing, even being forced to take holidays during the most expensive times of year.

'Knowing everything's fine with our little grape will be the best possible start to a new year,' Ray smiles, to a chorus of 'aaahhh's'.

'Grape? Surely that's not what you're calling it? It's almost as bad as Apple.' Liam looks horrified.

Issy giggles. 'I don't think we're going to go for anything quite that outlandish. We're not thinking about names yet, it's far too soon, but we'll probably go for a family name. Keep it traditional, you know. And Ray's only calling it Grape this week. It'll be Kidney Bean next week. I've got this pregnancy book that compares the baby's size to fruits and vegetables. He thinks it's hilarious,' she adds affectionately.

'Terms of endearment,' Ray corrects. 'It helps to get an idea of what's actually going on in there. I can't get my head around it, that we've actually made a real little person. It's incredible.'

'A miracle,' I agree.

I remember Liam's comment about not wanting children. I've always thought that I'd be a mum someday, somewhere way out on the horizon. What'll happen if we do get together? You can't compromise on things like that, there's no meeting in the middle. You're either a parent or you're not. Not that it's relevant, anyway, not yet but it's still there, buzzing away in my ear like a persistent fly, irritating and incessant.

'Hark the herald angels sing, glory to the new-born king.'

The sound of a jammed pub singing along to a traditional Christmas carol was far more moving than I could ever have predicted. It was like being at a concert. Not because it was melodious, because it was anything but, but it's easy to get swept along with everyone else as they throw themselves into the festive spirit. There's something special about being a part of this, a sense of togetherness in the now sticky (and frankly, quite sweaty) pub that sums up the true meaning of the spirit of Christmas. Although maybe the four gin and tonics I've had have gone some way towards contributing to my nostalgic glow.

Mike announces there's time for one last song before normal service resumes, although we all have a sneaky suspicion that he wants to get the singing wrapped up so people can focus on spending their hard-earned cash at the bar.

We all heartily join in wishing everyone and their kin a Merry Christmas and a Happy New Year; our arms wrapped around each other as we sing along to the optimistic tune. Things might have changed a lot over the past few months, but some things don't change at all. We're all still singing until our throats are sore and our souls are happy, exactly the way we originally set out to. But tonight we've grown in numbers, sharing the joy of singing with Mike's other punters. The pub is alive with the sound of music.

The Singalong Society. Tonight it's not just for Singletons – it's for everyone.

Chapter Seventeen

The following July – My birthday
Shrek – My choice*

'Oh my goodness.'

The scene in front of me is so totally new but at the same time seems like the most natural thing in the world. I've come to see Issy and Ray and meet the new arrival, although all I can see is a crinkly pink face swaddled in a waffle-weave blanket. Issy is radiant, every inch the proud mother. She has every right to be too. It wasn't an easy birth, according to what Ray had told me over the phone last night – thirty-six hours of labour doesn't sound like fun. But their little girl had been born just after midnight, and there's no one I'd rather spend my birthday with than their beautiful new arrival.

'Isn't she gorgeous?' Ray coos, leaning in to steal another kiss from his daughter, who looks snug and safe in the crook of Issy's arm. 'Just like her mum,' he adds.

I move closer, placing the soft toy I'd brought for the baby on the sideboard. The baby's sucking on her lower lip and she looks absolutely tiny. She wasn't a small baby, in fact she was a rather impressive ten pounds on the nose, but compared to the adults in the room she's like a doll.

'She's just gorgeous,' I beam, reaching out to stroke her cheek with the back of my finger. Her velvety skin is soft and warm against my hand. 'But then she was always going to be, wasn't she, with you two for parents.'

'Do you want a cuddle?' Issy offers.

'I thought you'd never ask.'

She places the baby and the layers of blanket (not really necessary – it's the height of summer – one of the blazing hot days that actually warrants that title) into my arms and I take in her face for the first time. Her eyes are scrunched closed, her rosebud lips constantly moving. Her button nose is twitching, so delicate and small. It's hard to comprehend that one day she'll be fully grown, slamming doors and giving her parents backchat. Right now she's so utterly reliant on Issy and Ray for everything, an absolute peach of a babe.

It's a struggle to drag my eyes away from her. She's perfect.

'Have you decided on a name yet?' I ask, gently swaying on the spot.

Ray and Issy look at each other, as if trying to decide who gets to reveal the much-awaited news.

'Yep,' Ray smiles. 'She's Isadora, just like her mummy.'

'Although we're calling her Dodie for short,' Issy adds quickly. 'It'd get too confusing if there were two Issy's in the house.'

'One Issy is enough for anyone,' I joke. 'But seriously – Dodie. That's super-cute. The old-fashioned names are really popular again right now but I've not seen any Dodie's on the class lists.' I'd been preparing books for the new intake of children that would be starting in September; the class that would be mine. There was an Edith and a Mabel and even a Gretchen, but no Dodies or Isadoras. Maybe they'd inadvertently chosen a unique name after all, even if it wasn't Apple or Grape.

I look at the baby cradled in my arms. Correction – I look at

Dodie cradled in my arms. The name suits her and I lean down to plant what's probably her thousandth kiss of the day on the top of her head. I take in her delicate scent. She smells amazing, like Marmite and baby powder and new trainers all rolled into one.

'I bought her a musical too,' I say. 'It's in my bag.'

Ray hands my leather satchel to Issy and she pulls out the case, the lurid green trim a clue to what's inside.

'*Shrek the Musical*,' Ray reads over her shoulder. 'Cheers, Mon. That'll start off her collection nicely. And she's bound to love musicals. Without them she wouldn't even exist.' He rips off the cellophane packaging and puts it straight on, the colourful fairy-tale characters springing into action on the TV. None of us are familiar with the musical, but its opening number couldn't be more perfect for today as the cast sing of a big bright beautiful world. For Ray, Issy and Dodie, it really is.

Shrek rumbles on in the background but the three of us are chatting away nineteen to the dozen, not really taking it in. It's an actual stage musical rather than a film adaptation, and it's never quite the same watching a recording of a live performance.

The doorbell rings and Ray gets up to answer. He leans over the Moses basket, where Dodie's still sleeping, reaching in to check she's still breathing. 'That'll be Uncle Liam,' he whispers to her.

My head jerks and I look sharply at Ray. 'Liam's coming?'

'He's working in Buxton this week,' Ray says, pressing the buzzer on the intercom to open the door.

I knew Liam was in a touring production of *The Wizard of Oz*, his biggest role to date. He'd earned the part of the Tin Man, a character who, like Liam himself, had so much going on beneath the surface.

Liam pops his head around the door as though he's playing peekaboo. 'Hey, everyone.' He comes in and leans against the arm of the chair I'm sitting on. 'Hi, Mon.'

I blush. It's been a while since I last saw him and he looks better than ever. His hair's a bit longer, his face a bit stubblier. 'Hi.'

'What're you watching?' he asks, although the giant green ogre should have been enough of a clue. He's more interested in the musical than in Dodie, as though he's forgotten the purpose of the visit. But then he's never been interested in babies, unless they're baby cats.

'*Shrek the Musical*,' Issy replies. 'Mon bought it for Dodie.'

He raises his eyebrows with interest at hearing the new arrival's name, but still doesn't move to look at her.

'I've got something for her too,' he says, handing over a present to Issy. It's wrapped in pale pink paper printed with small white hearts.

She unwraps the paper, pulling out a white baby-grow covered in treble clefs in every colour of the rainbow. 'Oh, Li, it's beautiful.'

He smiles bashfully. 'Don't sound so surprised. I thought it made sense to get something related to musicals and singing.'

'Great minds think alike,' Ray says, his gaze flitting between me and Liam until it rests firmly on his new-born daughter.

'We're glad you're both here together, actually,' Issy says. 'Because there's something we wanted to ask you and it saves us saying the same thing twice. We wondered if you'd be Dodie's godparents.'

'We won't be having a big ceremony,' Ray says, 'just family and close friends. But we couldn't do it without you two there and we hope you'll always be a part of our lives, and Dodie's too.'

'You're the obvious choices,' Issy continues. 'So what do you say? Will you do it?'

'Absolutely!' I beam. 'I'd be honoured.'

Liam's less sure. 'You know I'm not good with kids. I've never even held a baby.'

'Well, we can sort that out right now,' says Ray, gently lifting Dodie from the confines of her basket and placing her into a stunned Liam's arms.

He's rigid, scared to move for fear of breaking her. She looks so small compared to him and he so big compared to her.

'That's not so hard, is it?' says Issy with a wry smile.

Dodie fidgets then starts to scream at the top of her lungs. It's an ear-piercing scream and Liam's terrified. 'I knew she wouldn't like me,' he says, unsure of what to do to calm her.

'She doesn't know you,' Ray corrects. 'She doesn't know any of us.' He takes Dodie back in his arms as a familiar song comes out of the TV speakers.

' 'I'm a Believer' ', Liam says animatedly. 'Tune.'

'And I believe in you,' Issy says. 'You'll be a brilliant godfather to Dodie. Please say you'll do it?'

'How can I say no when you're flattering me like that,' he jokes. 'I'll do my best. And I can warn her off the boys who don't treat her right.'

'She's never having a boyfriend,' Ray says, shifting Dodie so she's in his other arm. 'Or at least, not until she's thirty.'

We sing along to the one song on the soundtrack we know just to keep to tradition, Ray bobbing up and down on the spot as he does so in an attempt to lull Dodie back to sleep. When it fails to do the trick Liam and I take it as our cue to leave. They're only just finding their feet as a family of three; we really should leave them in peace. If Dodie crying until her face is puce can be defined as 'peace'.

Liam and I are standing on the drive outside Ray and Issy's three storey townhouse, he's flipping his car keys over in his hand. 'D'you need a lift? I can take you back to Cardigan Close if you like?'

'Thanks.' I could have caught the bus but it'd mean changing in town and would take the best part of an hour. In the car it'd only take fifteen minutes. Connie wouldn't be home yet, she's teaching at the studio, so I'd be able to enjoy having the house to myself for an hour or so.

I belt myself in as Liam revs the engine.

'How's work?' he asks. 'Ready for the holidays?'

I laugh. 'I'm always ready for the holidays. But yeah, it's fine. I start teacher training in September.'

'Ray mentioned it.' I get a thrill of excitement from knowing they've been talking about me. I wonder who instigated the conversation, Liam or Ray.

'And the tour? How's life on the road?'

'Tiring, you know. We've not been in the same town for more than five nights in a row and it sounds glamorous, but staying in hotels and eating out every night's not all it's cracked up to be. I love the job, but it's hard being away from everyone.'

'I'd love to see the show,' I say, remembering how I'd felt like Dorothy in my gingham dress, and how I'd felt when Liam had complimented me on my style.

'I can put you on the guest list?' he offers. 'And anyone else you want to bring. Connie, Hope, Amara… I can sort it.' There's a twang of hope in his voice.

'I'd like that,' I say, sincerely. 'Maybe on Friday night? That's the last day of term and I'd do anything to get out of the pub. Teachers at the end of term don't know their limits. It's embarrassing.'

'Don't knock it, you'll be a teacher yourself soon enough,' he reminds me. 'And of course I'll sort the tickets. I'll put four aside for you at the box office.'

'Thanks.'

There's a pause.

'Do you ever see Justin?'

I shrug. 'Now and again. Not that often, though, since he got promoted.'

'So there's no big 'kiss and make up' on the cards for you two?' he enquires. He takes his eyes of the road, looking at me inquisitively as he waits for my reply.

'I don't love him any more.'

Liam looks back at the road.

*

It's not long until he's pulling up outside my house. The engine's still running as I unbuckle my seatbelt.

'Do you want to come in?' I ask. The tension in the car has ramped up since we were talking about Justin, the part of the conversation that hadn't been said hanging in the air.

He lets out a small laugh that sounds more like a cough. 'I want to.' His eyes catch mine. The way he's looking at me, as though I'm the last éclair on the pudding trolley, makes me weak.

'I want you to.'

I lean across the space between the seats. Without the constraints of my seatbelt I'm more easily able to move than he is, but he's inching towards me too until our mouths hungrily meet in the middle, somewhere above the gearstick. It's just like our previous kisses, an intoxicating rush where my senses are heightened. It's lightning bolts and Veuve Cliquot, fresh-cut grass and heavy metal. It's Liam's body melding into mine.

Then his phone vibrates; an inconvenient interruption.

'Leave it,' I murmur, my voice lazy with lust.

He disentangles himself from me. 'I can't,' he says looking unhappily at the caller display.

I wonder who it is that's tearing him away from me. Like we've not waited long enough already.

'Damn it!' He slams his hands against the steering wheel in frustration. 'It's my agent.' I hadn't realised he was in demand enough to need one. 'He's got me an audition, one we've been trying to wangle for weeks. I need to be in Manchester in an hour.'

My heart sinks.

'I wish I could stay, but it's a huge audition, Mon.' He looks

247

sort of reluctant, but his eyes are aflame. They're golden. Another of those quirky hazel-eye tricks. '*Les Mis*. A three-month run. Not Jean Valjean – but they need a Marius. I can't not go.'

I climb out of the car, rearranging my ruffled skirt as I do so. 'I wouldn't expect you not to.'

I walk to the window on the driver's side, already wound down to let some air into the car on this humid Sunday afternoon. 'Break a leg,' I say. 'In theatre terms, I mean,' I add, remembering all the times it had been me driving him to work after his tumble down the stairs. I lean in to give him a final kiss: shorter and softer but no less thrilling.

'I'll call you,' he promises. 'And I'll see you on Friday.'

'You will.'

'Oh, and one last thing. Happy birthday, Mon.'

Liam waves as he pulls away and I lick my lips. They taste of him, and I'm so content I feel I might explode. Right this moment it's as though everything's magical. Everything's perfect.

Epilogue

The following Friday
The Wizard Of Oz – Mine and Liam's choice*

'I loved it,' I say excitedly, clicking my heels together. 'Every bit of it.'

I'd dragged Hope with me to watch the performance and, to my surprise, she'd been thrilled to be asked. Amara's stuck at work for stocktaking and Connie's busy preparing a troupe of over-excited seven-year-olds for their Grade-1 ballet exam, so it was just the two of us.

'Me too. The costumes, the music – the whole thing was outstanding.'

'Liam was brilliant, wasn't he?' I add. He'd been fabulous, shining, and not purely because he was dressed head to toe in silver.

We're standing outside the stage door with a few enthusiastic autograph-hunters, waiting for him to emerge. My stomach's full of butterflies. I can't wait to see him, to tell him how much I loved what he'd brought to the role of the Tin Man.

Eventually he strides out, smiling as he stoops down low

and poses for photos with his fans. They're grinning from ear to ear at actually getting to meet him, asking him to sign their programmes with brand new permanent markers. It's crazy to think that they're all waiting for him, and his fan club will surely only grow once he starts in *Les Mis* in November. They'd be crying along with him as he sung 'Empty Chairs at Empty Tables' and I'd be joining them. He does things to me, Liam Holly.

The small crowd around him dissipates until there's only Hope and I left waiting.

'Hey,' he smiles, wrapping his arms around Hope in a friendly hug. 'It's good to see you.'

'You too, bigshot,' she jokes. 'Get you with the young girls hanging around the stage door begging for photos. Who'd want a pic of your ugly mug?' She grins. 'But seriously, you were fantastic up there. You stole the show.'

Liam rolls his eyes, but he looks secretly pleased to have won Hope's approval. Praise from Hope is a rarity that's given only on merit. You don't get it unless you earn it. 'Cheers. I'm glad you enjoyed it.'

He looks at me expectantly.

'You were incredible.' But he always has been. 'You blew me away.' But he always had.

'You don't know how good it feels to hear you say that,' he says with relief, wrapping his arm around my waist. I lean into his shoulder, resting my head against his chest. I can hear the beating of his heart, staccato and quick.

'I'm going to shoot off,' says Hope, nodding in the direction of the car park. 'Amara will be clocking off soon and we might catch last orders at the pub if we're lucky.'

'Thank you so much for coming,' says Liam, seeming genuinely touched that she made the effort. He squeezes my waist, and in hushed tones whispers in my ear. 'Are you going too?'

I shake my head and smile.

I've always considered myself a modern woman. That's why I'm spending tonight with Liam, who might seem like a tin man but actually has two hearts. His and mine.

THE END

Acknowledgements

An enormous round of applause and a raucous standing ovation go to –

My family, especially David and Zachary, for giving me the time, space and encouragement to keep on writing. I'm so lucky to have you.

Charlotte Ledger and Kim Young for believing Mon and co. had a story worth sharing, and everyone else at HarperImpulse for their enthusiasm for this book. I'm beyond proud to be part of the HarperCollins family.

Helen Williams, for the brilliant editing job. You had me tearing my hair out at times, but you were totally right. This is a better book because of your suggestions.

My incredible fellow Harper Impulse authors for being so generous with both advice and support.

The wonderfully talented team of Stuart Bache and Natasha Hughes at Books Covered for the stunning cover art. You absolutely nailed it.

My critique partners Emily Royal and Katy Wheatley for being there from the moment I decided to 'write something about a group of friends who watch musicals together', through the 'I don't know which tense to write it in!' stage and for eventually reading the manuscript almost as many times as I did. Without you two, there would be no book.

All my other writer friends, especially Brigid Coady, Kat French, Erin Lawless, Keris Stainton, and the Wordcount Warriors for keeping me going when I was running out of steam (and sense).

Everyone on Facebook and Twitter who put up with me talking

about musicals even more than usual. I'm sorry. I hope the end result makes up for it.

The bloggers, reviewers and readers who have been so supportive of my previous releases and shown excitement for my debut novel. You are fabulous, fabulous cheerleaders.

Janet Aspinall, Stephanie Cage, Anne Cater, Emma Doszczeczko, Michelle Jackson, Tallulah Wheatley, and Claire Wilson for loaning me DVDs. If you still haven't got them back yet, pester me.

The friends who get subtle mentions throughout this novel. You know who you are and I love you more than words can say.

And last but by no means least, a humongous thank you to *you*, for buying this book and allowing me to live my author dream.

Katey Lovell, Sheffield, July 2016